AN ARRANGEMENT WITH THE HEIRESS

KENTUCKY DEBUTANTES OF THE GILDED AGE

BOOK ONE

LISA M. PRYSOCK

WILD HEART BOOKS

Cover design by Evelyne Labelle at Carpe Librum Book Design. www. carpelibrumbookdesign.com

ISBN: 978-1-963212-02-0

*They claim to know God, but by their actions
    deny Him.*

— TITUS 1:16

*Whoever claims to love God yet hates a brother or
    sister is a liar. For whoever does not love their
    brother and sister whom they have seen, cannot
    love God, whom they have not seen.*

— 1 JOHN 4:20

CHAPTER ONE

A canter is a cure for every evil.
—Benjamin Disraeli

MAY 1901
VELVET BROOKS FARM, LEXINGTON, KENTUCKY

"You asked to see me, Pa?" Veronica Josephine Lyndon breezed into the library of her house at Velvet Brooks Farm. Arranging her riding skirt after sitting in the leather chair pulled up close to Joseph Lyndon's desk, she took in his gray brows and compressed mouth. Why did her father wear such a serious look?

"I did." Pa closed the ledger book where he tracked household and farm expenses. Setting it aside, he folded his hands together on top of the desk. "I wanted to speak with you about your future."

"My future?" She arched her brow.

He nodded. "Yes, your future."

"What's to talk about? I have it all planned out."

Pa cleared his throat. "Yes, well, that's precisely what I wanted to discuss. Your plans."

"What did you want to know?" She hadn't discussed any of them with Pa, but she had dropped a few hints. After graduating from finishing school at twenty-one, she'd mentioned she had no foreseeable plans to marry. During her recent twenty-third birthday dinner, when Grandmother Spencer had asked about her current beaux, she'd said she didn't have a beau or any plans to acquire one, but her grandmother and everyone else in the room had dismissed her reply with a few chuckles. Now she braced herself to defend her wishes to her father.

"Your mother is under the impression you wish to remain single and live out your days at Velvet Brooks." Pa leaned back in his chair.

"Nothing would please me more." Veronica thrived working with their horses, the lifeblood and legacy of the farm.

"That does present a problem. Your mother and I are concerned you won't have anyone to look after you later in life. You do realize, we won't be around forever."

"I know, Pa. I'll manage. I don't need looking after."

"The truth is, everyone needs looking after. We'd like to see you settled into a happy, secure marriage. Besides, we'll need some grandchildren to inherit Velvet Brooks someday." His thin lips spread upward.

Veronica didn't return his smile. Children? One could hardly have children without a husband. Gripping the arms of her chair, she sat up straighter.

"Before you say anything, hear me out. Your mother and I have spoken about this at length. Out of our concern for you, we have been in correspondence with my old university friend, Levi. You remember Leviticus Beckett and his wife, Gloria, and their four children. His eldest son, Edward, has recently graduated from Princeton. He is ready to marry and settle down. We've come to an arrangement regarding the two of you."

Had her parents lost their minds? They hadn't seen the Becketts in years. "Pa, you and Mama can't just marry me off to a perfect stranger." Where was her mother, as a matter of fact? Why had she left Pa to break this news? Probably best not to argue with both of them at the same time. But of all the cocka-mamie ideas...this had to top them all.

"You've met Edward before. He isn't exactly a stranger."

"I hardly remember that particular visit to New York, let alone him," she protested, releasing a nervous laugh.

"Still, your mother and I want you to have a chance for a happy, solid marriage and a family of your own who will love and protect you in the years to come. To be sure, we never thought for one moment that you would not have accepted any of the proposals from amongst your suitors, but here we are." He released a heavy sigh.

"I'm not marrying anyone, Pa." Veronica tilted her head. "I made up my mind. I don't see how a husband can make me any happier than I am right now."

"You say that because you are well provided for here at Velvet Brooks, but it's not the same as having your own family and a household of your own. In fact, it's all decided. Edward is aboard a train this very moment, traveling here with his father and brother, and with the understanding you will marry him. His train arrives the day after tomorrow. They'll stay at the Phoenix Hotel in Lexington, but much of Edward's time will be spent here, getting to know you better."

"I have no intention of entertaining your guests or getting to know Edward. I'm not interested in marrying anyone, Pa." She'd made up her mind about that years ago, after Henry Sullivan had run off and married her best friend. She would never open her heart to that kind of pain ever again. But Pa didn't need to know her reasons. He only needed to know she had a much better plan, but he rambled on about Edward.

"Nonetheless, it's an excellent match. He is highly sought

after, though my understanding is that he hasn't met anyone he is interested in marrying from New York. Furthermore, over the years, I've been able to add a tidy sum to the generous dowry your grandfather set aside for you. But if you don't marry before twenty-five, the majority will be lost to you and split between your sisters' dowries. I'm sure you don't want to see that happen any more than we do."

"Pa, I appreciate what you've done for me, and Grandfather's efforts, too, but I don't need the dowry. You can give it to Delia and Gladdie."

"No. I can't allow that to happen. It would place your entire financial future at the mercy of others. Your mother and I will not stand by and allow you to squander your chance for security and happiness." Pa entrenched his stance with a stern countenance.

She bristled, tilting her chin up, trying to think of something to say to make her father understand she remained firmly in the camp against any marriage. In fact, she could hardly believe her ears. "I didn't know a time constraint existed regarding the dowry, but that aside, it wouldn't change my mind. I have no intention of marrying anyone. Certainly not a man I barely know, and definitely not in an arranged marriage. Where is the love in that? I don't care if he graduated from Cambridge, Yale, *and* Princeton."

"Don't push your mother and me on this, Veronica. We've made up our minds after watching you turn away every eligible bachelor in Kentucky. You're running out of time and options, running recklessly into a lonely, unhappy future. If anything were to happen and we had to sell Velvet Brooks, you would have nothing left. No income. No husband. No children. No home. And no security in your future at all."

"Pa, I can't marry Edward Beckett. I don't love him, and I'm sure I never will." Veronica shook her head. Her father didn't understand the reason why she would never marry, and she couldn't explain it. Not without wounding her pride. To recount the reasons she'd lost Henry's interest to a peer and bemoan the extent of her broken heart asked too much.

Pa rose from his seat behind the desk. "You'll thank us later. That is all I have to say on the matter."

Arguing with him would obviously lead nowhere. Veronica fled from the library in horror. When she burst into the main hall, she nearly collided with her mother, Eleanor Lyndon.

"Oh, goodness me." Mama stepped back. "Are you all right, Veronica?"

Angry tears pooled in her eyes, blurring her vision. She took a step back, too, stunned. How long had her mother stood outside the library? How long had she known about the arrangement? Why had she left Pa to break the news?

Ready to explode, she didn't dare speak to Mama now. Veronica lifted her riding skirt and ran up the staircase to her room. The life-altering news she'd received from Pa had emotionally shattered her, leaving her in shock with no idea of how to defend herself.

Upstairs, Veronica slammed the door to her bedroom and locked it. She flung herself onto the bed for a good long cry amongst her pillows, allowing them to muffle her sobs and collect her tears. A little while later, she refused to answer her mother's knock or pleading to open the door and speak with her.

"I know you're upset with us right now, my darling daughter, but in time, you'll come to see this is all for the best. Your father and I have given this a great deal of thought and prayer. We'd like you to give Edward a chance." Her mother's gentle voice on the other side of the door reminded her they cared, but they would never understand the reasons for her refusal to marry. She had her own life to live, and it did not look anything like what had made them happy.

She didn't unlock the door for Delia and Gladdie either.

Had Mother sent them to do her bidding? They finally went away, leaving her to deal with her dilemma in peace, although anything but peace filled her soul.

Dinner came and went, but she didn't step outside her room. One of the servants, Grace Mitchell, brought a dinner tray upstairs. After knocking a few times, Grace left the meal outside the door. Food? The very last thing on Veronica's mind. No, this was war.

Instead, she alternated between fits of anger and sobbing. She cried, rocked, prayed, and cried some more until she thought she had reached the bottom of her tears. How dare her parents think they could control her life, forcing her into a loveless marriage? Their plan for her future was utterly ridiculous.

Marriage had crossed her mind a few times since her twenty-first birthday, but only briefly. Maybe if Henry hadn't run off with her best friend... But the hurt they had caused ran too deep. Remembering it caused her tears to start all over again.

Through the long night when sleep evaded her, she tried to think of reasons to offer her parents. Why couldn't things remain as they were? Living at Velvet Brooks made her happy. Why did she need to marry? What did she care about the dowry? She didn't want any of it and didn't imagine her parents ever selling the family farm, no matter what they said.

Her eyelids heavy, she finally fell asleep, emotionally drained.

When dawn broke, she prayed again as she dressed for the day, rehearsing words to convince her parents to abandon their disastrous plan. The servants began moving around on both floors, setting the dining room table for breakfast, knocking on bedroom doors to arrange hair and help the Lyndon ladies dress, but Veronica didn't speak much when she opened the door for Grace to style her hair.

Emerging from her room at seven o'clock sharp, she

joined her family for the morning meal, thankful when Gladdie poured a cup of steaming coffee and slid it in her direction.

"I hope you are feeling better this morning, Veronica," Mama began, unfolding a linen napkin and placing it across her lap over her gray silk gown. "Did you sleep well?"

Veronica glared at her mother as she stirred cream and sugar into her cup of coffee. Why did she speak as if the sky hadn't fallen yesterday? Indignation filled her heart, but she managed a calm, reasonable, rehearsed reply. "I would like to discuss this plan to marry me off to a perfect stranger. I'm sure I can do more good here, helping with the workload, than I can do anywhere else in the world. I believe my plan is best for all parties concerned. I can help take care of you and Pa as you grow older, and it is not unheard of for ladies to remain single in this day and age."

Mama absorbed her glare, listened to her words, and added sugar to her coffee. She stirred the cup painfully slowly. Then she set the teaspoon aside onto a saucer. "I know you received difficult news yesterday, and you must know how much your father and I sympathize with you, but we really do have your best interests at heart."

Her sisters observed the exchange with helpless but empathetic looks as they ate their breakfast. Pa glanced over the morning newspaper which Martin Everly, their butler, always supplied, his lips pressed into a firm, thin line. He exchanged a knowing look with her mother before taking a bite of his scrambled eggs.

"No, I don't think you do. If you did, you would respect my wishes." Veronica sipped her coffee, smoldering with renewed anger as someone set a plate of bacon, scrambled eggs, and a biscuit in front of her. But something told her any words she spoke would ultimately result in futility. Her parents behaved too calmly—too prepared, too united. Still, she had to try. They planned to dispense with her by marrying her off as if she were one of their racehorses.

Mama pinched off a bite of biscuit. "We do respect your wishes, but you must be sensible. Don't you see? Your younger sisters both have beaux. Once they are wed, you'll be considered an old maid, unmarriageable. Marrying Edward Beckett will resolve the issue and offer you the greatest chance of happiness."

"But I don't want to marry Edward...or anyone. I want to live here at Velvet Brooks, ensure its success, and help manage the farm." Veronica stated her case with a calm she hoped matched her mother's. "I don't want anyone to look after me when I could look after you and Pa."

"You can do that much more efficiently with your dowry in place once you are wed," Mama explained.

"But I don't love Edward. I would never marry for anything but love, and I don't care about the dowry. We don't need money to manage the farm. We only need good management of the resources we already have." Veronica carefully avoided delving into the real reason for her refusal. She had to protect her heart at all costs.

Pa folded down his issue of the *Lexington Gazette*. "I've been reluctant to disrupt your conversation with your mother, but frankly, Veronica, this has gone on long enough. As I said yesterday, our decision is final. This is all for the best in the end. You'll see."

Veronica stabbed some of her eggs with her fork. They'd come 'round to the same place in the discussion as yesterday, and neither of her parents put any stock in her reasoning. They wouldn't even speak about what she offered, other than to imply once she had her dowry, her offer of looking after them and Velvet Brooks stood on more solid ground. Did it all come down to greenbacks, then? She bit her tongue, biding her time about this aspect of the argument.

Martin handed Mama the morning's post. Her mother sifted through the letters and held up an envelope. "Oh, here is the introduction letter from your intended. Leviticus said Edward would send something before they set out on their journey, and it has arrived ahead of them." She handed the letter to Veronica with a pleasant smile, appearing unfazed by their discussion.

Veronica tossed it aside, resisting the urge to release a growl, a harrumph, any sign of her anger.

Mama prattled on, her countenance unaffected. "I'll plan a menu today for the duration of their stay. Something wonderful to welcome them into the family." As she lifted her coffee cup to her lips, she smiled again in Veronica's direction. "I expect you to treat Edward and his family with every kindness, Veronica. This is your chance to shine, to show your future husband all of your grace and poise."

"Mama, you aren't listening to a word I've said. I'm offering to take care of you, Pa, and Velvet Brooks when you grow older. The Becketts will expect me to pack my belongings and move to New York, spending all of my time and attention looking after a man I don't even love. How can I manage the farm from there?" Veronica reached for the butter dish and began slathering some on her biscuit.

"It's true. Lord knows Gladdie and I don't want to be stuck with all of the work," Delia put in as she reached for the cherry preserves.

Bravo, Delia! Veronica glanced at Delia with appreciation, noticing Gladdie nodding in agreement. In response, Pa barely glanced in her direction over the edge of the newspaper, but he turned a page and snapped it to keep the selected page firmly open.

"We have servants and employees to look after us. Love will come in time," Mama replied. "And you can visit us from New York whenever you like. They can even be long visits. You can bring your husband...and my future grandchildren. It will all be wonderful. Trust me. There is nothing more wonderful than holding your first baby in your arms."

Veronica glowered, aghast. Grandchildren? First baby? She hadn't yet agreed to the husband part, let alone New York. Or offspring. "You cannot possibly know love will come in time. Let Delia have my dowry. I'm not even sure I'm the marrying sort, let alone the mothering sort."

"I'll gladly accept her dowry if she doesn't want it," Delia interjected, glancing toward Gladdie before the two of them burst into giggles.

Lord, have mercy! Veronica leveled her narrowed gaze on her sisters. They should be helping her, not jesting about her situation. But at least the dowry would not go entirely to waste. Someone in the family might enjoy it, after all.

"I do not see the humor in your sister losing every chance for true and lasting happiness, girls." Mama shook her head and sighed, then sipped more coffee. When she set the cup down firmly, it clanked into the saucer, and she turned her attention back to Veronica. "You really have no idea how much of your future happiness is at stake, do you?" Veronica had rarely heard her mother use so firm a tone. "Give Edward a chance. He is your only hope at this point. And I simply refuse to hear one more word of this ridiculous refusal."

"Your mother is right," Pa said. "We will not continue this discussion. You will marry Edward. I have staked my word on it. You will not bring dishonor to the family."

Veronica rose, whipping her linen napkin from her lap, tossing it onto her barely touched plate. She stomped her foot, shouting, "No, I will not marry Edward!"

She marched from the dining room into the hall and through the front door, slamming it. At least they might hear the door, since they refused to listen to a word she said. Two slammed doors in less than twenty-four hours. Tears, yelling, arguments…but what choice did they leave her with? All the things she didn't like, truth be told, and moments she'd rather forget.

She headed for the horse barn, unable to face the four walls of her bedroom for another day, chiding herself for failing to make them respect her wishes. She must stick to her guns, no matter how much she despised the slamming of doors, shouting, and stomping. Her parents brought it on themselves, attempting to control her life with their meddling and matchmaking, turning all she held dear upside down.

They cited her future happiness and financial security, but what did they know about what made her happy? Clearly, they didn't understand, but when she refused Edward Beckett, the light of day would dawn.

Entering the barn, she turned away offers of help to saddle Gunpowder Fury from the Velvet Brooks groom, Carter Mitchell. "Thank you, Carter. I'll saddle him myself today."

"Yes, Miss Lyndon." He returned to a stool, wrapping the legs of Calamity June, one of their finest mares.

She had often helped Carter wrap the legs of any horses who exhibited signs of having tender muscles. Who would help him and their other employees keep up with all of the responsibilities at Velvet Brooks if her parents married her off to Edward Beckett?

Veronica spread a blanket over her favorite stallion. She hefted the saddle next. The remedy she sought during times of crisis usually included a good ride to soothe her soul and clear her head. Then she could figure out a plan to avoid Edward during his visit and convince her parents of their erroneous decision.

Yes, riding Gunpowder Fury—the remedy she needed for now. Tightening the saddle strip around his girth, she acknowledged one small glimmer of hope. Maybe Edward didn't want to marry her any more than she wanted to marry him.

After a long ride, she threw herself into various tasks around the horse barn. The staff didn't mind, accustomed as they were to her presence. She cleaned and polished every saddle Velvet Brooks owned. She mucked stalls, helped Carter wrap legs, turned horses out to pasture, and swept the barn's enormous floor. All the while, she formulated a plan to make Edward dislike her.

The next morning, after Pa left to fetch their guests from town, Veronica stuck to her usual routine, exercising several horses. Father's carriage returned from the Lexington hotel first, bringing a gentleman of about the same age as Pa. Leviticus Beckett, Edward's father, she presumed. Only much older than she remembered. From astride Gunpowder Fury on the eastern side of the property, Veronica simmered, watching them go inside the house together. But where were the Beckett sons?

Maybe they'd had a change in plans. Nonetheless, Mama would expect her to greet Mr. Beckett, appear on time for tea in the sitting room, and join them after for the luncheon. She planned to arrive as tardily as possible. She proceeded to finish another hard run on her horse, but not long into the ride, two figures in a fancy motor carriage took a wild, sharp turn onto the lane.

So the Beckett brothers had decided to make an appearance. Worst of all, in one of those noisy modern contraptions! She'd show them. She leaned farther over the mane of her horse. "Yaw!"

CHAPTER TWO

A horse gallops with his lungs, perseveres with his heart, and wins
with his character.
—Frederico Tesio

Edward James Beckett kept his hands firmly on the wheel of the two-seater Oldsmobile, breathing in the fresh country air as he and his younger brother, Rupert, left the growing city of Lexington, Kentucky, farther behind. The pastoral scenery along the winding dirt roads offered a refreshing change from the pace of New York and the busy streets of Manhattan. As the splendor of magnificent horse farms unfolded on their right and left, he could see why many called this the horse capital of the world.

If only he could enjoy the drive. Unfortunately, going along with this madness his father had arranged—expecting him to marry a perfect stranger—prevented him from reveling in any of it. The sky might look clear and as blue as the chicory wildflowers blooming along the sides of the road in clumps—not a cloud in sight, but Edward imagined dark clouds looming over his future.

Rupert had enticed him into renting the Runabout from the small selection next door to the Lexington livery at the motor carriage rental. It was the twentieth century, after all. He was a city boy. And he loved modern technology. What better way to express himself than by arriving in a shiny new red motor carriage? Plus, it might annoy his father who had yet to fully embrace the new contraptions.

After a few miles, Edward overcame the challenges of navigating the steering wheel while simultaneously operating the foot pedals. He liked driving the sleek contraption. His friend, Jack Curzon, had recently acquired a similar model. He and Jack had driven through some of New York's bustling streets in the machine, laughing as they gadded about to join other friends from their set at the rooftop terrace gardens at the Waldorf Astoria, frequenting one of their favorite tea parlors, and sometimes enjoying a drive through Central Park. Jack had even permitted Edward to get behind the wheel of his new mode of transportation once.

The whole family would soon need to curtail these sorts of outings if Edward didn't follow his father's instructions. Nonetheless, the experience had given him the confidence he needed for his present excursion. Except the conveyance began to sputter, something Jack's model had not done. Then it began to backfire, making all sorts of popping noises.

"What's going on?" Rupert's eyes widened while Edward debated about going faster or slower as his brother leaned forward, gripping the dashboard. "Maybe you should give the engine more fuel."

He didn't need advice from his spoiled younger brother. "You always think you know the answers to everything. Would you for once in your life just sit back and trust me to figure things out?"

He had already begun to speed up before Rupert had

opened his mouth. The automobile stopped sputtering and making popping noises.

"Whoa! What's your problem? I'm just trying to help." Rupert held his hands up.

His little brother, who wasn't so little anymore at twenty-one and now a Harvard student, crossed his arms over his chest and sat back in his seat, glowering. He had no idea of the price Edward would pay if he managed to carry out their father's plan, the enormous sacrifice he was about to make to ensure Rupert and their sisters had a good start in life. It didn't help any that his brother would always remain his father's favorite. The knowledge only made Edward work harder to please Leviticus Beckett.

Regretting his outburst, he sighed. "I'm sorry. That was uncalled for. I have a lot on my mind."

"Like what? You're going to see one of the most beautiful horse farms in the world, and you'll meet the girl of your dreams, Ver-on-i-ca." Rupert grinned.

Edward, in no mood for his shenanigans, shook his head. He clamped his mouth shut. The way his brother teased him, dragging out each syllable of her name, all because he'd caught Edward writing her name on a short letter he'd penned the morning of their departure from New York... "You really don't understand, do you?" He spat out the question. Hadn't Rupert picked up on any of his predicament during the long train ride?

"No. Why don't you just tell me?"

"We're in trouble, Rupert. Serious trouble." Edward kept both hands clenched on the steering wheel as they rounded a sharp curve in the road. Why did Kentucky have a bend on every other mile?

"What kind of trouble?"

"I don't know all the particulars, only that Father lost some money in a short sale that backfired. A lot of money."

"How *much* money?"

"I don't know exactly. Only that it's a large sum and it's all hush-hush so he doesn't lose his status as senior partner at Beckett, Reed & Johnston. I'm trying to figure out what's going on, but in the meantime, he's forcing me into an arranged marriage with Miss Veronica Lyndon so he can use her dowry to save the family coffers."

Rupert let out a whistle. "Wow! That is bad. I'd be steaming."

"Yes, I am steaming." Marrying a girl he hardly knew. Handing over most of her dowry to his father. Spending his future—week in and week out—in an investment office. Each mile they covered brought him closer to the dreaded reality of his situation.

He couldn't escape the office drudgery to do what he loved most of the time, but was there a way to escape a union with Miss Veronica Lyndon? He didn't know anything about the debutante except that her father bred, trained, and raced horses. She and her two younger sisters descended from Spencers and Lyndons, both of Kentucky. But these facts didn't help him see a way out.

Edward continued his rant. "And no, before you ask, there is nothing I can do except go along with Father's plan. He's threatened to cut me off if I don't comply."

"Cut you off? That is serious." At least Rupert sounded sympathetic.

"You can't speak of this to anyone, especially not any of the Lyndons. Mother doesn't know, and neither do our sisters. Father doesn't want us to worry them. He didn't want me to worry you either."

"Mum's the word. Cross my heart." Rupert made the sign of a cross over his heart. "We know Henrietta and Sophie can't keep a secret, but you can count on me."

"I could really use your support while we're here in Kentucky," Edward confessed. Perhaps after meeting Miss

Lyndon, a practical way to wrangle his way out of marrying her while still rescuing the family's finances would present itself. *Wrangle.* A term Miss Lyndon would surely know more about than himself.

He hadn't met her except once. Had he been sixteen? Seventeen?

"I meant what I said about not telling anyone, Rupert. If you let this out of your mouth to any of the Lyndon sisters or even one of the farmhands, Veronica will likely find out and bail." Edward gave his brother a stern glance. "Then you'll have to leave Harvard and your veterinary studies behind."

"I promise. I won't say a word. But isn't there someone you like well enough to marry in New York with a bigger dowry than this Kentucky debutante?"

He shook his head. "No, not anyone I'd want to marry. Besides, there are rumors about Father's financial troubles. Mother somehow caught wind of them too. Father assured her they weren't true. So even if I knew someone in New York society I'd consider marrying, chances are, they've heard the rumors as well. You know how fast gossip travels."

"Aha! So that's why Father brought us to Kentucky." Rupert gave him a sympathetic glance. "Why didn't you tell me when I first came home from my term at Harvard or on the train the next day?"

"Don't you remember? You were already out on a date with Mirabel by the time I arrived. And no, I didn't tell Mother about you and Mirabel." Edward raised his brow as he shot a look toward his brother. "After dinner, I went straight to my studio to finish a painting. Then I went to bed. We all awoke at five o'clock in the morning to catch the train. Father spent most of the journey waiting until you wandered off to the dining car to lecture me about my duty to the family."

"I had no idea. He said we were going to the horse races and visiting his old friend, Joseph Lyndon. Just how bad can this financial crisis be, anyhow? Father has lots of other stocks and investments. Can't he sell something?"

"As I told you before, he won't say exactly what his losses are, but I'm fairly certain he's trying to sell two of our tenement buildings to stave off creditors and keep our sisters in the latest fashions. I've never seen him act like this before. I'm accustomed to his lectures about us working at Beckett & Reed a few days each week every summer, but this is much worse. He's terrified Mother will find out. I guess he had a difficult time convincing her to consider this match with Veronica."

"Why?"

Edward shrugged. "Father said she believes it's social suicide to marry someone from Kentucky. He couldn't tell her he needed the dowry, and you know how adamant she feels about the ills of gambling, despite the fact Father enjoys the races. But in view of the rumors circulating around Manhattan, she reluctantly agreed with his plan."

"Can't you get out of it? What if Miss Veronica Lyndon doesn't want to marry you?"

He tapped the steering wheel. "I've tried to think of a way out, but according to Father, there is no other way. Mother concluded that me marrying someone from Kentucky is better than me not marrying anyone at all."

Rupert snorted. "Well, you are getting old. Twenty-eight. You're almost a confirmed bachelor."

"Thanks, Rupe. That certainly bolsters my confidence." Edward rolled his eyes.

"Speaking of Mother, when we had tea right after I got home, she mentioned she wants you to marry that daughter of her friend in New York, Amelia Hartford. I thought she'd given up on that idea a few years ago. She didn't mention Veronica."

"I think she's waiting to see how this visit will turn out. In any case, I'm not the slightest bit interested in Amelia Hartford." Edward shuddered at the idea of marrying the uppity debutante.

"What do you remember about Miss Veronica Lyndon?" Rupert gulped. "Gosh, I hope she's not...ugly."

While his brother roiled over with laughter, Edward shook his head and waited for the annoying display to subside. "Are you quite finished? She's not ugly. She can't be ugly. I've prayed she won't be ugly."

"That worried about it, eh?" Rupert slugged him in the arm good-naturedly.

He'd asked himself these same questions a hundred times since finding out about his father's predicament and proposed solution. What *did* he remember about Veronica? She'd been a pretty, shy, almost-teenager the last time he'd encountered her. Twelve or thirteen at the most. His father had mentioned she was now twenty-three.

He hit another bump in the road. Ack! They bounced up in their seats, jarring his already frayed nerves. Normally, he had nerves of steel, but the prospect of meeting Miss Lyndon had unraveled him. Dread and unanswered questions plagued him. Would she like him? Would she agree to the arrangement? What should he say when he greeted her?

Rupert changed the subject, chatting on about his hope of meeting an equine veterinarian during their visit to Kentucky, but Edward barely heard a word. He tried to ignore the fact he didn't possess the same anticipation about meeting Miss Lyndon. At least Rupert had stopped talking about his eagerness to attend the Phoenix Stakes at the Lexington Association Racetrack and his disappointment over the fact they had missed an opportunity to attend the Kentucky Derby at Churchill Downs in April. Edward had no desire to talk about horses, racing, or spending money they didn't have on gambling.

Rupert paused from explaining some technique concerning

the birthing of foals to glance down at the note he held. Their father had gone on ahead from the hotel with Joseph Lyndon, leaving his sons to follow the directions he'd penned about how to reach the Lyndons' horse farm, Velvet Brooks.

"We're supposed to veer left at the fork in the road after the big red barn coming up on the right. You might want to slow, or we'll miss it." Rupert folded the note and relaxed.

"All right. Hang on." Edward eased up on the pedal and then sped up around the edge of another bend in the dirt road while Rupert clung to the edge of his seat.

"How long on this road?" He ought to turn around and head for the Appalachian Mountains. He knew next to nothing about farming or horses, but that didn't mean Miss Lyndon might not share some of his interests. Would she like automobiles? Would she want a ride in his rented Runabout? Who was he kidding? The daughter of a horse farmer—she'd want to talk horses.

Rupert read more of the note. "This is Cornflower Road. Velvet Brooks Farm and your lady love should be located just up ahead on the left, about a mile or so." He reached across the back of the seat and patted Edward on the shoulder, chuckling. "All I can say is, better you than me, brother. I intend to remain a bachelor for as long as possible. And if I do marry, only for love."

"Thanks. That makes it so much easier, Rupe." Edward fought down a bit of resentment at the idea of his brother being able to marry for love when he couldn't.

"You're welcome."

Edward didn't dare glance at his brother, but he knew Rupert wore a smirk or an amused grin. "I've a mind to pull over and box your ears."

"That'll make a good impression, you showing up to meet your future bride with a black eye."

"You would do well to remember I learned a thing or two at

the military academy, but since I see the sign to Velvet Brooks up ahead, I'm going to let that last remark pass. But just because Father dotes on you, don't think you can get away with tweaking my nose, little brother." It briefly crossed his mind to push Rupert out of the Runabout and leave him behind, if only to teach him a good lesson.

In truth, he needed his brother by his side, today of all days. Who else would entertain Miss Lyndon's sisters while he attempted to get to know her?

"It's not my fault I'm more likeable than you."

Edward's jaws clenched. "Surely, you jest."

"Truth is truth, brother."

Edward reached out to slug him while keeping one hand on the wheel. When Rupert ducked, Edward missed slugging him by an inch, but he had to keep his eyes on the road. The farm came into view, stealing his breath away for a second. If he didn't regret and despise the situation so much, he could see himself painting the lush green meadows.

"Hey!" Rupe pointed to the lane lined with perfectly symmetrical sugar maples. "Watch where you're going. There's the drive."

Edward tossed his brother an evil grin as he swerved into the lane leading to a whitewashed, two-story house, making sure Rupert had to hang on if he wanted to remain in the Runabout. "Keep it up, little brother. You're one swerve away from eating dirt."

Rupert clung to the dashboard and his seat. "Fine. Fine, you win! Just get us there in one piece, would you? Can we call a truce, and can you drop the 'little brother' remarks?"

Had Rupert finally finished heckling him? "Fine. Since we're nearly there."

Movement on his left caught Edward's attention as they progressed up the drive.

A woman riding a chestnut stallion raced toward the main

house, cutting across the lawn at a remarkable speed, her white scarf trailing behind her hat in the wind. A blaze of purple skirts and white petticoats, she leaned low, stretching across the horse's mane with the expertise one might expect of a trained jockey. She didn't ride sidesaddle, defying the convention and the dictates of society as she flew along over lush bluegrass astride a glorious stallion.

Rupert sat up straighter in his seat. "See if this machine can beat her horse to the house."

"I'm guessing it can." Edward shrugged, then pressed the pedal to the floor. "Why not?" He hadn't seen anyone in front of the house to lecture them—or her.

He cast his gaze on the lady racing across Velvet Brook Farms at an alarming speed while he pushed the Oldsmobile to its maximum capacity. He hadn't seen a horse run so fast. The fellow they'd rented the conveyance from had warned him the auto could only reach up to twenty miles per hour, and when they sped up, the dark-haired beauty on the horse had to be riding nearly double their speed.

Within seconds, she—whoever she was—and her stallion, surpassed them, reaching the front porch before the automobile finished sputtering along to the end of the lane.

Rupert let out a low whistle. "I guess technology has a way to go. She's quite a rider, and that horse!"

Edward turned the automobile to their right and parked beside the terrace where the lady, still astride, offered her horse the reward of patting and sweet words. Before he had a chance to respond to his brother's remark, the machine backfired.

The horse reared up and neighed. Edward, fumbling to turn the engine off, watched in horror as the woman struggled to keep her seat. What had he done?

CHAPTER THREE

A difference of opinion is what makes horse racing and missionaries.
—Will Rogers

Veronica grasped the saddle horn and reins with all her might. She leaned forward, using every bit of her expertise to hold onto her seat as Gunpowder Fury neighed and reared up, protesting the loud popping noises and rumbling emitting from the modern mode of transportation parked directly behind them. Of all the nerve...but she didn't have time to consider the actions of the men now. She had to hang on for dear life or land in the dirt, possibly be trampled...

"Whoa, boy! Whoa!" She managed to find her tongue as Fury's front legs danced in the air. The stallion brought his hooves down hard, but what sounded like one last backfire released from the horseless carriage.

She bounced in the saddle as her mount skittered forward, neighing, only to rear up a second time.

"Down boy, down!" Veronica wrapped both reins around her wrists and clung to the horn of the saddle. "Whoa! Steady, boy. Down!"

This time, Grandfather—the stable nickname they'd given Gunpowder Fury—brought his front legs down, then he scampered sideways. Gunpowder Fury was by no means a grandfather, but the nickname suited their need for humor in the barn. Especially given the horse's tendency to act like a born champion.

The driver behind Veronica finally turned the engine off.

"About time," she muttered, rolling her eyes. City boys! She patted the horse, exhaling in relief. "Good boy, good boy." Veronica scrambled down, careful to maintain a firm hold on the reins until Carter Mitchell reached their side.

"Are you all right, Miss Lyndon?" Out of breath from racing toward the circular drive, he began patting Grandfather, too, speaking soothing words from the other side of the horse.

Veronica caught sight of their visitors stepping out of their conveyance. "I'm fine, Carter. Thank you." She tossed their guests a hard glare. "He's terrified and breathing pretty hard."

"I'll be sure Grandfather gets some extra loving care," Carter assured her as she handed the reins over, satisfied her favorite horse wouldn't run away.

She took a calming breath and turned to meet their unwelcome guests.

~

*E*dward reached the lady rider. He tried not to stammer and stumble over his apology. "I'm so sorry. We didn't mean to cause you or the horse any distress. Are you all right, M-Miss Lyndon?" He held his hat in his hands, turning it 'round and 'round. He'd certainly mucked up his chances for a good first impression. *Mucked.* Another word Veronica Lyndon should know more about than him.

She spun around to face him, hands on slender hips. He

didn't dare ask which Miss Lyndon stood before him, but if she was Veronica, or if Veronica resembled her, instant relief concerning her looks washed over him. But what a start, meeting her like this. She'd certainly defied odds and managed to hold onto her seat in the saddle like an expert horsewoman. Not only could she race well, but she could maintain control under duress.

"Rule number one on a horse farm. Don't frighten the horses and endanger their riders with reckless behavior in your modern contraptions."

Miss Lyndon offered no greeting—to be expected after what his actions had caused. She spoke with fierce disapproval in her tone, one booted foot tapping. Fire behind those narrowed brown eyes. Clearly, this was someone who would not put up with one bit of nonsense.

A breeze caused the long white scarf dangling from her hat to flutter around her fashionable riding habit. Rosy cheekbones, an adorably turned-up nose, and cherry-red lips competed for Edward's attention.

As if transported to some other realm for the briefest of moments, he couldn't think of a single reply. He had no excuse for his actions. What had he been thinking, racing his rented Runabout up the Lyndon drive, then parking behind her horse?

She sure was mad at him. Maybe she even hated him right now, but what a beauty!

"It's all my fault." Rupert came around the motor carriage and stopped at Edward's side. "I pressed him into racing against your stallion to see if the Runabout could beat him to the house. I didn't think it would backfire...and scare the horse."

Edward glanced at his brother, stunned that he tried to take the blame. But Rupert had forgotten to remove his hat. Edward swiped the tweed cap from his brother's head and handed it to him. In the presence of a lady, they'd done enough to forget their manners. But at least Rupe had tried to salvage some of Edward's dignity and his chance to marry into the Lyndon family. Maybe, if he was lucky, this wasn't Veronica Lyndon.

Before he could inquire, she turned on her heel, disappearing inside the house with a flurry of skirts. The door closed, but at least it didn't slam or draw further attention. They'd done enough to highlight their ignorance of horse farms. If Father had noticed the backfiring or the agitated horse, Edward would never hear the end of it.

Leading the disgruntled stallion toward the row of barns, with the horse's tail flicking as if to shed more disdain upon them, the groom left them standing there awkwardly. Edward sucked in a deep breath and drew himself up taller. If the lady rider had indeed been Miss Veronica Lyndon, he certainly had a long road ahead to win her affection. She did not look one bit happy—not about the manner of his arrival, or his presence.

Brows raised, Rupert settled his cap back on. "You're in so much trouble."

"Thanks, Rupe."

He chuckled, shaking his head. "She is never going to marry you."

"If that was even her..." Edward raked a hand through his hair.

"You have a point there. Could've been a sister."

"That's not much better. A sister will inform Veronica what idiots we are."

"Come along, Princeton. Don't let her intimidate you. You've much more to offer than first meets the eye." Rupert dug an elbow into Edward's side.

"All right, Harvard. Let's do better." Edward mustered his courage, turning his attention for the first time to the house.

Black shutters on the windows contrasted nicely against the white siding. Plenty of chimneys for a modest home, indicating a spacious and comfortable size and number of rooms, but mainly, he noticed the four grand columns spread across the front of the covered terrace-style veranda.

To his far right, where the groom had wandered off with the horse, a row consisting of several barns and four-board fences hemmed in the property. In the distance, he spotted several thoroughbreds grazing in the meadows…and a racetrack. The Lyndons must be fairly loaded to own their own racecourse. It all reminded him of portraits he'd seen in museums of other picturesque horse-farming landscapes.

But now they had to go inside. And try to salvage the mess he'd made. Had he just destroyed any possibility of marriage and ruined his entire family's future?

Edward drew in a deep breath as he and his brother crossed the front porch, reaching the main doors of the house. He paused, straightening his jacket, pulling his vest down a notch, and tugging on his tie. Before they could knock, the door swung open to reveal a butler.

"Edward and Rupert Beckett?" the employee asked. They nodded. "Mr. and Mrs. Lyndon and your father are expecting you. Right this way, gentlemen."

Edward's throat began to constrict. Soon, someone would introduce him to his future bride. Maybe Mrs. Lyndon would offer a cup of tea to wash away how dry his mouth felt at the prospect. Rupe followed him past a staircase and through an arch beyond it. They turned right before reaching the rear of the house, where a heart-shaped piano stood.

Glancing ahead through the windows, Edward could see a small flower and shrub garden beyond a covered porch. The charming country farmhouse held an appeal their posh New York townhouse didn't offer. The servant opened a set of double doors on their right to reveal a family sitting room. Relief washed over Edward at finding his father gathered with the Lyndons…far from the front of the house. Maybe they hadn't heard his automobile backfire or the horse neighing in distress.

"Edward and Rupert Beckett have arrived," the butler announced before stepping aside to grant them entrance.

Edward glanced around at the faces seated in the pleasant room as Joseph Lyndon stood to welcome them with a firm handshake. Where had the fiery southern belle gone? Did he detect a pang of disappointment at not finding her there? He had a feeling they had already encountered Miss Veronica Lyndon, but time would soon tell.

They'd met Joseph Lyndon at the train station, and Edward had instantly liked the man, vaguely recalling him from their first meeting long ago. He returned a greeting from Mrs. Lyndon before nodding to his father and sitting down on the sofa with Rupe. Two young ladies who resembled the one he'd met so disastrously outside occupied chairs across the room.

"I see you've finally made it," Father said without rising from his chair. "I was beginning to think you were lost."

How should he reply to that frosty tone? Should he apologize for arriving later than his father? Did the stiff greeting infer he should not have taken time to rent the Runabout? Or had his father heard about the incident outside, after all? "No, not lost, just enjoying the countryside, Father."

"Would you like sugar in your tea, Edward and Rupert?" Mrs. Lyndon asked, leaning toward a silver tea service on a table before her.

"Yes, please and thank you. We both take sugar in our tea, ma'am." Edward nodded toward an older version of the three brunette ladies he'd seen thus far on the property.

"Call me Eleanor, boys," Mrs. Lyndon said as she prepared their tea.

"Your directions were spot on, Father." Rupert shot a glance at their father on their left, breaking the ice with him, even earning a smile. "Lots of fresh country air. We passed a few other horse farms too."

"Refreshing change of pace from city life." Edward accepted

a cup of tea Mrs. Lyndon had poured, delivered to him by way of Mr. Lyndon on his right. He passed it on to Rupert as another came for himself.

"Your father said you rented one of those new horseless carriages," one of the ladies on the sofa said, causing Edward to freeze. She continued. "Was it a Runabout model? Delia and I would love a ride in it sometime."

Edward sighed inwardly with relief as he took in the face of the youngest-looking Lyndon sister. She practically held her breath with excitement evident in her eyes as she glanced from Edward to Rupert, awaiting a reply.

Before he could answer, her mother spoke up. "These are our two youngest daughters—Delaney, our middle daughter, and Gladys, our youngest, but please call them Delia and Gladdie as we do. After all, we're about to become family. Veronica will be here shortly. I'm not sure what has delayed her..." Mrs. Lyndon's smile fell flat as she glanced toward the double doors to the room.

So Veronica *had* been the one on the horse. Ignoring the way that realization hollowed out his stomach, he offered Mrs. Lyndon a forgiving smile before he nodded toward the young ladies. "Yes, it was a Runabout, and we'd be delighted to take you out for a spin."

"Veronica has probably been out riding. You know how she loves Gunpowder Fury," Gladdie said before sipping her tea, glancing toward her mother. Then she directed her gaze to Edward. "And thank you. I'm sure we'd enjoy a spin in your automobile."

Her sister nodded, looking shy and demure as she stared at the floor.

"Gunpowder Fury?" Rupert repeated, leaning forward. "That's an unusual name."

"Our newest champion stallion," Joseph Lyndon explained. "Or so we hope. He's a descendant of Colonel Blaze."

Edward perked up at the topic. Anything to avoid a discussion of what had happened earlier in front of their house. Why hadn't he accepted Joseph Lyndon's offer to ride from the Phoenix Hotel to the horse farm in his carriage? "I assume this Colonel Blaze was a noteworthy stallion. Do tell us more." Perhaps he could at least give Miss Veronica's father a decent impression of his potential as a son-in-law.

"Well, since you ask...Colonel Blaze won the Kentucky Derby and the Belmont Stakes during my father's days here at the farm. Though my father has retired to live in town now, he visits frequently. Anyway, Gunpowder Fury is a grandson of Colonel Blaze, sired by Blaze of Glory."

"His stable name was Glory," Mrs. Lyndon informed them.

Was this the same horse his Runabout had frightened? Great. Just great. He could now accept responsibility for traumatizing their next champion horse.

"Glory won everywhere *except* the Derby in his prime," Gladdie added.

"I can imagine how exciting it would be to watch one of your horses win at such a prestigious track as Pimlico or Churchill Downs." Hopefully, Edward's reply demonstrated the right amount of enthusiasm.

Rupert flashed his charming grin. "Yes, Edward and I are looking forward to the Phoenix Stakes Race."

"We are too. Every race feels like the first one I've ever watched. I get caught up in the excitement and forget everything else, but I will never forget when Colonel Blaze crossed the Derby finish line to victory." Mr. Lyndon let out a sigh. "Those moments are rare and thrilling."

"You have a fine horse farm with a stunning racing record, Joseph. I look forward to our tour and meeting some of your horses after our luncheon. And I, too, am excited to attend the Lexington race." Turning to his sons, Father added, "In addition to training his own horses for thoroughbred racing, Mr.

Lyndon also trains horses for several local horse farms. Isn't that right, old friend? I always knew you'd be successful, even back in our university days."

The double doors opened, and the beautiful lady Edward had nearly caused to fall from her stallion breezed into the room. He held his breath as she settled into a seat across from him between her sisters and the conversation continued. She didn't even glance in his direction—surely, a sign of how much she disliked him at this point.

～

*V*eronica's late arrival constituted another act of defiance. She smoothed her skirts, determined to show Edward how little he mattered to her by not looking in his direction. She had changed into a suitable day dress in a shade of pale yellow, and Grace had freshened her updo with additional hairpins, but she had already endured a lecture from the faithful housekeeper and didn't need any disappointed glances from her mother. That meant she must also avoid the gazes of her parents, seated to her left in two armchairs near the fireplace where Mother poured her a cup of tea.

When Veronica tried glancing at her sisters, Gladdie cleared her throat as if to say, *it's about time you arrived.* That left precious few places to look.

"Thank you, yes," her father was saying to Mr. Beckett, "we do train a number of horses for some well-known farms in the area, but I always knew you'd be a Wall Street success from the first time I met you, Levi. There's just one thing I've never understood, though. Why did you leave Harvard to attend Cornell?"

"That's easy to answer," Mr. Beckett replied as Delia passed a cup of tea to Veronica. Too bad she hadn't sat beside Edward where she could startle him by spilling it all over him, the way he'd frightened her stallion. "Well, you know I wanted to be in banking and stocks."

Veronica stiffened. Banking. Just like Henry Sullivan, who'd broken her heart. The Sullivans owned Sullivans Savings & Loan, one of the few banks in town. Bankers could not be trusted.

Mr. Beckett continued. "Of course, Cornell opened in Ithaca in 1868, where I had been offered an entry-level, part-time job writing down the stock market prices on a chalkboard for a small trading company. *And* they were the only university to allow us to choose our own course of study. I wanted to study banking law, and Father wanted me to earn my own way. So off I went to Cornell."

Father's face lit up. "I'm so thankful we met there. You know I had gone as far as I could in my studies at Kentucky University and how my parents said it wasn't safe to travel through the whole blasted war. I couldn't wait to get out of Kentucky."

Mr. Beckett grinned. "I remember looking out the windows during lectures and thinking how lucky you were to spend so much time in the university stables instead of being stuck inside the classrooms with the rest of us."

"I had my fair share of lectures to listen to and medical books to study."

As the elder gentlemen monopolized the conversation, Veronica couldn't help but steal a few glances at Leviticus Beckett's two sons. Unfortunately for her plan to avoid a betrothal, they were both quite good-looking. She assumed the one with dark-brown hair and blue eyes must be Edward Beckett, the one they intended her to marry. The younger one who looked like a replica of Edward must be Rupert. Hadn't Pa said Mr. Beckett called him *Rupe* in his letters?

In any case, the three Becketts appeared fashionably dressed in their light-colored spring suits. Yet another reason she decried the match—they were no more than upper-class snobs trying to impress her. Didn't her parents see through their facade?

"A week after I arrived home in South Carolina with my degree, my Gloria and I were wed. A year after our wedding, Edward was born, the first of our four children." Mr. Beckett turned to gaze at his sons with pride, but his florid color and stiff posture revealed an unexpected tension. Likely from the stress of city life and his high-powered business dealings. The way he looked down at his tea and pressed his lips into a firm line, Veronica had the sense he had something more on his mind than college memories and family history.

Edward shifted in his seat and exchanged a glance with his brother. A concerned glance? Was their father unwell?

Basking in the nostalgia of the reunion, Father seemed impervious to anything amiss. "And I came home to Velvet Brooks and promptly married Eleanor at the end of our first summer, one of the greatest decisions I've ever made in my lifetime. Three years later in May, our darling Veronica was born, right here in this house." Father smiled at her.

Martin stepped into the room, sparing Veronica from becoming the subject of conversation. "Luncheon is served."

Could she have some sort of coughing fit and retreat to her room? Fainting wouldn't work since she'd never fainted before. And if she did manage to faint, no one carried smelling salts these days, so she could potentially lie there for an embarrassing amount of time, unrevived. Dread filled her, but she couldn't think of a single reasonable excuse to skip the meal.

"Thank you, Martin," Mother replied, rising. "Let's adjourn to the dining room where we can continue our conversation. I'd love to hear more about your train journey from New York. Was it a pleasant one, I hope?"

Veronica breathed a sigh of relief as everyone else stood. Thankfully, no one had drawn any undue attention in her direction or attempted to awkwardly introduce her and Edward to one another.

"A fine journey, Mrs. Lyndon. Beautiful mountain views and countryside." Edward responded on behalf of his family as they all began to move toward the hall.

"I'm so pleased to hear it. Veronica, let me introduce you to Edward," Mama insisted, raising her voice just enough and dashing Veronica's thoughts of escaping through the front door to the barn.

Drat! She wanted to pretend she hadn't heard, but since everyone else filed out of the sitting room ahead of them, Veronica found herself trapped. Now she had to acknowledge him.

She turned to him with a forced upturn of her lips. "Yes, I believe you met me and my horse at the veranda."

"The pleasure was entirely mine. A lady of unrivaled beauty astride a fine stallion." Edward returned a genuine smile.

Did she detect a hint of wonder in his eyes? He bowed his head and then stood up taller. His formal, stiff greeting reminded her of an officer doing his duty.

Perhaps he, too, felt the pressure of family bearing down. Perhaps he tried to find the honor in fulfilling it, while she found no pleasure in it at all. The way he clamped his lips together and waited for her mother to step around them made it clear that he wished to avoid discussion of their first encounter.

Veronica hurried away, slipping out into the hall and ahead of him to gather her composure before facing the luncheon. She felt like a heel. Her tardy entrance and accusing manner had fallen barely short of insulting.

He, on the other hand, had chosen not to point out to her mother that Veronica had lacked any display of hospitality. She couldn't speak to that bit he'd said about unrivaled beauty. Beauty was too subjective. It remained in the eye of one's beholder. But grace was the one thing she had definitely not shown him or his brother. Yet he praised her in front of her mother.

No matter how chivalrously he'd behaved during their introduction with Mama hovering nearby, she had to find better ways to make him dislike her. It simply could not be helped.

CHAPTER FOUR

You can lead a horse to water, but you can't make it drink.
—Saying about horses

Veronica caught up to Gladdie in the hall, terrified Edward would offer his arm as her escort to the luncheon if she wasted any time in reaching the dining room. However, upon arriving, she realized Mother had outsmarted everyone. Not only had she outdone herself with using their finest china, silver, crystal goblets, and the best linens, she had also instructed Martin and Grace to use place cards. Why hadn't Veronica seen that coming? She hadn't expected Mama to use assigned seating, but when Edward found his name on the card directly across from hers, she tried not to groan.

Mama took the seat on her right, Delia the one on her left, and the handsome older Beckett son took his place between his father and brother on the other side of the table. Gladdie, sitting down at the end of the table near Rupert, snickered like the horses in their stables at Veronica's predicament. Seated across from Rupert, Delia elbowed Veronica, showing no sympathy whatsoever. Her sisters would enjoy entertaining

Rupert while Veronica struggled through making conversation with Edward and their parents.

Pa took his seat at the head of the table with Mr. Beckett on his right and Mama on his left. Veronica sank into her seat and kept her eyes planted on the first course, a bowl of steaming beef consommé. Why did she feel like a lamb to the slaughter, and seated close enough for Mama to clutch her if she tried to escape? Mama could also nudge her if she made any wrong moves.

Pa said a prayer, but Veronica could hardly focus on it. As the meal began, she avoided making eye contact with Edward or participating in the small talk her parents exchanged with Mr. Beckett. Why make Edward feel warm and welcome?

She needed a strategy to survive this elegant luncheon designed to impress their guests. What else could she do except show him she could not possibly be a suitable match? If Leviticus Beckett, and especially Edward, thought she had no training befitting a bride for an eligible bachelor from Manhattan, perhaps they would find some excuse to abandon the visit and return home.

The last to taste her soup, she lifted the spoon to her lips and tested her strategy with a long slurp. She did not have to look at her mother to know Eleanor Lyndon wore a face aghast. Veronica repeated the procedure. Dip spoon, lift, slurp. Predictably, Mama patted Veronica's skirt under the table.

Veronica cast a wide-eyed glance at her. "Did you need something, Mama?"

"Why, no, my dear. I wouldn't dream of interrupting your enjoyment of the first course."

She disregarded Mama's reply and sucked in more of the soup, creating another long slurp, suppressing a giggle at the looks exchanged all around.

Mr. Beckett peered at Veronica. "The soup is so delicious. I can see why she likes it."

"It does have good flavor," Pa agreed, but his brows furrowed.

Mr. Beckett returned his attention to the broth, seemingly unfazed by her table manners. But Veronica considered it a win. She'd garnered his attention. Her sisters looked on in horror at first, but they soon began to snicker and joined her in making the slurping noises. Even though her sisters doubtless only slurped to spare themselves from boredom and entertain Rupert, who broke into a wide grin, Veronica reveled in the sense of solidarity in protest of the idea of any of them forced to endure an arranged marriage. If she could figure out a few more stunts as effective as slurping, perhaps the Becketts would leave on the very next train bound east. Mama shook her head and held a linen napkin to her forehead.

Pa exchanged looks with Mama and gave her a subtle wave of his hand, no doubt meant to discourage her from reprimands.

Edward shifted in his seat, and Veronica's eyes briefly met his, but he locked his gaze on the bowl of consommé before him and did not join in the slurping—unlike his brother. Maybe he feared he could prevail, seated beside his father, or maybe he considered himself above such ill manners. Meanwhile, Mr. Beckett and her father did an admirable job of discussing the weather.

Her back stiff as a ramrod, Mama beckoned Martin and Grace to her side and leaned toward them. "You may serve the next course, and please begin with my daughters."

Martin and Grace nodded and began the rescue for Mama's attempt at a New York high society luncheon. Veronica didn't dare look at Grace or her mother as Grace removed her remaining soup. The faithful servant dutifully replaced the bowl with a plated salad of spring greens and hard-boiled eggs lightly drizzled with poppy seed dressing.

Veronica frowned. Their family typically ate a lunch of cold fried chicken or ham-and-biscuit sandwiches with the farm's employees gathered around two long picnic tables under the shade of several oak trees behind the kitchen. Willamena, their cook, would serve most of the meal on one or two plates. The second plate might contain a slice of apple or cherry pie.

Mama had read in the *Lexington Gazette* about luncheons of multiple courses of smaller quantities of lighter fare served at restaurants like those in the Waldorf Hotel. But really, couldn't her mother simply have found a new recipe for an ordinary casserole? Impressing Edward and his family certainly did not top Veronica's list.

Mama leaned toward her. "Perhaps you could ask Edward to tell you something he likes about Manhattan while Father and I chat with Mr. Beckett, Veronica."

Drat! Since the remark had been loud enough for everyone else to hear, avoiding a discussion with Edward would prove futile. She sighed. "Do tell me something you like about Manhattan, Edward."

Edward's brow arched. "Manhattan?" He paused. "I like the many rooftop restaurants and gardens. They are thrilling to visit in the evenings with the stars twinkling in the sky and the city lit up below."

Rooftop restaurants and gardens sounded romantic, but she refused to admit they did. "I can almost imagine it." Hopefully, her remark sufficed. Would he resume eating, and would Mama find satisfaction in her attempt to speak in a civil manner to their guest?

"And you? Tell me something you like about Kentucky." His head tilted to one side.

Her brows furrowed, and she resisted the urge to drum her fingers on the linen tablecloth. There was much she liked about Kentucky, but what should she divulge to a man she did not want to converse with? Relenting with a slight heave of her chest, she toyed with her spoon, refusing to look at him except for a brief peek through her eyelashes. "I like the local night races amongst the younger set."

"Ah, that sounds entertaining." Edward leaned forward. "Do tell me more. Are these frequent events?"

"Nothing to tell, really. Folks used to race right through the middle of town, but authorities put a stop to it with the institution of fines. Now, people our age have taken to racing in the countryside, usually in the evenings, where innocent bystanders are less likely to be run down. If it gets a little late, after sunset, we use lanterns and torches for light. They're quite exciting, if I do say so myself."

"And Veronica Jo has won her fair share of those races...I should add," Gladdie interjected, her voice fading when Veronica cast her a quelling look.

She didn't need Gladdie to brag about her racing ability, but she softened when she realized Edward and his family might consider her participation vulgar. She'd have to thank her sister later.

"How intriguing." A contemplative and almost perplexed look appeared on his face.

If only he didn't sound so intrigued, nor so well versed at making polite conversation. He didn't even bristle at her involvement.

"Good harmless fun for our young people," Mama said, trying to smooth over Gladdie's faux-pas.

Veronica stared at the eggs on her plate and twirled her fork for a few moments. Hmm. If she pressed the utensil hard enough onto an end of one of her eggs, perhaps it would perform some stunning acrobatic feat. That would surely send the Becketts running.

She pressed on one end of the egg nearest to the edge of her plate, and it went flying. It landed with a splash directly in Edward's consommé, startling everyone, including herself. He jumped back, and Martin, standing behind him, the next course in hand, froze.

"Oh dear...pardon my egg." Veronica smothered a nervous laugh. Perhaps she had gone too far. "I don't suppose I could make a repeat of that spectacular landing, but I won't try it again since Mother will faint." Veronica hadn't expected the egg to so fully cooperate. She had hoped and aimed for a middle-of-the-table landing, not a splash into his consommé.

All eyes wide and mouths agape, everyone waited on Edward's reaction.

Please be cross with me. Please have a foul temper so my parents will change their minds at once.

He recovered quickly, lowering his raised brows and leaning forward again. "Beef consommé is so much better with an egg."

The corners of his mouth curved upward, revealing a smile *and* a sense of humor. The others laughed. Not exactly the reaction she'd hoped for. He'd taken it in stride, graciously behaving like a perfect gentleman. Why did he have to look so handsome and forgiving when he smiled at her?

"Would you like the next course, Mr. Beckett?" Martin inquired.

"Yes, but I'll finish the soup. You may leave both courses here." Edward winked at Veronica as Martin complied. Edward sliced into the egg drowning in his soup, tasted it, and then looked up with a charming smirk.

"Veronica Josephine Lyndon, I don't know what has come over you," Mama chided her, but Mr. Beckett began asking about the size of their chicken flock, diverting Mother's attention.

Veronica refused to consider her efforts at sabotage a defeat. She must believe she had done enough to plant seeds of doubt about her suitability as a bride. When their guests returned to their hotel, Mama would reprimand her. But that was a small price to pay with her entire future and freedom at stake.

"Veronica, perhaps you could ask Edward about where folks go to experience the countryside when in New York?" Mama encouraged when she'd finished her discussion with Edward's father.

Here we go again. Veronica sighed. "And where do you like to go to experience the countryside when in New York, Edward?"

He shifted in his seat. "We head to the Adirondacks or our estate on the coast of South Carolina to enjoy the beach."

Both locations sounded terribly appealing, but Veronica replied, "What a pity you must travel to enjoy the peace and nature the Lord has freely given us." Veronica avoided eye contact with him.

Edward's brows furrowed, and he clamped his lips into a firm line. Sitting back in her chair, she made no effort to extract more information, but her sisters began asking the brothers about both locations. The city boys admitted to having gone hiking, boating, and fishing in the Adirondacks. Somehow, Veronica couldn't picture Edward putting a worm on the hook.

When Delia asked what he did at the beach, Edward said he enjoyed taking walks at sunrise and sunset. Rupert commented that they both enjoyed playing badminton in the sand with their sisters and friends. In truth, the activities the Beckett boys mentioned sounded lovely, and Veronica struggled not to smile.

Next came a course of tiny oyster-and-cracker sandwiches alongside delicate ham slices topped with mint jelly, served on small triangular slices of brown bread. Beside these tiny sandwiches, each plate displayed two cucumber slices topped with a teaspoon of chicken salad and one freshly baked scone. Joined crystal bowls containing clotted cream and blackberry and raspberry preserves—boiled down from berries picked on their own farm—made their way around the table.

Best to approach her next act of sabotage with a bit more subtlety. She heaped extra jam and clotted cream on her scone.

It might make Edward think she'd become quite fat in her old age. She took an unusually large bite of the scone and let some of the blackberry preserves decorate her face.

Then she leaned forward to draw Mr. Beckett's attention. But instead of addressing him as *Mr. Beckett*, she would use his first name—something she would never do under normal circumstances, even if he invited her to at this stage of their acquaintance. "Do tell us more about Manhattan, Levi. I suppose you have a great many balls, parties, and afternoon teas to attend."

Everyone looked at Veronica with raised brows and horrified expressions, as though they were watching a comedic play that had turned into a tragedy. No doubt Mama simmered beneath her cool and calm exterior. Edward's eyes widened, but he clamped his lips together.

Mama waited for Mr. Beckett to finish the response he managed to give about their busy social calendar. Then she could clearly take no more. "Veronica, you are...I was going to say a mess...but at this point, I concede. Why not invite the chickens into the dining room?" She sighed deeply and again pressed her linen napkin to her forehead.

Veronica refused to let Mama's exasperation ruin her strategy. "I do miss having them wander freely about the house. Do you have chickens in New York, Levi?"

"Veronica..." Pa's tone was stern, but Mr. Beckett cleared his throat.

"No, someone delivers eggs, butter, and milk," the man answered, his brows furrowing as he surveyed Veronica's appearance. "Would you mind passing those preserves? They look quite tasty."

"Certainly." Veronica smiled. Reaching across the table for the crystal trio dish of preserves and clotted cream, she nudged her glass of tea toward Edward, spilling it in the center of the table. "Oh dear, I am so sorry."

Edward pushed his chair away from the table to avoid the rush of sugary brown liquid running toward his plate. The preserves somehow made it to Mr. Beckett in the ensuing chaos. Grace and Martin jumped into action to soak up the mess with extra linens from the buffet. Edward survived the ordeal without a stain, but after the servants stepped back to their places, he eyed Veronica with a wary look. Edward slid his seat forward and resumed eating, and she cheered silently, assured of victory at last.

Veronica took a large bite of her scone and, with her mouth full, muttered a somewhat distinguishable apology. "How clumsy of me." Then she licked jam from each of her fingers and took another bite of her scone. Unfortunately, Rupert's occasional chuckles indicated he might find her amusing, but the wrinkled forehead Edward wore made her think her plan might actually be working.

Mr. Beckett chuckled and nudged his son. "I haven't had this much fun in years. My boys—Edward here in particular—used to spill something weekly at the table. Gloria would go into hysterics half the time, but I always found it amusing." He turned toward Veronica's father. "Remind me to tell you about some of our best stocks to help set you up for a fine retirement, Joseph—when we are not in the presence of such fine ladies, of course."

~

Fun? Fine ladies? His father's disingenuous description of the present company only made his determination to overlook *Miss* Veronica's theatrics more obvious. And if memory served, Father had never found messes amusing. Not only did Edward's mother frequently display hysteria if any mishap ruined a meal, but his father had raised his voice on a number of those occasions, dismissing the child to blame from the table.

His father's congeniality irked him. Especially since in private, Leviticus Beckett seldom spoke so nicely. In fact, he frequently turned into a gruff, stern, and unforgiving version of himself, lecturing Edward and his brother about this, that, and the other.

Thankfully, the servants had reacted quickly enough to spare him from a cold tea bath in his expensive summer suit. He didn't dare lose his patience with Miss Veronica lest his father grumble and complain endlessly at the hotel.

He had to admit, however, that Veronica looked adorable with jam smeared at the corners of her mouth and a little on the prettiest nose he'd ever seen. She certainly kept him on his toes wondering what she might do next.

Yet Father excused everything she did with a wave of his hand as if none of it mattered. His mother would have been horrified and snubbed a girl waging war on her parents, now that he thought about it. If Edward didn't know better, he'd think his father might have something else in mind in addition to getting his hands on Veronica's dowry. The way he spoke so nicely to his old friend and overlooked Miss Veronica's lack of table manners... And now his father indicated he had some investment tips for Mr. Lyndon too.

But what else could he want? A good horse, maybe? Race-track betting advice? Or the most likely scenario, and in keeping with his mention of stock tips, perhaps his father wanted Mr. Lyndon to invest in stocks at Beckett, Reed & Johnston.

Miss Veronica used her dessert fork to attack her potato salad, stabbing each bite vigorously, accompanied by a clanging of the fork tines on the china. He half expected her to shoot the olives at him like marbles or stuff the thinly sliced roast beef and butter cheese into her mouth all at once.

He *had* hoped for a more refined bride.

When the butler appeared from the kitchen ready to serve the dessert course consisting of crystal bowls of custard garnished with nutmeg and strawberries harvested from their garden, relief washed over Edward.

Miss Veronica eyed the tray of desserts in the butler's hands. "I'll have two servings, Martin."

My, how slim Miss Veronica's waistline appeared in comparison to her appetite.

"Just give it to her, Martin. If she wants to..." Mrs. Lyndon's voice faded, and the servant did as commanded, setting two bowls of custard before Miss Veronica.

The young lady proceeded to gulp down the desserts—a Kentucky debutante and finishing school graduate who had gone out of her way to prove otherwise.

"I haven't seen such a healthy appetite in a girl in years," Father marveled aloud. "In fact, I'd like two servings as well, if you please. Then let me tell you about the best stock I've found to make a rich man richer."

There Father went again, dismissing Miss Veronica's unusual behavior and managing to mention stocks in the same breath.

Edward almost missed Rupert attempting to exchange glances with him. They had all noticed Veronica's audacious antics, but had his little brother noticed father's odd behavior too?

~

*V*eronica could hardly wait to make her exit. She had done as her parents asked. She had appeared for the introduction and the luncheon. Her only regret was the extra work her sabotage attempts would cause Martin and Grace—who faced piles of dishes thanks to Mama's determination to give the Becketts a fancy dining experience. Poor servants. They already looked worn out.

Veronica intended to keep herself busy during the tour of Velvet Brooks following the meal, far away from Edward Beckett, no matter how handsome and intelligent and annoyingly polite he might be. Hopefully, he would now want nothing to do with her.

The time had come to escape. Rising from the table, she urged her sisters to join her by nodding toward the hall with a stern but silent look. To the others, she announced, "If you'll kindly excuse us, I have a matter to settle with Delia and Gladdie—on the racetrack."

Her sisters dutifully rose, following her lead for one final act of impoliteness.

CHAPTER FIVE

Money, horse racing, and women: three things the boys just can't figure out.
—Will Rogers

Veronica imagined Mama's eyes popping wide open at the mention of the word *racetrack*, right along with her mouth. Before Mama could sputter a response, chairs scraped back from the table, and Veronica's sisters followed her out of the dining room, murmuring similar excuses. They clustered in the foyer, putting on hats they'd left at the hall tree. No need for one, though. She'd only lose it in the race.

"Where are we going, Veronica Jo?" Gladdie asked as she tied bonnet ribbons beneath her chin.

Before Veronica could answer, Edward's voice carried from the dining room. "Thank you for the delicious meal, Mrs. Lyndon. Rupert and I will join the young ladies and then catch up with you all on the tour of the farm."

Oh no! Must the New Yorkers follow them?

"As I said, the racetrack." Veronica swung the door open and stepped outside. The girls spilled onto the veranda. She stood there for a moment, breathing in the fresh air and releasing as much tension as possible. Sight of the mares grazing in a nearby corral gave her a sense of freedom. She had survived her duties, unscathed thus far. Surely, out here with a hundred places to hide, she could slip away unnoticed once their parents caught up to them for the tour.

Avoiding the trap of spending time with Edward remained high on her priority list. Hadn't he figured out how much she disliked the idea of this arranged marriage from her behavior in the dining room? If not, hadn't she at least proven she lacked the necessary etiquette for the kind of bride he needed?

Maybe the stakes for the race would prove it. Perhaps he would finally realize she and her sisters were entirely the wrong kind of females to present to his circle of refined society.

Edward and Rupert caught up to them, and the veranda became too crowded near the front door. Mother's containers of petunias, phlox, pansies, and snapdragons wafted in the air. It had paid off to plant them from seeds indoors, well in advance of the first signs of spring. They had fragrant blooms everywhere to enjoy, including the window boxes, where a few tender sweet potato vines draped amid the velvety petals. Too bad there was nothing poisonous planted that she could offer in a bouquet for her guests. It was unlike her to think such a thought, but she had been pushed beyond her limits. Even morbid humor kept her from unleashing her temper at this point.

She sighed and led them toward the stables.

"Remind me why we're going to the racetrack again." Delia finished tying the bow of her wide-brimmed straw hat to one side of her jaw and wore a questioning look, but she dutifully followed along.

"I remember." Gladdie laughed, taking the lead with a bounce in her step, looking pretty as a picture with the puffed sleeves and bodice of her fashionable white tea party dress, its periwinkle skirt matching the bow in her braid. Of course, Gladdie looked carefree. She wasn't being married off to a perfect stranger. "We're racing to decide who sits with Grandmother Spencer at the Phoenix Stakes. Whoever comes in last will have the honor."

"Yes, that's right. Because we know it's *not* an honor." Veronica picked up her pace to fall into step beside Gladdie lest she end up paired off with her tall and handsome guest. Bravo to Gladdie for clarifying the stakes. Had Edward heard their unladylike quest? Hopefully, he found the reason for their race completely inappropriate.

"It's not fair to race against Veronica Jo. She always wins," Delia complained, a pout appearing on her face.

"Not *always*." Gladdie smirked. "Sometimes I win."

"You've won before, Delia." Veronica took her sister's arm, effectively closing out the handsome fellas behind.

She didn't care how handsome Edward J. Beckett appeared —she still would refuse him. Only because she'd received a very short and bland letter from him stating that he looked forward to getting to know her and bearing his signature did she know his middle initial was *J*. What did it stand for? Jonathon, Jared, Jason, or James, perhaps? James would be nice with a name like Edward, but what did she care about his middle name? In fact, she hadn't penned a reply because his letter had only arrived the day before his train did, and now she had no need to respond to it. Why encourage him? The dandies. He and his brother dressed so fine for a tour of their stables, they would surely decry a speck of dust messing up their fine suits.

"I don't win often enough. You always seem to choose the best horse in our stables to ride." Delia sighed, persistent in pouting.

"It goes with the territory when you're the oldest. If you'd stop hiding your nose in a book, you'd know which horses will beat my choices more often. Besides, it's not always the horse alone. Sometimes it's how you ride the horse, as Father has said many a time." Veronica elbowed Delia, hoping Edward saw her as less than refined in so doing. She looked forward to their race. A good race always took her mind off stressful situations, such as the fact her entire life might be falling apart before her very eyes.

"I suppose you're right." Delia checked her skirt. "Bother. I forgot my gloves. But I'll go ahead with the race because I don't cherish the duty of playing companion to Grandmother again. I sat with her through the Derby, and she had me fetching one thing after another."

"So it's decided. Whoever comes in third will sit with Grandmother on race day." Gladdie pulled two pairs of riding gloves from a pocket hidden in her skirt. "Here Delia, you may use my extra pair. And I don't mind sitting with her. I may lose on purpose. She makes me laugh, and she has an uncanny ability for predicting the winning horse."

"I'll give you that. Thank you for the gloves. Who are you planning to ride?" Delia asked Gladdie.

"You know I like Diamond Comet, and he likes me." Gladdie rolled her eyes at having to remind her sister which horse she preferred.

"But last week you liked Midnight Sunburst," Delia protested.

Couldn't they just hurry along and pick a horse and race so Veronica could get away from Edward? Then she would find a way to disappear from the tour and leave her sisters and parents to entertain their guests.

"That was last week. Which horse are you going to ride, Delia?" Gladdie pulled her elaborate braid over her shoulder as they passed the carriage house.

"I'll ride Silver Streak." Delia's lifted chin and firmed lips showed her competitive side.

Neither of them asked which horse Veronica would ride, nor would the groom or any of the stable hands. They all knew she would ride Gunpowder Fury, and their jockey and trainer would always let her—or any of the Lyndon daughters, for that matter—unless illness, injury, or a strict training regimen due to an upcoming race prohibited them.

"An excellent choice, Delia. He's beaten Gunpowder Fury several times." Veronica quickened the pace. If they didn't saddle up soon, she might burst. She toyed with a plan to confront Edward and tell him she had no plans to marry him, especially since he insisted upon tagging along.

When the group neared the open horse barn, Edward circled around to face them. "We'd enjoy observing your race, ladies, if you'll pardon our intrusion."

Veronica bit her tongue. Couldn't Edward and Rupert take a hike? Plenty of trails existed at Velvet Brooks. She ought to point them in some other direction.

Gladdie tossed a sideways glance at Veronica and Delia. When neither offered a reply, she smiled pleasantly at the gentlemen on their behalf. "Sure, we don't mind."

Veronica certainly did mind, but she couldn't exactly say so, could she? Shrugging, she kept her eyes forward. "Whatever suits our guests is fine with me."

"Thank you. We're looking forward to your race," Rupert said as he caught up and adjusted his tweed English cap.

Edward offered a genuinely warm smile.

Before Veronica could kick herself for not being a little friendlier to their guests, Gladdie spun around to face them with a wide grin as they entered the barn, walking backward but leading them to the center of the barn. A mischievous look of excitement in her eyes, she asked, "And how far shall we conduct this race?"

"Hello, ladies. How are you all doing on this fine spring afternoon? Did I hear the mention of a race?" Carter Mitchell greeted them with a friendly expression. The rest of the staff in the horse barn ambled forward to see to their needs—except for Hank Parker, the farm's manager, who remained at his desk, always jotting down something or another about one of the horses into their records.

"One mile and a quarter, or a longer race of perhaps a mile and a half?" Delia rested her hands on her hips, looking from Veronica to Gladdie.

"We're fine, Carter. Thank you for asking." Although Veronica didn't feel fine in view of her predicament. She turned to answer Delia. "One mile and a quarter," she said firmly, stepping toward Gunpowder Fury's stall. "It's spring. You know as well as I, Delia, they're not ready to race for much longer after being cooped up most of the winter." She reached up and patted the stallion's nose, producing an apple slice she'd swiped from the luncheon out of her pocket. She held it out to him on the palm of her hand, and he nibbled it right up, nudging her hand for more. "I have more of these for you if you win today, my sweet friend."

"Will the gentlemen be riding today?" Carter nodded toward Edward and Rupert as they admired the horses in the stalls, each compartment bearing a metal engraved nameplate and generous piles of golden straw for bedding.

"No, not today, but thank you. We'll enjoy observing the ladies race for now." Edward spoke gently to one of their horses. The change in his tone from strong and confident in his reply to sweet and gentle with the horse caused Veronica to slowly turn toward him. She hadn't expected this from the city boy.

"No side saddles for us today, Carter," Veronica instructed.

"I know you ladies could race side saddle as well as any jockey, but I agree, it's safer to race on a regular seat." Carter liked a good race but always kept their safety in mind. The trainer for Velvet Brooks, Rutherford Brickman, whom they called "Red," brought a saddle over for Gunpowder Fury, and Veronica opened the stall for him.

"Thank you, Carter." Delia stood on the tips of her toes and patted Silver Streak's mane. "I'll ride this beauty today. He's looking a bit frisky and ready for some fun."

"A fine choice, Miss Delia." Carter grinned and headed toward the tack.

"That's far more bedding than we keep in our Charleston stables," Rupert commented in a quiet voice to his brother, pointing at one of the stalls in front of them. "See the way the straw is tufting? It fills almost half of each of these stalls. Must be a Kentucky thing."

Plenty of clean straw made for a more comfortable environment for their horses. A more comfortable environment meant better rest. Better rest meant healthier horses and better performance. For as long as Veronica could remember, Hank had always kept the stalls filled with more bedding than other horse farmers did, but her father said it constituted just one of many of their trade secrets.

Delia and Gladdie looked as though they would burst into giggles at overhearing the observation, but Veronica gave them a stern look in time to save their guests from embarrassment. Once she worked up the nerve to speak her mind to Edward J., it would be hard enough on the man.

Come to think of it...why was she delaying? It was so obvious Edward did not belong here.

Veronica began putting on her riding gloves and stood as tall as her five-foot-two-inch frame would allow. "Just so you know..." She waited until Edward met her gaze to continue. "I appreciate the fact you and your family have come all this way, and I'll play along with the charade so we don't cause a scene with our parents, but I'm not for sale like one of my father's horses. There will be no wedding. You can relax and enjoy Velvet Brooks and all Kentucky has to offer."

Red brought Gunpowder Fury to her, saddled and ready to ride. Veronica accepted the lead and mounted her horse in a flurry of skirts and petticoats, settling into the seat.

All eyes and ears focused on them. Hank had abandoned writing his notes to lean in the doorway of his office, staring at them with an arched brow. Nathaniel Hartley, a burly, large-framed stable hand, stopped saddling Diamond Comet for Gladdie. Carter, taking his sweet time selecting a seat for Delia from the tack corner, looked their way, his mouth hanging open.

Edward had taken up a confident and relaxed stance, his hands in his pockets, one foot crossed over the other as he leaned against the stall near him. Did he exude a calm, aloof, indifferent, or arrogant demeanor? She couldn't tell, but something about him drew her attention. As she had done, he waited until Veronica's gaze met his from astride her horse. For the first time, she took in how blue his eyes looked, how tall and lean he appeared, possessing a sense of steadfastness and easy strength.

"I can't imagine your father would think he could succeed in making such a transaction. You are a woman of far greater value than a horse, and one who knows her own mind. I'm sure he has your best interests at heart, but he and my father are sidetracked with their own notions and motives. I can't imagine a lady like you happy anywhere but here."

The barn grew so quiet, everyone could surely hear her accelerated heartbeat as she tightened her hold on the reins. Gunpowder Fury flicked his tail and did a bit of a sidestep, his hooves clicking on the new cement floor Pa had ordered installed last spring, breaking the silence.

Maybe Edward could understand her position. Although she could have spoken privately to him, she had to live at Velvet Brooks amid the looks and whispers about Pa orchestrating her future as if she were a horse. And why let Edward have his hopes dashed if he intended to acquiesce to the arrangement?

He'd taken the high road in returning a compliment in the face of her declaration, but instead of him bristling at her statement, did he appear relieved to have the ice broken between them? She couldn't tell if Edward intended to pursue a courtship with her or not from his reply. Maybe he, too, felt cornered into compliance because of his father.

Either way, nothing more could be said now...given their attentive audience. She tilted up her head and clicked her tongue, urging the beautiful bay forward.

Once outside the barn in the warm sunlight, she tugged the reins gently to lead Gunpowder Fury toward the one-mile oval dirt racetrack her father had installed beyond the corral, a pricey endeavor. And one Veronica did not take for granted. She steered her horse to the starting line and patted his neck. Thankfully, she'd have a chance to recover from the exchange with Edward while waiting for her sisters.

Charlie Ford, their jockey, leaned on the rail from the outer edge of the track as he talked to one of their other horses which would participate at one of the many races the day after tomorrow at the Phoenix Stakes. Judging by the way the rider grinned, the horse had just completed a successful run around the oval. Most jockeys had to train their racehorses at the Lexington track, but not Charlie.

No doubt, the jockey would hear about her announcement to Edward in the barn before the race with her sisters came to an end. News traveled fast at Velvet Brooks. So long as it didn't reach the ears of her parents, she didn't care.

How could her father ever think she would find any happiness at all in marrying a stranger from New York high society? She had imagined living out her days at Velvet Brooks, eventually marrying someone who appreciated horses as much as she did—when love came her way through an encounter of God's perfect timing.

She had to give Edward some credit, though. Not only did his remarks convey a talent for diplomacy, but his response seemed on target. Their fathers had notions and motives, indeed, and they had overlooked her wishes, and likely Edward's too.

Still, it would take more than a compliment and good looks to win her heart. If he didn't know it before, he knew it now.

CHAPTER SIX

Forget the prince, I'll take the horse.
—Unknown

E dward, shadowed by Rupert, leaned over the rail as the
horses of the Lyndon daughters galloped around the first
turn. His father, accompanied by Mr. and Mrs. Lyndon, had
reached them in time to see the race begin.

"Step up to the clubhouse turn, Levi." Clad in a tweed
sports coat, Mr. Lyndon motioned Father toward the fence.
"You'll have a front row seat for the finish."

"The clubhouse turn." Father chuckled, grasping the edge
of the rail. "I like that. Would you place it here, before the finish
line, if you built one?"

Mr. Lyndon nodded. "I probably would."

"Now don't go putting grand ideas into Joseph's head, Mr.
Beckett, not with three daughters and three weddings ahead of
us." Mrs. Lyndon shook her head, but a smile on her face
conveyed her sense of humor intact.

Most of the men Edward had met in the horse barn had
also lined up along the rail. A jockey-sized fellow began to

mention the performance of a horse with Mr. Lyndon, but most of Edward's attention remained on Veronica as she leaned low over the neck of Gunpowder Fury. She had a feisty temperament and...dare he say he found her downright interesting? The glorious bay stallion moving beneath her had already taken the lead in the race, and all he could see now consisted of a flash of petticoats and skirts fluttering in the wind as the three daughters urged their horses toward the finish line.

The one they called "Red" stood at the quarter-mile marker with a white flag bearing the farm's emblem, ready to wave it when the winner crossed into victory. Edward had seen the same emblem embroidered on the corner of several horse blankets and a few other items around the barn. The design consisted of a chestnut horse jumping over a blue river cutting through two green meadows. Atop the horse rode a figure wearing a pink-and-gold silk jersey—which must be the family colors. The shelves of a display cabinet in the family sitting room had displayed trophies, ribbons, and horse memorabilia behind sparkling glass doors. How would he—a city boy, a stockbroker's son from the banking world of Manhattan—ever fit into this horseracing family and the legacy they'd built? If he could spend time getting to know the horse farm and Mr. Lyndon, perhaps he could slowly win Veronica over.

The horses rumbled around the track, approaching the final turn before the last quarter mile. They kicked up clouds of dust and dirt as they thundered toward Edward and the other observers. Veronica only had to hold onto the lead to secure a win.

"Look at Gunpowder Fury go!" Mrs. Lyndon didn't seem worried about her daughters falling off the horses or becoming injured. No, on the contrary, her smile told Edward she thoroughly enjoyed the race and had accustomed herself to such antics among her offspring.

"Delia is edging in closer on Silver Streak." Carter crossed his arms over his chest. "It's going to be a close one."

"Sure is. Gladdie on Diamond Comet is almost neck and neck with Delia," Nathaniel said approvingly. Pride rang in their voices—in the farm and the expertise of the Lyndon girls.

A few seconds later, Red waved the white flag as Veronica flew past where he stood. The trainer checked the time on his pocket watch as each of the Lyndon girls brought their horses across the marker.

Mr. Lyndon stood up taller. "Another victory for Gunpowder Fury! I love that horse."

"He has so much potential, Joseph," Father said. "And what a treat to see a race we didn't expect today."

"What did our daughters race for as a prize?" Mr. Lyndon looked toward his wife.

"I'm guessing it's all about who will escort my mother, their Grandmother Spencer, at the Phoenix Stakes." Mrs. Lyndon opened her parasol to block the sun.

"I should have known." Mr. Lyndon turned toward Father. "The girls help look after my mother-in-law and fetch things for her on race days. She's still quite...active for her age." He didn't take his eyes off their horses, now breathing heavily from the exertion.

Father chuckled. "I see. Well, a bit of sibling rivalry is only natural and seldom hurts anything."

Edward's father's remark struck a chord. His folks hadn't sent Rupert to a military boarding school. No, they'd kept him at home with fine tutors and spoiled and indulged him, like Edward's sisters. It would seem Edward and Veronica both contended with sibling rivalry. Maybe the topic would prove useful for a future conversation with her, if she'd ever give him the time of day.

He pushed darker days and memories aside, turning his attention toward Veronica as she exited the track astride the winning horse, pacing Gunpowder Fury at a canter, then a slower trot, and finally, easing the stallion to a stop.

The groom and some of the middle-aged farmhands met the sisters as they dismounted. The employees, after congratulating each of them and consoling Gladdie for coming in last, took the reins to walk their mounts toward the horse barn. And doubtless, they would cool them down with extra walking to prevent their muscles from tightening up and stiffening. That much Edward knew about horses, but he had so much more to learn.

"After we congratulate the winner of the race, shall we begin our tour of the rest of the farm?" Mr. Lyndon turned to Edward's father, who nodded as they strolled toward the three girls—all of them windblown, an air of breathless excitement about them.

"Yes, yes, I'd like to see as much of it as we can. The fresh air out here in the countryside does me good."

"Well done, Veronica Jo! A fine race, Delia, Gladdie," Mr. Lyndon said, embracing each of his daughters. They received similar adulation from their mother and then shook hands with Edward's father. Then, showing good sportsmanship, each of the sisters shook hands with each other.

Gladdie, with hands on her hips, offered a magnanimous smile toward her sisters. "It appears Delia and I shall both look after Grandmother at the Phoenix Stakes since we've nearly tied for second and third by a nose length."

"A fair assessment and a good race." Delia handed her sister the borrowed gloves.

Edward hung back with Rupert, waiting for his turn to congratulate each sister, but particularly the winner. Since the eldest Miss Lyndon had held onto first place, she would be free to observe the Phoenix without having to tend her grandmother's needs. If he did not make some attempt to pursue her, Father would only nag and pester him.

Perhaps he could find a way to ask if she would permit him to escort her to the race. If she said yes, it ought to satisfy their parents and show they had at least put forth an effort. Not that he would necessarily dislike having Miss Lyndon as a wife, but she seemed...how should he put it? Rather feisty. Though she was also rather adorable in her petulance.

Finally, she stood before him, and he shook hands with her. "Congratulations, Miss Lyndon. A splendid race." If only he could think of something more to say...

She barely looked at him, though she said, "Thank you, Edward." As she moved on to shake hands with his brother and then fall in with the others on their way to look at the horse barn, he hung back near her.

He couldn't help but wonder if she had any other interests besides horses. He aimed to find out before he ruled a marriage with her completely off the table. Never mind the fact she had made it clear she would not consider him only moments before the race. He would take things one step at a time. First, he had to learn more about her, and he only had two weeks in which to do so before returning to Manhattan with Rupert and his father.

Except now, as he opened his mouth to ask her a question, she made a beeline escape toward the house. Should he attempt to catch up with her? But no, she had disappeared around the corner of the horse barn before he could blink an eye. His plan would have to wait. The woman had dogged determination to steer clear of him, and he would need to step up his game to catch a moment alone with her.

~

*E*dward stared at the front door of Velvet Brooks the very next morning and gulped. Would Veronica like the flowers he'd brought her? The Lexington florist hadn't much to offer this early in the season. If he could get her to simply tell him one thing about herself, he'd consider it a small step in the right direction. At least parking the Oldsmobile out front hadn't frightened any horses today. He'd learned his lesson, parking a little farther away from the door than yesterday.

Mr. Lyndon had invited them to spend as much time as they liked at the farm over the next two weeks, even going so far as to offer some of the guest rooms, but Father had assured him they would remain at the hotel and continue to make the drive into the countryside as needed.

He tucked the flowers under his arm and tugged on the vest under his suit jacket. Then he buttoned one button of the suit and, thinking the better of it, unbuttoned it. Shouldn't he try to blend into the farm and look casual? Finally, he knocked on the door.

When the butler opened it, Edward offered what he hoped was a relaxed smile. "Hello, Martin. Nice to see you again."

"Thank you, Mr. Beckett. Do come inside. I assume you are here to call upon Miss Lyndon." Martin opened the door wide and beckoned him into the foyer.

Edward stepped over the threshold, casting a glance around. "Yes, I'd like to call on Miss Veronica Lyndon." Best to specify which Miss Lyndon, just in case.

"I believe she's out in the garden with her art instructor. Right this way." Martin led him through the main hall, then through the music room to the set of French doors leading onto the rear covered porch.

An art instructor? Had he heard Martin correctly? Did Miss Lyndon enjoy art?

Edward spotted her at once through the windows. Seated on a wooden stool before an easel in the middle of the garden, she looked lovely dressed in a shade of violet, surrounded by spring blooms, basking in the morning sunshine.

The butler's voice interrupted Edward's thoughts as he took in the glorious scene. "I'll leave you to it."

"Thank you." Edward straightened his tie as the employee hurried away to tend some other task. He opened the door and stepped outside onto the porch, waiting for the right moment to address Veronica, almost wishing the butler would have at least announced his arrival.

~

*V*eronica glanced at the timepiece pinned to her reception dress. Nearly eleven o'clock already! Her art instructor, the elderly Isaac Brennan, would soon depart, although she never wanted him to since she enjoyed his classes so much. He always had a new technique or some idea or another to broaden and challenge her artistic abilities.

"Yes, that's it, Miss Lyndon. I dare say you have mastered pine trees. You can see how fanning out the bristles of the brush works well if it is a very stiff brush." He leaned closer to her canvas to inspect her work as he spoke. "I believe you've got the hang of it."

Veronica smiled at his praise. "Thank you, Mr. Brennan. I do find this technique helps a great deal. I'm terrible at pine trees, but now I am able to build the appearance of a forest line or a cluster of trees with merely a few strokes of the brush."

"Yes, it is a wonderful technique. No, don't get up from your easel. I don't want to disrupt your progress with your spring landscape, but I must be on my way to my next pupil."

"I never know what you will teach me next. One week, ceramics, the next pottery, sculpting, sketching, painting on canvas, shading with pencils..." She glanced at her supplies, an assortment of at least a dozen tin tubes containing oil paints in various shades of violet, red, blues, greens, orange, pinks, and yellows. "I will continue to find ways to add the colors of God's glorious rainbow to my landscape and master this brilliant technique."

"Yes, next week at the usual time." Mr. Brennan gathered up his supplies.

She refrained from flinging her arms around his neck to thank him for helping her master the challenge. It would only cause him to blush and become flustered. Every now and then, the aging fellow became forgetful, and then his lessons sounded a little repetitive, but she still enjoyed his instruction. Watching her silvery-white-haired instructor pick up his satchel and hurry away, she caught a glimpse of someone standing on the porch with hands clasped behind his back. Edward!

The smile of contentment disappeared from her face. Had he been there for long, observing her in their private garden? Why hadn't Martin announced his arrival? She didn't want him to know anything more about her, least of all invade her creative space.

"Oh, Edward, hello." She forced herself to greet him, but his appearance did not invigorate her aspirations.

"Hello, Miss Lyndon." He stepped forward, offering a bouquet of flowers. "These are for you."

She couldn't refuse the offering he thrust into her hands, and as he had somehow managed to bring her favorite Virginia Bluebells, she supposed she couldn't avoid spending some time alone with him forever. The offering softened her a little. Reluctantly, she motioned him toward the stool in front of her instructor's easel. "Would you care to sit down for a few moments?" If he overstayed his welcome, she would simply tell him she had an important obligation to attend.

He joined her beside the easel and perched on the stool. "Thank you. It's nice to see you again too. I didn't know you liked to paint."

She had no desire to tell him about her artwork, but as it

was too late to hide the fact now, she muttered a response without looking at him. "Yes, I do very much enjoy painting." She drew in the scent of the flowers, closing her eyes as she breathed in. She set them aside on the table next to her tea service, palette, and other painting supplies. She should probably show him she possessed civilized manners, but it defied every bone in her body to do so under the circumstances. "Would you care for a cup of tea?"

"No, but thank you."

She tried not to rejoice at the indication he didn't intend to pester her for too long. Unless the other Beckett men were with him...in which case she might be forced to entertain them as well. "And where is Rupert today? And your father? Did they accompany you?" She resumed her work, picking up a brush, dipping it in some purple from the palette to make a pansy on her canvas.

"I think they are touring a museum today in Lexington not far from our hotel and joining us here later for dinner. I won't take up much of your time. I've only come to make a proposal."

"A proposal?" Veronica's heart dropped, and her brush streaked the canvas with a swath of purple. Did he plan to make a formal offer of marriage, right then and there? Now, in her family garden, after she'd told him only yesterday she absolutely would not marry him?

What trouble this man brought to her life! Now she'd ruined her spring landscape. She drew in a deep breath and bit her lower lip, ready to explode with the anger about to boil over from deep within. Laying the brush aside, she stared at the mess she'd made.

Edward glanced at her damaged portrait and then at her, holding up a hand in his defense. "No, no, it's not what you think...not that sort of proposal. More of a plan, and one I think you might like, if you'll hear me out."

"Oh." How silly of her to jump to conclusions. Goodness,

she really must stay calm. She'd have to wait for the streak of purple paint to dry for a few seconds and cover it with a great bunch of flowers. Maybe turn it into a large dark-green shrub with pink blooms.

"Go on." She cast a wary glance at him before picking up her paintbrush again. "Tell me your idea."

He studied the progress on her canvas as he spoke. "Seeing how neither of us are thrilled about the idea of an arranged marriage, I figure our parents will only become agitated if we don't spend time together and show we are making some sort of effort to go along with their plan while I'm here in Kentucky."

"I had considered that, too," she admitted, keeping her eyes on the canvas, but she did glance over at him and nod after completing a few brushstrokes in a shade of forest green to cover the purple streak. "I only found out about this whole ridiculous idea a few days before your arrival, and to be honest, I'm still trying to sort through what my parents are thinking and why."

"I understand. I haven't known about it for long either. I thought perhaps if I could escort you to the Phoenix Stakes, and if we could plan a few other excursions, our parents wouldn't be able to say we hadn't at least tried."

"You aren't suggesting I ride in that noisy Runabout, are you?"

"Not if you don't want to." He paused. "I could rent a horse and carriage from the livery if you prefer."

"I see." Veronica set her brush aside in a mason jar filled with a little turpentine to dissolve the paint. She swiveled on the stool to look directly at him. His plan did make a bit of sense. And hiding from him had thus far proven an inefficient way of convincing her parents their union posed a threat to her happiness. "What exactly did you have in mind?"

CHAPTER SEVEN

If you look the right way, you can see that the whole world is a garden.
—*Frances Hodgson Burnett*

Feet planted apart on the brick terrace amid the Lyndons' garden, Edward crossed his arms over his chest. He sat up taller where he perched on the wooden stool while he pondered the answer to Veronica's question, leaning back a tad to keep his balance. He'd nearly caused her to throw him out by using the wrong word when he'd said he had a proposal. The feisty woman had curbed her temper and let him stay a bit longer, but he didn't want to scare her with poor ideas for their outings. Talking to her felt like holding a butterfly. Best to pace his answer slowly, though he couldn't blame her one bit for feeling the way she did.

"We have a family dinner tonight. The Phoenix Stakes is tomorrow. We may as well fill in a few of the other days." He caught sight of the extra easel beside his stool, and he dropping his arms, sat up straight. "Seeing that we both enjoy oil painting, I could acquire another canvas in town, and we could paint for a few hours some morning next week."

"You like to paint?" Her brow arched as if she didn't believe him. And the surprise in her tone told him they needed to remedy not knowing much about each other even if they would only become better friends in the end.

Come to think of it, he hadn't mentioned anything of note about himself in the letter he'd sent ahead of his visit. He'd kept it short, but now seemed a good time to remedy the faux pas. "I have a garret art studio at both of our family residences."

"Surely, you jest." She smiled at him for the first time, the loveliest of smiles he'd ever seen. "I'm sure I have an extra canvas you could use..."

He'd worked hard to earn her smile, and for a moment, it took his breath away. The way her light-pink lips shimmered in the sunlight with some kind of glossy cosmetic, for a moment, he wondered what it might feel like to kiss her. He dismissed the thought and heard himself say, "Maybe we could go on a picnic and horseback riding some other day."

"You know I won't turn down an opportunity to go horse-back riding, and I do dearly love picnics. A carriage ride might be nice one afternoon." Another smile played on her lips.

"That sounds good. I have to admit, I'm enjoying my time in the country. I can see why you love it here, Miss Lyndon." His eyes came to rest on a white trellis where rich purple morning glories and their curling vines twined. Rose blooms spread velvety petals toward the sun in shades of yellow, orange, and bright pink. A hint of fragrant spring blossoms hung in the air, and a pair of white doves with silvery wings fluttered in the branches of a dogwood, cooing contentedly. He could stay there the whole day, enjoying the tranquil garden. "But do you enjoy going into the city occasionally too?"

"Of course. One has to do a bit of socializing and partake of local culture."

"All right. How about attending a play at the theater and dining out in Lexington one evening?" He would look forward to seeing her dressed in an evening gown and spending a few hours over a fine meal discussing theater.

Veronica nodded. "Those outings seem sufficient. I suppose if we become bored in the company of our parents and siblings, we could spend an evening reading books in the library, and I might consider playing the piano sometime, but I'm not as proficient as I'd like to be. Do you like to sing?"

"It pains me to admit that as much as I enjoy it, I'm better at reading the notes than I am at singing them, but I do try, and I could turn the pages on the sheet music for you." He grinned, heat rising up from his collar. "My love for music reaches far and wide."

Her sweet laugh resembled a delightful melody. He hadn't seen this side to her until now. "I like our plans." She paused, and her smile diminished. A serious look replaced it. Then she spoke gently but with firm resolve. "I will agree to most of the outings we've discussed for the sake of keeping our parents from pestering us, but mind you, I have no intention of marrying anyone right now. I'm enjoying my life as it is, and I plan to make my parents face the truth at some point."

Edward, on the other hand, couldn't see a way out of his father's plans, but as he, too, felt trapped, he could agree to all she'd said. At least they'd not waste a chance to get to know each other a little better. "I feel much the same way. An arranged marriage isn't my idea of a good way to begin a lifetime commitment."

"What time will you pick me up for the race tomorrow?" She pursed those pink lips that shimmered in the sunlight.

"Does eleven o'clock sound good? I heard the activities begin around noon and last most of the day." Hopefully, the weather would cooperate. He didn't relish spending tomorrow drenched by rain or seeing the horses race on a sloppy track, but they'd have to make the best of it no matter what the weather might do.

"Eleven o'clock is fine. We can dine at the clubhouse between races if you like," she suggested.

Edward rose. "A meal at the clubhouse sounds wonderful." Best to keep their garden meeting short before he ruined his success. He would see her again at dinner. "Well, I'll be on my way. Can you tell me where I might find your father? He promised to show me more of the farm today." If he hurried, he could make the noon appointment with a little time to spare. "We only toured the horse barn and livestock barn yesterday before my father grew tired."

"Ah, yes. He's probably in the library, but he could be out with our jockey, Charlie Ford, discussing Gunpowder Fury's chances for the race tomorrow. The first door on your left before the front door." She swiveled on her stool and pointed behind her. "See you this evening."

He bowed slightly. "See you then."

His heart pounded as he left her there. Nothing could have prepared him for seeing her in such peaceful and beautiful surroundings, doing what he most loved.

The Kentucky debutante tantalized him with her love for art, her vivacious beauty, and her temperamental ways. Completely different from ladies in New York. Maybe a glimmer of hope for them existed, after all. He'd hold onto that for now. One step at a time...

But what if, after three or four outings, he fell in love with her...but had to return home without her agreeing to marry him? Would he have a broken heart on top of bearing the burden of responsibility for his family's downfall into poverty if he didn't find a way to win her hand? His father would heap loads of blame on him if he failed.

$\sim$

*E*dward arrived in a rented carriage with two beautiful horses to pick Veronica up for the Phoenix Stakes Race, driving them with ease to the Lexington Association Track on the east side of town. Their first date—if she could refer to it as such. The rain held off, and he asked her more about the races and what they did to prepare their stallion for the day.

The ride passed pleasantly enough. Then he escorted her to the clubhouse where Lexington's most notable families feasted at linen-covered tables while wearing their finest fashions, catching up on the latest news. After a long winter of the residents being cooped up at home, the clubhouse fluttered with excitement, the clanging of forks, and a constant flow of conversation as waiters dashed about to deliver gourmet meals to their guests.

Most of her family had arrived earlier and had already eaten with Rupert and Mr. Beckett. They greeted Veronica and Edward before heading out to the stands to observe the horses, leaving the counterfeit couple to themselves. All four of her grandparents stopped at their table before they placed their orders, and Grandmother Spencer winked at Veronica, causing her some embarrassment when she said, "You've captured a fine gentleman, Veronica. When's the wedding?"

Veronica flushed, but Edward only chuckled good-naturedly, taking the remark in stride.

"Don't mind my grandmother. She simply wants more grandchildren," she mumbled, watching her grandparents retreat to their box in the stands with the rest of her family. Hopefully, others hadn't heard the bold remark, but her sisters had. They cast her apologetic looks and shrugs as they hurried away to catch the next race.

On the arm of an eligible bachelor so impeccably dressed, and a mystery to Lexington society at that, Veronica drew a great deal of attention. She dutifully introduced Edward to the Sullivans, the Breckenridges, the Picketts, the Harpers, and everyone else who mattered or wanted an introduction. Even Henry Sullivan stopped at their table and shook hands with Edward, forcing her to admit to herself how much smarter, more self-assured, and more fashionable Edward looked in comparison.

Edward kept the conversation moving along nicely during their meal of roast chicken, mashed potatoes, buttered green beans, rolls, and salads. He asked about her favorite horses for each of the day's races, asked how they'd selected Charlie Ford to become their jockey, and paid attention to the important families from the area when introduced. Most of all, everyone liked him. It all tugged on her heart, leaving her struggling with remorse that she had rejected him when, in fact, he behaved like a perfect gentleman.

Then, joining their families in the grandstands, they cheered on Midnight Sunburst to a second-place finish. In the next race, the biggest race of the day, the glorious moment when Gunpowder Fury crossed the finish line to take first place left them all elated. Two victories in one day had everyone floating on clouds of joy. How proud Father looked to have two of their finest steeds place as Charlie bounced along in the saddle to congratulate the second-place winner atop his horse, a champion called Freezing Frank. Even their horses seemed to know they raced in front of important family guests, urging Veronica to consider her future and her choices carefully.

After the race, Veronica and Edward slipped away from their families and the crowds so he could return her to Velvet Brooks.

Edward stopped her with a hand to her arm before they

exited the gate. "Would you like to return home in the carriage or the Runabout?"

Her eyes went wide. How did he know she did actually want to try out the new contraption? Yet she quirked her brows together. "But the carriage is waiting outside in the parking lot. How would we retrieve the Runabout?"

"It's parked in the hotel's lot, so we could have a bit of fun and exchange them if you like before leaving Lexington. The livery for the horse and carriage is right next door..."

She flashed him a grin. "Let's do it."

Once tucked inside the Runabout, she held on for dear life. The ride made her laugh as they took the curves and turns on the country roads while pushing the machine to its limits whenever it seemed safe to do so. By the end of the drive, she had to admit she'd thoroughly enjoyed their day together. The best part—he promised to let her drive the shiny red automobile sometime before returning to New York.

～

*B*efore the Sunday morning church service began, Veronica glanced over her shoulder to spot Edward quickening his pace and making a beeline in her direction with his brother and father. He reached the area where she sat and proceeded to nod politely at the other gentlemen buzzing around in the center aisle near the end of her pew, all of them making polite conversation with her about the previous day's race. Upstaging all of them, he leaned close and asked if he could have the honor of sitting beside her. Of course, she said yes, since their parents would appreciate their efforts to get to know one another.

Once he'd settled into the hard wooden pew, the other gentlemen sulked away. He whispered in a low voice, "Shall I put my arm around your shoulders?"

Veronica's eyes widened, and she shook her head. "My parents will think it's much too early for something of that sort," she whispered. "Plus, they won't believe it's a genuine gesture. You've only known me for a few days."

"All right, then, maybe next Sunday."

"Maybe next Sunday." She kept her eyes on the empty pulpit while she waited for the pastor to step into his place and lead them in the song portion of the service. Had she detected a little eagerness in Edward's voice? A tingle of anticipation stirred within, surprising her.

After church, he offered to drive Veronica to Velvet Brooks in his Runabout while their families piled into two of her father's carriages to take them home for the midday meal. Grandmother and Grandfather Spencer and Grandmother and Grandfather Lyndon—called Colonel Lyndon by all who knew him—would join them. Though she loved them dearly, their presence only reminded her of their deceitful ruse. She shoved the thought aside, too weary to contend with it. After all, her parents had pushed her into her current dilemma. What else could she do?

Once everyone had gathered around the dining room table, they feasted on a meal Willamena prepared consisting of a first course of chilled oysters, followed by a second course of creamed asparagus soup. The gentlemen landed on a discussion about the price for a bushel of oats, but she only listened with half an ear, praying none of her grandparents would make remarks about what a handsome couple they made. Or worse, asking when the wedding would take place.

Martin and Grace began serving the sliced cucumber and onion salad course while a crystal relish tray circulated around the table. Veronica once again sat directly across from Edward near the middle of the table. Her grandparents flanked the far end, the younger folks in the center. Mr. Beckett and her parents kept the conversation flowing from the head of the table.

No, she wouldn't send any eggs flying this time. It would only distress her grandparents. She had narrowly escaped a reprimand from Mama for her behavior at their first meal together, and she certainly knew better than to think she would escape a second display of temperamental antics. Instead, she should pay attention to the conversation and try to behave now that she and Edward had arrived at a plan of their own. Never mind the fact her conscience twinged frequently about the ruse.

"Your twenty acres of oats would fetch a fine price at forty-nine cents a bushel if you didn't have all of this fine horseflesh to feed," Mr. Beckett remarked to her father. "At least you don't have Rupert at your table too. He loves his oatmeal every morning."

"Father..." Rupert shook his head.

"I'm grooming the boys to take over my place at the firm one day. Edward shows great aptitude there. Of course, he will also eventually inherit our coastal vacation home. There's a real threat in that since I suspect he will retreat to his painting at Chesapeake Manor when I'm dead and gone. But you see, I have a plan." Mr. Beckett held up a finger even as Edward shifted in his seat. "Edward will need to entice Rupert away from his veterinary pursuits so Rupert can run the company when his brother is painting."

"You have one thing right, Father." Rupert leaned forward to look at his father from his seat. "Edward is the mathematical genius in the family. He can predict which stocks will do well before I can. He should inherit the entire stock-trading business, and I should find clients who need my veterinary expertise near our South Carolina estate. Tell us, Edward—how much would Mr. Lyndon profit if he sold all twenty acres of those oats out there in his fields?"

Edward cleared his throat and leaned back in his seat. His brow furrowed in concentration. "Let's see. Twenty acres at an average yield of seventy bushels an acre, which I only know because Mr. Lyndon told me he expects about seventy bushels per acre this year...that's about thirty-four dollars and thirty cents per acre at forty-nine cents a bushel, times twenty acres. You'd profit six hundred and eighty-six dollars or about seven hundred dollars if you sold the whole crop."

Veronica gulped. How quickly he rattled off those numbers. Edward *was* a mathematical genius compared to her struggle with figures! But Rupert's argument did little to help his brother's plight. From what she could tell, a man who very much enjoyed being an artist also existed inside Edward. Maybe Rupert's desire to escape a life of office work overshadowed any of Edward's ambitions. Apparently, he thought since Edward was the elder brother, inheriting the family stock investment business should fall to him instead of both of them.

But did she observe some degree of surprise on Mr. Beckett's face? He recovered quickly, offering a mere grunt.

Rupert's ploy contained a weak approach. If he had used an example pointing to Edward's artistic ability, and if he had insisted their father recognize his love for veterinary work, maybe they could all put their heads together and find someone else to handle the stock trading. He might have convinced his father to reconsider, but he had only cemented the fact that Edward's grooming was perfect for taking his place at the helm of their New York business.

The main course came out next, a traditional Sunday roast. Along with it, sliced tomatoes, green beans, and early spring peas. But Veronica barely noticed the delicious meal wafting beneath her nose as Martin set a plate before her. She felt sorry for Edward and Rupert—sorry for how both of them were trapped at their father's stock firm in the city.

By the time Martin and Grace began serving slices of apple

or peach pie with a scoop of vanilla ice cream, and coffee or tea, Veronica's heart ached for Edward's predicament. She'd begun to see a side of him she hadn't known existed.

She must keep her empathy at bay. They had only agreed to an alliance to thwart their parents, but the more she discovered about him, the more likeable he seemed. She had best keep her heart and mind in check.

CHAPTER EIGHT

Jesse Beery had a charming personality. He could always make
friends with the most savage horse in a few minutes.
—Percy F. Thorn, Author of Humane Horse Training

After the delicious meal, the elder adults gathered to sit
on the back porch facing the creek, the tree line, and the
garden. Veronica led Edward to the piano in the music room,
inviting him to sit with her on the bench. Her sisters and
Rupert occupied a few chairs in a corner of the room, talking
about yesterday's race and some of their other horses.

Edward's voice rang out as nicely as it had during the
singing portion of the service at church, and he joined her in
playing some of the notes, his hands gliding effortlessly along
with hers over the keys. But sharing the piano bench with him,
and sitting so close their hands and knees occasionally bumped
into each other, did not help matters. An undeniable kind of
magnetic appeal kindled between them. With her heart soft-
ening toward him, physical attraction in such close proximity
amounted to the very last thing with which she wanted to
contend.

She could not let this man worm his way into her heart, but part of her enjoyed the experience. Maybe because she so loved sitting at the piano in their lovely home, her childhood home, the only place she'd ever lived. The place she loved so much. Maybe some of it had to do with the many memories she'd collected over the years, sitting at this very bench. And then, when her sisters joined in the last two stanzas of one of her favorite hymns, "Nearer My God to Thee," nostalgia brought moisture to her eyes.

"Do you know 'In Haven,' composed by Elgar?" Edward asked when they finished singing the hymn. "I believe he changed the name of it from—"

"'Love Alone Will Stay'...?" She flipped through some of their sheet music until she found it. "Ah, here it is."

She could have stayed there with him at the piano for hours. The way Edward looked at her, serenading her as he sang the words, his blue eyes alight as his voice blended with her playing—it certainly stirred something in her heart.

She could not, would not, allow herself to fall in love, despite enjoying his companionship. Despite finding him so attractive. Despite him being a perfect gentleman thus far. Despite everyone around her appearing to like him. Despite the fact he liked artwork. Despite the fact he had a wonderful singing voice and could play piano well enough to make her heart feel all warm and happy inside. She needed to stop finding things she liked about this man.

Danger lurked if she continued sitting so close, singing romantic melodies, so when the song ended, she agreed at once to his suggestion for a buggy ride. This left the use of his automobile for Rupert and Veronica's sisters to follow behind or drive slightly ahead as their chaperones.

"Would you and Rupert like to hitch up the buggy?" Veronica began tidying the sheet music and sliding the bench forward. "Most of our employees are off for the rest of the day, being a Sunday and all. You'll find our conveyances parked in the carriage house, farther down from the barn."

Edward's eyes widened, and he scratched his head as they abandoned the music room and began walking down the hall toward the front door. "Hitch up the buggy? Sure..."

Of course, he must be doubtful about finding his way around on a farm foreign to him. And he probably had servants or a livery close to their home for attending to such matters, living in the city. She offered a reassuring smile. "My sisters and I will wait for you here on the veranda."

Ten minutes turned into fifteen as Veronica and her sisters paced outside the front door. Veronica fussed with her bonnet, Delia remarked about the weather, and Gladdie smoothed her gown as often as she sighed.

"I wonder what's taking them so long." Delia gazed toward the barn with an arched brow.

"I don't think they know what they're doing." Gladdie paused in her pacing to tap her foot.

"Let's give them the benefit of the doubt. They hardly know where we keep things, since they are visitors," Veronica pointed out. "Maybe they had to find someone to help."

But fifteen minutes stretched into twenty. By the time the brothers appeared with the buggy, Edward holding the reins behind one of their oldest mares, and certainly not one Veronica would have chosen, her sisters had to smother a good chuckle.

"This is going to be one endless buggy ride," Gladdie mumbled. "Millie is slower than molasses."

"Shall we change out the horse?" Delia asked.

Obviously, Edward and Rupert had done their best. Veronica didn't want to embarrass them. "No, let it be. It's taken them long enough. Millie will probably enjoy the exercise if we don't stay out too long."

Rupert led her sisters to the Oldsmobile, and Edward came around to help Veronica climb into the buggy.

Once they'd turned onto Cornflower Road, the others crowded into the Runabout and following at a slower than slow pace, Veronica wondered if the machine would sputter and stall. She turned to look up at Edward as she rearranged some of the pins in her favorite hat with its piles of cream-colored chiffon so she could see his face better. She smoothed her best Sunday gown, a matching cream chiffon concoction with criss-crossing panels over the bodice and a slender but flowing silhouette with a modest demi-train trimmed in cream lace.

"I'm curious, Edward J. Beckett. Why haven't you married before now? I'm sure you're popular among the ladies with your good looks." She made a mental note to ask him later about what his middle initial stood for.

Edward grinned and tossed her a glance. "You think I'm good looking?"

"Of course," she said with a teasing smile, "but don't let it go to your head."

"Why haven't I married?" He let out a whistle. "That's a good question. I haven't fallen in love yet. I suppose I once knew a girl, Ava, I liked a little more than the others, though I can't say we fell in love. But her father purchased a hotel in California, so she moved to the west coast with her family. I had my studies at Princeton. With a double minor in economics and history, plus my fine arts major, it didn't leave much time for anything beyond the usual campus social activities. I have spent my fair share of time escaping my mother's matchmaking efforts with New York society belles. She's always introducing me to someone or insisting I dance with someone's daughter. Let's just say, I've fine-tuned the art of hiding at social events."

Veronica laughed. "I can just imagine you hiding in curtained alcoves at balls and all of the ladies searching for you."

"It would not be far from the truth, although I do enjoy dancing now and then. What about you? I saw a dozen beaux swirling around you at church this morning."

She smiled and looked out toward the countryside, busying herself with pulling her cream gloves on more snugly as the mare plodded along the country roads around her home. "I wouldn't say there were that many, but yes, I suppose I've had my fair share of beaux. The only one I ever really loved was Henry Sullivan, but his brother Percival pestered me to death with unwanted affection. Once one of my dearest friends betrayed my secret and informed Henry of my feelings for him, he didn't care if I existed. He dismissed me as a silly, lovesick girl."

"It must have left you feeling as if you'd lost both a trusted friend *and* a possible future love."

"Yes, it broke my heart more than I care to admit. There were a few other gentlemen callers over the years who have asked for my hand, but I couldn't marry any of them knowing it wouldn't be for love. Of course, each time I declined a marriage offer, it threw Mama into a tizzy, but I am determined to marry for love or not at all. In fact, I would prefer to live out my days right here at Velvet Brooks. Right where I belong. I do not need a husband to ensure my happiness. I'm perfectly happy the way things are."

Veronica fidgeted with the elegant lace trim on her right sleeve, tilting her chin upward a little for emphasis on the last phrase. She needn't tell him her heart had been broken so badly, she could never let herself open to embrace love again. If she ever did, it would take far more than someone singing a few sweet songs or accompanying her on a few outings.

"I can certainly understand and agree," he said in a gentle, calm voice. "I mean, not wanting to marry for reasons other than love."

The conversation lulled, and she imagined they both

pondered the many reasons they shouldn't marry each other. She had a life she loved in Kentucky. Other than her suspicion about him preferring artwork to helping his father's business, he seemed content with life in Manhattan except for the occasions when his family retreated to their South Carolina coastal estate, Chesapeake Manor. She'd heard his father speak about the home they kept for summer vacations and getting away from the snow for a few weeks at Christmas, and though she imagined it a grand place, one where she could become the future mistress if she agreed to marry Edward, the fact remained—they didn't love each other. They barely knew each other. Though they had a strong mutual interest in artwork and books, he behaved like a fish out of water around a horse farm. She didn't know much about city life, much less about maintaining two grand homes.

Still, she had to know..."And do you have ambitions to become a full-time artist, Edward? Or do you look forward to inheriting your father's investment company one day?" Why not bring it up?

"Nothing would make me happier than the pursuit of my artwork, but my father considers my art and Rupert's interest in animals as hobbies, not careers. He has only permitted us to pursue our fields of interest at our respective universities so we would obtain an education, with the requirement we would each minor in some sort of business, finance, or banking. He fully expects both of us to work at Beckett, Reed & Johnston for the rest of our lives. When he retires, I am to inherit his shares of the company and become a senior partner."

"I see. Perhaps you will find a way around working in stocks someday." She had to say it, although she didn't hold out much hope for him. Clearly, he was trapped, just as she'd suspected.

Yet another reason she shouldn't marry him. He may know all about the stock-trading market on Wall Street, but if it didn't truly make him happy, he had only days of misery ahead.

She knew about horses—breeding, training, and racing them. She came from generations of the horse-racing world. She remained close with her family, but the way Rupert had not defended his brother's dream of becoming an artist, the way Edward seldom addressed his father, and the absence of his mother and sisters made her wonder if perhaps his family lacked close bonds.

And what of Edward's passion? Where would his dreams fit into his life? What a shame to waste Chesapeake Manor while slaving away at Beckett, Reed & Johnston when he could use their second home to inspire his artwork. And would he end up holding down the fort at the investment company while Rupert found a way to work in some rural community as a veterinarian?

Veronica glanced at Edward's handsome profile. Had the man given up on his dream for the sake of responsibility, sacrifice, and loyalty?

Goodness, even though she would never wish unhappiness in his future, those were also admirable traits.

She needed to look harder and find more things she did not like about this city boy.

CHAPTER NINE

*One who believes that he has mastered the art of horsemanship has
not yet begun to understand the horse.*
—*Anonymous*

After their Sunday afternoon ride, Veronica didn't see
Edward again until Monday morning. He arrived
promptly with more Virginia Bluebells at eleven o'clock to
paint in the garden with Veronica. Mama had answered the
door in Martin's absence and couldn't have worn a wider smile
when she led him to Veronica's side.

She tried not to roll her eyes at her mother's smile, turning
her attention to laying out plenty of art supplies on their easels
instead. So long as her mother thought she and Edward made
an effort, ultimately, he would return to his life in Manhattan.
When nothing more came of their alleged romance, what could
her parents do but admit defeat?

"I see you've set up the phonograph." Edward eased onto a
stool at his easel.

"I thought we could listen to a few songs. I have a small
collection of records we can choose from."

Soon, they'd settled into their artwork, but she frowned and pouted a bit in her struggle to create a realistic sky.

"Having trouble with something?" He paused to observe her work.

"Yes. It's my clouds. They aren't right." She looked over at his progress. "Goodness, you do have a knack for this. Look at you, painting a close-up sign to Velvet Brooks surrounded by all of those flowers, with horses and meadows in the distance."

"Thank you. I can share a technique I've used before to help with your clouds. It gives a kind of layering effect to make them appear like perfect, fluffy clouds in the blue sky. See, like this one."

"Those are brilliant clouds." She frowned at the difference between his clouds and her flatter ones. "I must learn how to make mine like yours. What is this technique you speak of?"

"Here, I'll show you, if you'll permit me. First, dip more paint on the brush." He rose from his stool, standing slightly behind her but maintaining a proper distance between them.

She added more white paint to the tip of the brush as he instructed. "Is this enough?"

"A little more..."

"All right, more."

Once she had the right amount of paint on the brush, he placed his larger hand over her slimmer one, guiding her brush, helping her master the technique on the canvas. In a few moments, perfectly fluffy clouds appeared.

"Now those are clouds," she said, laughing.

They took a moment to admire each other's completed paintings, then cleaned their paintbrushes and palettes and moved to the porch swing facing the garden.

"While dining at the hotel last night with Rupe and my father, the concierge told us 'Sag Harbor' is playing at the Lexington Theater," Edward said.

"It sounds like a great play, one that could have some

humor." Veronica chanced a peek at him as the swing glided forward gently. "Delia said it's about two brothers vying for the same girl."

"Shall we go this evening or attend the family dinner here at the house?"

"Let's go into town and see the play." She hadn't meant to sound so wistful, but she did not relish Pa and Mama spying on their progress of getting to know each other. "I'd rather have dinner in town, too, away from the family. It will give our parents something to talk about when they see you pick me up for an *actual* date."

"All right, I'll see you at seven. That gives us an hour to drive over and find our seats. The play begins at eight, and maybe we can dine at the fine French restaurant across the street from the theater afterwards." Edward sounded as if he tried to contain his enthusiasm. "I believe it's called *La Parisienne*."

"I'll be ready." Hesitation marked her words. It had begun to feel all too natural to be in his company. Maybe she could even get used to it.

Later that afternoon, Grace styled Veronica's hair in a fancy updo and helped her dress in an emerald-green satin evening gown with a swishing demi-train, a shimmery gold-fringed wrap, and elbow-length black gloves.

"You'll be the most glamorous belle in Lexington this evening, Miss Veronica Lyndon," Grace said when she surveyed her final look. "Now mind you don't go breaking that gentleman's heart like you have all the others."

"I have not broken anyone's heart, Grace. Not like ..." Her voice faded as a fleeting thought of Henry passed through her mind.

Did she still have a faint longing for Henry Sullivan? No, she did not. But the pangs of a heart once broken would never permanently erase, no matter how much she tried.

Edward arrived promptly. She had agreed to riding in his

Runabout for their excursion. Veronica's father had sent the carriage to fetch Mr. Beckett and Rupert from the hotel and they, along with her whole family, gawked from the hall as she descended the staircase while Edward gazed up at her in approval. Oddly, it made her heart beat faster. She hadn't felt a stirring like this in a long time. Excitement took over at the prospect of an evening on the town with a handsome, approving gentleman at her side.

The family spilled outside to wave goodbye, abuzz with hopeful whispers. Edward helped her settle inside the Oldsmobile and circled around to climb in behind the wheel. Then they sped away for a dreamy evening, leaving their families to dine at Velvet Brooks on an old-fashioned meal of fried chicken.

They chuckled before the play began about how well their ruse had gone. During the performance, they laughed at all the same moments, their eyes locking on each other. Their shoulders brushed several times, an altogether enjoyable sensation. At the restaurant, they talked about the play, Edward's days at Princeton studying fine art, his life in New York since graduating, and about her former studies at a local finishing school. After they realized the restaurant would soon lock its doors for closing time, Edward paid the bill and left a tip while Veronica freshened up in the powder room.

When she met him outside the front door, he gestured toward the sidewalk, hat in hand. "Would you care for a short stroll? The whole city still seems alive."

She tilted her head to consider it as a carriage drove by and other couples enjoyed a walk along the boardwalk in both directions. "A stroll sounds nice." When he extended his arm and she placed her hand on it, she smiled. How natural and easy their relationship had become since the pressure of marriage had faded a little from their minds. But then her smile faded too. Soon enough, Edward would return to New

York, while she remained at Velvet Brooks. Life would go on as it had before. "I confess, I feel a little guilty, pretending to acquiesce to our parents' expectations when we have no intention of following through."

He shrugged. "Don't feel guilty. It's not an easy situation. We're doing the best we can to muddle through it and avoid further disastrous confrontations with our families. You have a good heart, Veronica."

"Thank you. You're right—I don't want to hurt anyone. Truly, prayer is the only thing I know to do in our situation." She grimaced but then turned to search his face. "Do you spend time in prayer, Edward?" His lack of conversation about spiritual things had led to yet another reservation she'd harbored.

"I do, but there was a time in my life when I couldn't pray. These days, I find myself praying during my artwork time in the mornings, and of course, at the end of each day." He hesitated before continuing. "I don't want you to have guilt because of our outings. These were my idea in the first place."

"I guess the guilt stems from the preacher's granddaughter in me. Grandfather Spencer spent years in the pulpit before he retired, long before our current minister took his place. My grandfather has always said to tell the truth, even when it's hard. And it's one of the ten commandments of Exodus—that we shall not lie. My parents shaped this truth inside my heart, too, but for some reason, they aren't making it remotely easy to tell them the truth. In fact, they told me they won't discuss it again until they choose to. They are treating me like a child when I'm a grown woman." Veronica kept her focus on her steps, trying not to stumble in her lovely evening gown. But also trying not to look at her handsome escort again. Maybe some of her guilt originated from the fact she actually liked Edward, but she did not want to put herself in a situation where the outcome could ravage her heart with so much pain.

"I am sorry for the impossible position your parents have put you in, but it may be your faith is stronger than mine." Edward's tone had grown serious. "My family raised us in the faith, but I still have so many questions. My parents have always been more reserved about their beliefs."

"Didn't they tell you it's wrong to lie?" Veronica gaped at him. Surely, he could understand why she still struggled with guilt over their ruse. And yet...she had never been fully honest with her parents that her reasons for avoiding attachment stemmed from her own heartbreak. And did not withholding truth equate to telling a lie? Here she was talking about lies being wrong when she had failed to recognize the mote in her own eye.

But didn't most rejection lend itself to some degree of shame? And who wanted to bare one's soul to anyone but God in those cases? Maybe at some point, she would feel ready to share her losses more openly. For now, perhaps she should consider laying her shame and guilt at the foot of the cross. She needed to apply her faith, too, that somehow the Lord would work all of this out and protect her heart from breaking in the future.

How had talking to Edward led to so much self-discovery?

His chuckle snatched Veronica's attention back to the present moment. "Yes, of course, and we were properly disciplined if we were caught telling a lie or misbehaving. When I was a child, it meant going to bed early or the loss of a privilege. As a teenager, I found myself in some trouble one summer when a few of my friends coerced Rupert and me into gadding about the countryside, setting the local farmers' chickens loose. Rupe wanted to inspect one of the chickens with some sort of wing trouble. Of course, my brother got away with it, but I was caught. He could run faster."

Veronica laughed, picturing that. "Oh no! What happened?"

"Before I could blink an eye, my parents sent me off to a

military academy...boarding school. Father paid the debt of the missing chickens to the local farmers for my part in the ordeal, but my life changed drastically."

"We had boarding school, too, but for finishing school. By the time we were sent away, we wanted to go. Military academy as a young teen sounds a bit harsh in comparison."

He shrugged, nodding. "I learned my lesson. I disliked military school intensely. I'm an artist, not a military strategist. I wanted to go home, but my parents wouldn't give in to my pleading no matter how many letters I wrote to them about it."

Veronica's heart twinged with sorrow for him at the pain and bitterness she discerned in his eyes. "It must've been a terribly difficult time in your life. Did you lean on the Lord to help you through it, or do you think it pushed you away from God?"

"In retrospect, I know it pushed me farther away. I didn't have anywhere else for my anger to go. As I said, my family didn't talk as openly about their faith as you and your family do. I heard your father thanking the Lord for giving him the second-place and first-place finishes, for instance. He said it out loud for everyone seated around us to hear."

Veronica chuckled at Edward's astonishment, affection warming her chest. "Yes, he does that sometimes."

"I like his attitude of seeing all things as coming from the hand of the living God. No, my parents are reserved and formal, too concerned with etiquette to express their emotions about spiritual things. It's been good for my father to be here with your father, as well as good for my brother and myself. Enjoyable, robust discussions. And I've been learning more and more about horse farming from your father too. He asks us about stocks, and we ask him about horses."

Veronica smiled. "I'm glad my family has made a favorable impression. I'm sure our families will remain friends for years to come." But the idea of their families remaining friends when they parted twinged, leading her to acknowledge the fact she might one day regret the loss of Edward's attention, knowing what could have been. Instead of dwelling on this, she said, "Tell me more about your mother and sisters."

"My mother is busy with managing the household and keeping our social calendar full. My sisters, Henrietta and Sophie—they are silly girls. Maybe you'll meet them again someday, and my reclusive Aunt Lavinia, in South Carolina."

Summing up his closest female relations in one or two brief sentences? How typical of a man. It gave her pause. She wanted to ask him more, but the hour had grown late, and the lovely evening came to an end.

After a drive home in companionable silence, Edward stepped out of the Oldsmobile and came around to help her out of the conveyance. At the door, they stood awkwardly beneath the soft lantern light until he surprised her when he reached for her hand and kissed the back of it, a gentle brush of his lips against her skin.

"Good night, sweet Veronica Josephine," he said in a low voice.

She raised a brow. Had her parents mentioned her middle name to him?

"Good night, Edward J. Beckett. Maybe you'll tell me *your* middle name one of these days..." His breath and kiss still warmed her hand. Dare she want him to warm her cheek or lips with a kiss one day? Fancy her wanting more before he returned to New York. She shouldn't desire such a thing.

He offered a half smile. "James."

She liked the name, however mediocre his expression suggested he might find it. "I was hoping it might be James. It's one of my favorites. Good night, then, Edward James. You can call me Veronica Jo. Everyone usually does, except when elite guests visit us from Manhattan."

At her teasing smirk, he laughed. "I wouldn't consider us elite. My family may think they are, but I wouldn't."

"We'll save that debate for another time, since my father is likely waiting up for me in the library. He won't rest until all of his chickadees are safely home. Thank you for a memorable and enjoyable evening."

Edward smiled with a farewell nod and, jamming his hands in his pockets as he so often did, headed toward the driver's side of the automobile. He climbed in and waved. "See you tomorrow, late morning, for a horseback ride and a picnic—hopefully, with some of that fried chicken we missed."

She couldn't help but smile at his mention of Willamena's fried chicken.

He fired up the engine and drove away, a trail of dust kicking up as he sped down the lane. Rarely had she found such a comfortable and easy friendship with a gentleman before, and his good looks certainly attracted her, but she didn't dare admit anything of the sort to her parents. Giving them an inkling of hope would amount to a recipe for disaster.

CHAPTER TEN

There are few things so pleasant as a picnic lunch eaten in perfect comfort.
— *W. Somerset Maugham*

V eronica gazed out over the creek banks where she and Edward sat on a quilt after their horseback ride as he bit into another piece of the fried chicken leftovers. Willamena and her kitchen assistant, Frances, under Mama's watchful eyes, had packed a feast for two into a large picnic basket. They had added a corked pottery jug of sweet tea to the meal. But the look of amazement on Veronica's face when she withdrew two long-stemmed goblets from the basket had made him hastily ask, "What's wrong?"

"This definitely isn't a normal picnic." Veronica's brow had furrowed. "We usually get tin cups, wooden plates, and mismatched odds and ends utensils in case anything is lost or broken. That is, unless the meal takes place closer to the house...or if it's for one of our horse competition events. On those occasions, our staff will dress up our tables in the garden or under a big tent."

"Nothing wrong with your mother trying to do something nice for you."

Veronica was still pondering that as Edward took another bite of the potato salad before returning to taste more of the chicken he held with his other hand.

"Your family has the best cook." Edward eyed the spread on the quilt as he finished his plate of food. "I think I'm ready for a slice of that sweet potato pie."

Veronica served the dessert and offered it to him on a small plate.

He reached for it, then dropped his hand. "Well, maybe after two more of those pickled beets and one more pickled egg."

Laughing at his hearty appetite, she took the plate back, added the pickled items, and handed it to him. As she did, a thought struck. "Maybe all of this isn't my father's doing at all. Maybe it is Mama's."

"You mean your father packed all of this?" Edward waved his fork over the spread.

Veronica giggled. "No, silly. If he'd packed it, we'd have a chunk of ham and a pocketknife. And no napkins or dishes."

Edward laughed so hard he had to set his pie down. When he finally recovered, she continued.

"I mean, I just realized maybe it's my mother influencing my father to arrange a marriage between us. I've been struggling to understand Pa's insistence on financial security. But Mama...she has always cared a little too much about what her New York and Baltimore society friends think."

An image of running into her mother in the hallway after her father first mentioned the arranged marriage returned to her mind. Had her mother eavesdropped on the discussion? Had it all been her idea in the first place? Hadn't she attempted to meddle and make matches a few other times when eager suitors appeared on the doorstep?

"I didn't realize she traveled in New York and Baltimore circles." Edward put his fork and plate aside, turning his attention fully toward her.

"She does, occasionally. Usually only during an out-of-state race when she might attend with my father. I've accompanied them for a few important races myself, but my mother maintains extensive friendships with some ladies back east. She receives letters in the mail from her friends and has visited some of them before, sometimes even with my sisters and me in tow."

"I see." Edward shifted his position. His brows furrowed. A pensive look appeared on his face, and he tilted his head. "I wonder if my mother and yours may know some of the same friends."

"Possibly so. In any case, I keep coming back to something my father mentioned when he said our marriage would secure my place in New York society. I didn't even know he cared about New York society, but I believe my mother does. Of course, like most fathers, he usually goes along with everything Mama wants, for the sake of peace in the household."

"Aha." Edward sliced into another bite of the pie with his fork as she picked up a piece of chicken. "The plot thickens."

"Yes, indeed." Veronica waved the piece of meat. "She probably gave him this whole cockamamie idea." She sighed, then caught herself and returned the chicken leg to her plate, untouched. She'd lost her appetite.

"Are you going to eat the last pickled egg?" Edward eyed said item with a raised brow.

"You can have it." She handed the egg to him. "What about your father? What are his motives?"

Edward finished the last bite of the egg as he held the dessert plate with his slice of the sweet potato pie. "Money. It's always about money with my father."

Veronica bit her lower lip and crossed her arms over her

chest. "I am not a horse they can simply trade in some grand, old-fashioned, outdated dowry scheme."

"I hate to say it, but you're actually looking at that all wrong."

"What do you mean?"

Edward finished the pie and set his plate aside. "The higher the dowry, the more esteemed and valuable the woman. It signals the man in pursuit of her that she is beloved, highly sought after, to be protected..."

She inhaled a quick breath as she considered his statement. "I hadn't thought of it like that before."

The burble of running water in the swift creek provided an underlying soothing sound, nature's embrace relaxing her as his statement had. She let out her breath.

Their horses, tethered to an oak tree nearby, nibbled on the luscious blades of grass, content to look in their direction from time to time. Green leaves had returned to the trees in the thick wooded area on the other side of the water, and the rich soil along the banks contrasted nicely with the foliage. Wildflowers clumped along the tree line. Blue chicory and white bloodroot blossoms with their yellow stamens peeked up from the earth. Soon, summer lilies and daisies would bloom too.

She looked up into his face. "Is that how you think of me, Edward?" She had to know.

Edward scooted closer, resting his hand over hers. "Absolutely. Of course, I do. In truth, I'd like to spend far more time with you now that I've had a chance to get to know you better. I'd like to take you to New York and South Carolina to meet the rest of my family in our environment. But we'd have to be willing to become engaged because it's what my father expects. It's the arrangement our fathers have, and in matters like these, we'd have to show solidarity to their plan."

She looked down at his hand resting on hers. "If I didn't know better, I'd think you were proposing marriage to me. Are you inviting me to come to New York as your fiancée, Edward James Beckett?"

"Yes, I think I am." He turned to gaze into her eyes. "You are the only woman I've met who has managed to capture my attention. I would maybe go as far as to say I think I'm falling in love with you, but you'd doubtless feel it was too soon for that. And then I might become discouraged. So I won't say I'm falling in love with you yet, but I think I could easily fall in love with you."

Veronica flushed and bit her lower lip. Her heartbeat had risen, flooding her with all kinds of emotion. "I must admit, I've enjoyed our time together more than I thought I would. I've grown quite fond of you, if I do say so myself, and I'll certainly think about all you've said, but please don't get your hopes up too high, Edward."

He smiled, and they abandoned conversation for the rest of the picnic, taking in the scenery and enjoying the warm sunshine. But Veronica's thoughts raced. After all her efforts to evade a match, was she considering his offer to come to Manhattan as his fiancée? Except for her reservations about leaving Kentucky and her desire to avoid having her heart broken the way Henry had broken it, he had slowly worn down all of her protests.

Did he genuinely find her valuable? She hadn't known him long enough to tell for certain, which was why the extra time together and chance to meet the women of his family might be needed. So far, he seemed like a man of not only integrity, but a man of his word.

❧

*A*fter the picnic, Edward returned their horses to the barn. He'd wanted to admit the truth to Veronica— that he'd fallen for her. He had hopelessly fallen for her. He chided himself for not telling her so clearly. He'd hem-hawed about it instead, because as usual, talking to her about matters of love and marriage equated to holding a butterfly which might take flight in an instant.

He also chided himself for not bringing proper riding clothes to Kentucky. He'd packed a leisure bag with the items, but somehow, it hadn't made it onto the train. He needed to remedy that matter. After turning the reins over to Carter, he paused and rested his elbows on the top rail of the four-board fence outside of the barn to take in the view of horses grazing in the meadow.

He had wanted to kiss Veronica at the picnic, and he almost had, but she continued to speak so adamantly against marriage. Of course, he couldn't admit his discouragement. He adored her feisty personality—her beauty, her confidence.

He found himself falling fast for everything about her.

Sure, he liked fast cars, and she liked fast horses. She liked the countryside, and he liked the city, but he could picture himself in a place such as this, able to concentrate on his painting and artwork. He could certainly see why she was so happy here. He *didn't* see how he could convince her to travel to New York with him, and he had little hope she would accept his ridiculous proposal to come as his fiancée.

He sure had messed that opportunity up. He should have presented her with a diamond ring or something, though it was doubtful that would have worked either. At least he'd asked her to join him in New York. Maybe she'd think about it, but why did it seem as though he was headed straight for a broken heart? How could he turn the tide? Did he have any chance with her?

He spotted Joseph Lyndon walking across the lawn from the main house to join him and turned to greet him.

After reaching his side, Mr. Lyndon shook hands with him

and patted him on the back. "Nice to see you, Edward. How are things going with you and Veronica?"

"I don't exactly know, sir."

Mr. Lyndon harrumphed. "If that isn't a classic answer in response to a question about a woman, I don't know what is. I don't know how things are going with Eleanor half the time, either, if it makes you feel any better."

Edward chuckled, but he didn't feel like chuckling. In fact, he felt downright baffled. He removed his hat and raked a hand through his hair. "I don't think Veronica will marry me, to be honest, sir. In fact, I don't think she'll marry anyone." Though Veronica had mentioned marrying for love, how could she ever surrender her heart with so many internal guards up? He stood at a crossroads in his relationship with her, but truly, something bigger than the reservations she had given him seemed to be blocking them from moving forward.

"Funny you'd say that. It's the same feeling Eleanor and I have had ever since... well, ever since Henry Sullivan broke her heart."

Edward stood up taller. He recognized the name—and recalled meeting the fellow at the Phoenix Stakes. "Yes, she mentioned him. It did sound like a situation that could have disturbed her more deeply than perhaps she cared to discuss with anyone."

Mr. Lyndon nodded. "She's fiercely loyal, and she's always had a bit of a stubborn and independent streak, but we think she suffered such a terrible break of the heart, she flat out decided not to ever try to love again. We're rather hoping you can help her past that, but it will take some patience, a whole lot of love, and maybe a great deal of persistence."

Could this truly be the answer? Edward blew out a breath. "It does make sense. Thank you for sharing this with me. I was ready to give up. I've been so baffled."

"Don't give up. She'll come around for the right person, and

Eleanor and I happen to think that person is indeed you, especially after seeing the two of you together. We've never seen her let anyone as close to her heart as she has you, not in a long time. The way she looks at you...it's different than with the other fellas. We have faith in you, son."

"Thank you, sir. That's all I needed to know." He returned his hat to his head. "I had no idea, but now I must say, you've bolstered my courage. I won't give up yet."

"Staying for dinner?" Mr. Lyndon asked.

"Yes, and looking forward to it. Thank you, sir." Edward smiled, relieved to have a clue to the puzzle of Veronica. "One more thing—do you happen to have some extra riding clothes around here? I hate to admit it, but they didn't make it onto the train."

"Riding clothes? I'm sure we have plenty of spare riding clothes. Just tell Martin to find something for you, and Rupert, too, if needed."

Edward brightened. Things were looking up. "Thank you, sir."

He watched Mr. Lyndon continue on toward the horse barn. Maybe Edward could turn things around, after all. But would Veronica be able to trust him, and how long would it take him to prove his trustworthiness? And how exactly could he prove she could trust him not to break her heart?

$\sim$

*V*eronica pondered Edward's invitation to visit New York at the dinner table later that evening, remaining somewhat quiet and distracted. She had enjoyed her outings with him, and their time together would end in less than a week. She had grown fond of him and had to admit, she hated to think about him leaving, but he had an entirely different life waiting for him in Manhattan. And she had her life here at Velvet Brooks. Things would return to some semblance of normalcy when he left, and hopefully, her parents would forget about Edward. But would *she* ever forget the tall, dashing, and debonair gentleman who'd been so sweet and kind to her?

They left their families to finish their dessert and coffee at the dining room table, heading into the library to select books to read from the collection her parents had acquired over the years. Thaddeus Sullivan had also dined with the family, but after the meal, he joined Delia on the back porch swing, leaving Gladdie to entertain Rupert with a game of chess. The adults ended up in the sitting room, and Veronica reveled at having Edward to herself—another strange thought.

As Edward turned page after page in the book he'd selected by Thoreau, she found herself unable to concentrate on Charlotte Brontë's words in the volume she held. Her mind wandered instead to what Edward had said during the picnic. Did she want to spend more time getting to know him? She had to admit, the trip to New York sounded fun, as well as the idea of meeting the rest of his family.

She could picture him showing her Manhattan on his days off, around the work for his father a few days a week and his artwork. However, she could not see herself leaving Velvet Brooks to live in New York. A city girl she was not and would never be, not for any serious length of time. Visits, perhaps, but to reside in New York, so far away from everything she held dear? No, she couldn't imagine it.

She glanced over at Edward, stealing a peek at him. He looked perfectly content at the moment. But wouldn't a husband expect her to live near his family? What if he expected her to live *with* his family? She blinked, shaking her head, and returned her attention to the book in her hands.

The next morning, they took a drive in the Runabout, her

hair blowing in the wind as they sped along on the country roads surrounding the farm.

"Ready to try driving?" Edward pulled the Oldsmobile to the side of the road.

"I thought you'd never ask." When the automobile stopped, she gathered her skirts and practically leapt from the passenger side.

Edward traded places with her, and once he'd settled into the passenger seat, said, "Press the pedal there. There you go. You're a natural."

"I'm driving! I'm driving!" Veronica laughed as the car sped along.

"It's better to learn out here in the countryside. New York wouldn't be a good place to learn if you agree to come to the city and marry me."

She darted him a narrow-eyed glance. "Who said anything about me living in New York? I thought I'd made it clear I could never leave Velvet Brooks."

His mouth hung open, and he raked a hand through his hair. "I just assumed you would live in New York since my work is there."

Veronica didn't know what made her angrier—the thought of living in New York, the thought of leaving Velvet Brooks, or the topic of marrying him. Hadn't she debated this very thing with herself last night in the library? And yet, hearing him make this grand assumption about where they would live somehow seemed so much worse. It all made her so angry that as she stared at him, she steered his rented horseless carriage right into an enormous honeysuckle shrub, no less than a quarter mile from where she'd begun driving.

Veronica gasped and sat up in her seat, craning her neck to peer at the hood. "Oh no, have I done any damage?"

"It's all right," Edward said patiently, though the nose of his rental had completely disappeared into the branches of the bush. "No major harm done. It has reverse."

"We're on the edge of the Sullivan farm. They don't like trespassers. They might shoot at us."

"Not if we back up and get out of here."

"Right. How do I do *that*?" Veronica burst into a fit of nervous giggles as Edward helped her shift the automobile into reverse. Meanwhile, two bumblebees began buzzing between the windshield and their faces. She tried to swat them away. "Oh dear, I'm allergic to bees." Looking up into the bush, she spotted a few more bees buzzing around, and her eyes widened. "Reverse, reverse!"

"Step on the clutch," Edward hollered.

As soon as she'd managed it, he shifted the gear. She mashed the pedal with all the force she could muster. The vehicle shot backward, jerking them three times.

"Brake, brake!" He reached out to help her steer the wheel, navigating them onto the road as she slammed her foot onto the brake pedal, jerking them again.

One of the bees landed beneath her right eyebrow, and a sharp prick made her jump. She screamed and cupped her hands over the sting. Somehow the automobile came to a complete stop in the middle of the road. Tears welled in her eyes.

"Are you all right?" Edward leaned toward her. "Did you get stung?"

"Yes, yes, I did. Maybe you should drive, Edward. I'm terribly allergic to bees. I might die. Truly. Do let's hurry."

His brows flew up. "I'll trade places with you. Stay where you are, and whatever you do, keep your foot on the brake."

She sniffed, holding her hand to her brow. "I don't understand what all of these pedals are for. I think I should stick with horseback riding."

"Fear not. It takes some practice. I had similar problems the first time I drove."

When Veronica took her foot off the pedal to allow Edward to take over behind the wheel, the automobile stalled. Had she damaged the engine for good? "Oh dear. I think I've broken it."

"It's all right," he said as she scooted over on the seat. In seconds, he had fired up the Runabout, turned them around, and sped them along toward Velvet Brooks.

Her brow area throbbed. Edward kept both hands on the wheel, but the frequent glances he sent her conveyed his concern.

"If I pass out, it's because of the bee sting." In fact, she had done so once before. "I'm not really the passing out type, except when it involves bees." She couldn't let him think of her as one of those damsel-in-distress types who needed perpetual rescuing.

He sped up a little more. "We're almost there. Keep taking deep breaths."

"Good idea." She gripped the edge of the seat as he took a sharp turn into the long, tree-lined drive and floored it up the lane. Before she could do as he suggested, everything faded to black and she slumped onto his shoulder.

CHAPTER ELEVEN

We should regret our mistakes and learn from them, but never carry
them forward into the future with us.
—*Lucy Maude Montgomery*

E dward parked outside the front door as Veronica leaned
on his shoulder, passed out. Holding her steady while he
slipped out of the conveyance, he then scooped her into his
arms. He hurried across the veranda to the front door, opening
it with some fumbling.

Now what? Where was Martin? Veronica weighed about as
much as a feather, but the longer he looked around wondering
what to do, the heavier her limp body grew.

"Martin? Grace?" he called out. He thought he heard voices
in the kitchen, and someone upstairs...but the kitchen was no
place for someone passed out, and he couldn't very well barge
upstairs.

The sofa in the parlor seemed like the best place, so he
hastened down the hall. Hurrying across the sitting room, he
stumbled, tripping on the carpet and plummeting toward the
sofa. A sharp pain shot through his ankle, but he righted

himself and held on without dropping Veronica. Wincing, he somehow managed to gently place her on the sofa.

He limped to the door and bellowed, "Mar-tin?"

Still no answer.

But Veronica began to stir. Signs of her returning to consciousness were good, but oh, his ankle! Thumping pain declared the joint most definitely hurt as he hobbled toward the sofa again. Groaning, he sank onto the far end beside her feet.

"Ed-Edward..." Veronica's eyes fluttered open. With one of her arms extending over the other end of the sofa, she drew in a deep breath. "Wh-what happened?"

"You passed out," he managed to say, strain evident in his voice. "But I'm very glad to see you are awake."

"Passed out?" She shifted, and her hand flew to the site of the bee sting, which had begun to swell and turn red. "H-how did we get here?"

"I carried you. But I tripped on the rug and twisted my ankle." He bit back a groan.

"Oh dear, are you all right?" Veronica managed to sit up and rearrange her skirts.

Finally, approaching footsteps and voices streamed from the kitchen. Martin appeared at the door, Grace hovering on his heels, her arms full of linens.

"Pardon the interruption. Everything all right?" Martin peered at them, eyes wide, his brows arched.

"No, Veronica needs help." Edward grimaced. Why did his ankle have to throb at a time like this? He needed to focus on helping the lady in distress. He would not mention his own condition, at least not yet. Martin would think him a clod once he knew he'd tripped on the Lyndons' carpet. "She was stung by a bee on our drive and passed out."

"Oh no." Martin's eyes grew wide as Grace followed him into the room for a closer look.

"Another bee sting! I'll get my medical bag." Grace shoved the stack of linens she carried into Martin's arms and dashed toward the kitchen.

The butler looked around for a place to set the linens. "How did this happen?"

"I remember now. I'm a bit foggy, but I was driving the Runabout, and..." Veronica gulped. Then she rolled her eyes, shaking her head. "I somehow drove us into that huge honeysuckle on the edge of the Sullivan property line."

"You're both lucky to be alive." Martin drew closer and peered at Veronica. "The Sullivans have been known to shoot trespassers."

"I've heard." Edward grimaced. At least that hadn't happened. The fellas in the barn would've laughed him right out of the state.

He'd felt so heroic carrying Veronica into the sitting room—until he'd made a clumsy fool of himself. He took comfort that she hadn't seen him trip. But the truth was, Kentucky boys didn't endanger their women, frighten their stallions, hitch buggies to retired mares, or stumble on rugs.

What would Veronica think of him now?

$\sim$

*V*eronica held some ice wrapped in linen over a glob of soda paste applied to her brow. Though she must look ridiculous, she tried to think of how she might console Edward, who currently held his booted ankle with both hands, his shoulders slumped.

They had endured a steady flow of inquisitive help from the household and staff. Mama had been most insistent about sending for the doctor, dispatching Rupert, Delia, and Gladdie on the errand. Meanwhile, Edward had acted—did she dare say?—embarrassed about the whole ordeal.

He hadn't wanted to divulge how he'd injured his ankle or even admit that he had injured it. All he'd said was that he'd rolled his ankle while carrying her inside. Perfectly understandable, in her opinion. Could happen to anyone. But there he sat on the far end of the sofa, stewing, while Mama went with Martin and Grace to prepare the guest room for him.

Though Veronica could hardly see past the ice she had to hold over half of her face, she smiled weakly, a chuckle escaping her lips. "Aren't we a fine mess?"

"Indeed." He scooted a little closer, likely noting her struggle to focus on him.

She softened her voice. "I hate to admit that I agree with Mama, but it won't hurt for the doctor to have a look at your ankle when he checks my bee sting." Earlier, he wouldn't even permit Martin to remove his boot for a better look.

Edward didn't offer a response, but he didn't argue either. A few seconds later, he slipped his arm around her shoulder and drew her closer in a sweet, comforting way. Weak from her fainting spell, she allowed his embrace.

Someday, her parents would install a telephone at Velvet Brooks. But now, with nothing to do but wait for Rupert, Delia, and Gladdie to return with the doctor in tow, she would content herself in the moment, snuggled beside her city boy.

In spite of the day's precarious events, she had to admit one thing. Nestled beside Edward James Beckett, she rather liked the way his strong arm felt around her shoulders and how she fit perfectly under his arm, close to his side.

When had she begun to think of him as her city boy?

~

*D*r. Avery assured Veronica she would not perish from the bee sting, and only then did she finally put her concerns to rest. He closed his medical bag and offered a comforting smile. "You would have experienced a worse reaction by now if you were going to die, Miss Lyndon, but it's good you escaped from the other bees. I would be more concerned if you had suffered multiple stings. Now, if I might check on the young man's ankle..."

"Thank you, Dr. Avery," Mama said as Veronica sighed and sank into her pillows with a great deal of relief sweeping over her and a fresh cold compress with ice to hold against her head. "If you'd please follow me to our guest room..."

The doctor trailed her out of Veronica's room. Reaching the second floor had been no easy task for Edward, who had barely made it up the staircase, hobbling the whole way while gripping the railing, with one arm slung over Martin's shoulder.

The doctor confirmed what Edward needed most amounted to plenty of rest and time for his ankle to heal. Mr. Beckett and Rupert agreed it best to keep Edward at Velvet Brooks for a few days, and after dinner, Edward's brother brought his personal items from the hotel.

Martin carried meal trays upstairs to him, while Frances brought Veronica's meal trays up so she wouldn't have to appear downstairs with soda paste above her eye or cold compresses held to her head.

The next day, she experienced less throbbing, and she guessed her Manhattan friend might enjoy it if she read a book to him during their afternoon teatime. Not to mention, she had missed Edward's company over the past twenty-four hours. Grace went across the hall and confirmed Edward would accept her offer to read when Martin brought tea upstairs.

"Shall I return to style your hair then?" Grace offered.

"Yes, please. And I'll wear my best afternoon tea dress."

"All right, but this time, I'm not removing the baking soda paste. The doctor said you'll heal faster if you keep the paste on for a few days."

Veronica knew better than to argue with Grace. When

teatime rolled around, she knocked on Edward's open door in anticipation of her visit. "Hello from across the hall," she called out before popping inside.

"Come in, come in." He grinned sheepishly at her from atop his bed. Grace had apparently made up the covers, and he'd dressed for the occasion, though he didn't wear a suit jacket. Despite having his foot propped up on pillows, he wore a bowtie with his freshly ironed shirt, suspenders, and trousers.

"How's your ankle today?" Veronica positioned herself in the corner armchair, poised to read aloud a chapter from the recently published novel *The Crisis* by a fellow named Churchill. But she was all too conscious of the glob of paste on her brow, so she held the book up high before her face.

"Better. Still sore. And how's your...?" He pointed to her brow area as she peeked over the edge of the book.

"It's not throbbing as much as yesterday. Would you like tea?"

"Yes, please."

She set the book aside and poured them both a cup of the hot drink. "I wonder where my sisters are today. I wasn't told where they were going, but I heard the carriage leave."

"Martin told me your father, Delia, and Gladdie are meeting Rupert and my father in Lexington. They are headed to a museum at Ashland," he said, accepting the tea. "They'll return for dinner."

"Ah, I see. No wonder the house is so quiet. The museum is one of the best. All sorts of relics from the war." She stirred two teaspoons of sugar into her brew. "I do hope you won't mind having someone read to you with a glob of baking soda paste above her eye."

"I think it only makes you more adorable," he remarked with a sly grin on his face, causing her to blush.

"I shall leave if you call me adorable again." Veronica gave him a stern look.

"Tossing the word adorable into the waste bin forever," he promised, pretending to do so with a wave of his hand. "Now, tell me about the book you've selected."

Veronica sipped some of her tea and settled into the chair, holding the book up high again. It pleased her to think he considered her adorable with paste on her brow, but she didn't intend to let him see too much of her condition. Instead, she plunged into an introduction of the book. "I think we'll enjoy this look back at the Civil War. There are characters on both sides of the divide, and Abraham Lincoln is yet a rising star as the story unfolds."

"Ah, very good. I'd like to hear your sweet voice reading the story." He sat up straighter, still wincing each time he moved his ankle. "Maybe it will help me forget I sprained this ankle just walking between the front door and the sitting room. I'm sure the boys out in the horse barn will have a good laugh about that."

"I don't think they will laugh about your injury, Edward. Hush, now. Let us not think such thoughts." She turned to the first page.

"Very well, but only if you promise not to hide your pretty face behind that book."

She sighed, flushing again, lowering the book, and began reading the first chapter. How could she resist this gentleman? She had to admit to herself, if to no one else, she'd begun to fall for the city boy. She couldn't say she was head over heels in love, but she did acknowledge a strong fondness for him.

The idea of him leaving for Manhattan soon, and without her, gnawed at the pit of her stomach. Should she consider going with him? Wouldn't she miss all of the time they shared and the attention he lavished on her?

But how could she leave Velvet Brooks? And what if he couldn't leave New York to live at Velvet Brooks? Could they split their time between the two places somehow? Would he agree to marry her even if she didn't fully love him?

Torn by so many questions, she couldn't bring herself to discuss any of it with him.

Worst of all, what if he turned out to be like Henry? What if she fell for him hard and he left her with a broken heart? Could she face that kind of pain again? The answer she kept coming back to was no, she could not.

~

*T*he last few days of the Beckett visit approached. Neither Edward nor Veronica spoke any further about his invitation to accompany him to Manhattan as his fiancée, but the idea swirled around in the forefront of Veronica's mind. Her bee sting healed after a few days, and she no longer needed to apply the baking soda paste, but she continued to read to Edward each day for afternoon tea. Though Rupert and his father traveled daily from the hotel to the farm, Edward remained in the second-floor guest room at Velvet Brooks.

There, he had the best of 'round-the-clock care and attention from the household employees and Veronica's family. Martin, Grace, and Frances insisted on spoiling him, bringing tea and meal trays upstairs, as did Veronica when the staff grew too busy. Levi and Rupert even went upstairs to visit him, and they spoke of the possibility of delaying their return to New York. After four days of rest, though, his ankle healed enough for him to walk with only an occasional limp.

The day before Edward's departure, Mama turned her attention and that of her daughters toward the visit of Aunt Eliza and Aunt Ida. Their mother had two older sisters, both spinsters. Aunt Eliza and Aunt Ida lived together in a small cottage down the road from Grandmother and Grandfather

Spencer and wanted to meet the Becketts before their return to New York.

The aunts sat on one of the two small sofas in the sitting room. Edward's father and Rupert hadn't arrived yet, but Edward sat in an armchair near Veronica's father. The men only drank a few sips of tea before excusing themselves. Edward used a cane for the long walk to the horse barn.

This left Delia and Gladdie seated on the other sofa opposite their aunts. At the end of the room nearest the fireplace, Veronica sat beside her mother to assist with passing out cups of tea. Mama poured from her best tea service while Veronica wished she could escape to the horse barn too.

"Did you hear the dreadful news about Miss Julia Baldwin?" Aunt Eliza asked.

"No, I don't believe we have. What has happened to Miss Julia? She was a fine governess for our three daughters for many years here at Velvet Brooks." Mama added some sugar to her tea and stirred.

Aunt Ida leaned forward and lowered her voice. "She was jilted at the altar on her wedding day this past Saturday."

Veronica gasped, her eyes widening. Poor Miss Julia!

"Oh no, that is dreadful news." Mama's cup clanked in its saucer, and she set it aside, sorrow in her eyes.

"Yes, it is. Such a nice gentleman, too, or so we thought until this happened." Aunt Eliza clucked her tongue and sipped more tea.

"Yes, and we're sorry we couldn't arrive earlier during Edward's visit to meet him. We might have had the pleasure sooner if we could have made it to church, but we've had some sickness in the house. Early summer colds, you know." Aunt Eliza sniffled into her handkerchief, dabbing at her nose. "We're only now well enough to enjoy a buggy ride out to Velvet Brooks. It did us some good, did it not, Sister Ida?"

"Oh yes, I very much enjoyed the buggy ride." Aunt Ida

sipped some of her tea, but the cup and saucer trembled and clinked in her hands.

Her poor aunts. They lived with only each other for company. A good deal older than her mother, how had they managed to content themselves with what seemed a dreadfully boring and somewhat lonely existence?

Why had they never married? Without marriages, they had no children or grandchildren. And now Miss Julia might experience a similar fate.

The room began to close in on Veronica. Her throat constricted.

"I'm so sorry to hear the news about Miss Julia," Mama said. "But I'm very glad to hear you're feeling better."

"Very sad news about Miss Julia," Delia repeated, exchanging glances with Veronica and Gladdie as their aunts prattled.

Veronica's hands tightened on the arms of her chair, and her eyes widened as she truly glimpsed the reality of an elderly spinster's life for the first time. Struggling to breathe, she did her best to maintain her composure. Did the room seem exceptionally warm?

"Yes, but on a brighter note, the fresh air and getting outside to come and visit all of you has improved our health and revived our spirits so much. Sometimes our bones creak now, and Ida's arthritis flares up, and of course, we have the usual aches and pains that come with old age, but we're managing." Aunt Eliza set the crumpled handkerchief in her lap and picked up her tea.

Veronica squeezed her eyes shut for a few seconds, trying hard not to think of growing old and having arthritis. Yet a vision of past visits from her aunts repeating in much the same manner danced before her. Their faces loomed up close in her memories. First, Ida's face, then Eliza's, then her mama's face telling her to marry someone, then Ida again. Only, the sea of faces swirled in front of her like the hands on a clock, spinning. Tick, tock, tick, tock… The faces continued to spin to the left for a few moments and then to the right—all the while, seconds and minutes of life dwindling away at a rapid pace.

"We're enjoying the lovely weather we've been having as June is nearly upon us." Veronica barely heard her mother's comment. The mention of June only made her warm and dizzy. Thankfully, Mama snapped her fan open and for a moment, Veronica had temporary relief.

"I agree, Eleanor. It's been so nice lately with the flowers all in bloom, but with my gout and arthritis, I don't get out often enough for my daily constitutional." Aunt Ida gestured toward the window with a wrinkled hand displaying bony fingers.

Remembering she had her own fan lying in her lap, Veronica picked it up and deployed it with barely contained desperation. Come to think of it, she couldn't remember a time she hadn't heard Aunt Ida complain about her arthritis and gout. The words echoed in Veronica's mind, and their faces began to spin up close in her thoughts again. Gout, Ida whispered. Arthritis, Eliza's scratchier voice added. Creaking bones. Veronica gulped. Did those whispers contain a warning of her future?

"I just hope and pray we don't have another cholera epidemic like the other epidemics Lexington suffered through in the past." Aunt Eliza sniffled into her handkerchief.

Veronica nearly choked on her tea. Would she end up like her aunts ten, fifteen, or twenty years from now?

Mama sipped some of her tea calmly and returned the cup to her saucer. "You don't really think we'll have another cholera epidemic, do you? It's been years …"

Veronica's fan slipped to the floor.

"Are you all right, Veronica Jo?" Delia inquired from her perch on the sofa.

Gladdie turned her head as Veronica started trembling. "You do look a little pale, Veronica Jo."

Veronica set her teacup aside with quivering hands and blinked, shaking her head, hoping to dismiss the visions dancing in her thoughts, to stop the walls of the sitting room from closing in on her. "P-pardon the interruption, b-but if you'll excuse me, I think I need some fresh air. I don't feel quite right."

She rose and hurried out into the hall, dizzy, clutching any furnishings along the way until she found the front door and opened it wide. She stepped out onto the veranda. The tension in her body released, and she breathed in the fresh air. The dancing and spinning visions of the faces of her aunts and mother vanished.

Glancing over her shoulder toward the house, she collided directly into someone's arms. Veronica gasped and turned to look up into Edward's pleasant blue eyes with a flood of relief and safety.

His strong arms clasped her forearms and held her gently but firmly. "Hello, there. Are you all right, Veronica?"

"I—I think so..." What on earth had just happened?

"I came to see if you could escape for a horseback ride. I had a feeling you'd had enough tea for now, or I was hoping. Perhaps a slow ride, what with my ankle just beginning to feel better..."

"Oh, Edward! Edward!" How handsome he looked in his borrowed riding boots and proper riding attire, even with a cane draped over his arm. "Yes, Edward, yes, take me to Manhattan with you."

Edward took a small step back, dropping his hands. "Truly? You mean it?"

Veronica gulped and glanced down at the sleeve of her dress, fiddling with it. "Purely as a test of our relationship, mind you, as to whether or not we might have a future together. I mean, I'm not entirely convinced we do, but perhaps we should continue getting to know each other. And then, we can decide if any more should come of it, of us." She peeked up at his face. "Do take me with you. Say you'll take me with you."

~

*E*dward stood up taller as he looked down at Veronica, his brow arching in wonder. What had caused her to have a change of heart, and should he care why at this point? Perhaps he should just be elated that she was willing to go with him. His father had been pleased at the prospect of him being cooped up close to Veronica—though not happy he'd injured his ankle—and he'd thought it a brilliant way to make the most of his few remaining days with Miss Lyndon. And Edward had enjoyed the past few days, reading books with her and seeing her pretty smile whenever she checked in on him.

He hadn't seen her like this before, though, so willing to give the two of them a chance. He'd thought she would be happy to see him leave so her life could return to normal, but something had shifted. Having sisters, he knew women could sometimes radically change their minds. Maybe it was best not to try to figure this out, but to just thank the Lord above for small miracles.

Recovering, he stammered in delight. "O-of course, yes, I'd very much like to take you to New York, and later, our South Carolina estate."

"That would be very nice." She looked up at him with a genuinely warm smile. "I'd very much enjoy the opportunity to see your studio and meet the rest of your family."

"I've hoped you would give us a chance for some time now. In fact, I've thought of little else since the first day I saw you, racing across the front lawn of Velvet Brooks, all grown up into a beautiful woman with a mind of her own."

Veronica collapsed into his embrace. "Oh, thank you, Edward. Thank you."

"May I kiss you, sweet Veronica Jo?" If he didn't breathe, maybe she would say yes.

Her smile widened, and she tilted the side of her face up toward him. "Yes, you may kiss my cheek, Edward."

He brushed her cheek with his lips. How soft her skin was! And the gleam in her eyes...contentment? Did he detect she may have actually enjoyed his kiss? Indeed, a slight blush tinged her cheeks a rosy pink shade. But she hid her eyes from him, looking down, fiddling with her sleeve again.

"I could get used to this," he admitted, trying to tilt her chin upward with a gentle touch of his finger to view her expression and better gauge her feelings.

Veronica did smile, but only briefly before she spun out of his arms. "Yes, well, that's enough kissing for now. I've got packing to do."

Edward laughed, amused with her escape. "I suppose I can wait until we're in New York. I will try to restrain myself on the train, but do plan on more kissing in New York." His chuckle dwindled as Veronica paused at the door. Hopefully, she realized he was teasing her. Although...maybe it would also help prepare her to open up to him. It would certainly be interesting to see his country beauty react to the city.

She lingered with her hand resting on the doorknob as if she had something else to tell him.

"What is it, Veronica Jo?" he asked gently.

She turned to him, clasping her hands behind her back. Her playful smile reassured him she had indeed realized he teased her. "As for the arrangements when we are in New York, I believe Mother will require that I stay with my Aunt Mae, and I'm sure she'll insist upon my having a travel companion."

"Of course." He nodded.

Before he could say another word, she disappeared inside

the house. He resisted the urge to toss his hat into the air. He could hardly wait to tell his father and brother she would accompany them to New York, after all, but most of all, he had hope. Hope they might indeed marry, if he didn't mess this up. It didn't matter that it had all started out as his father's plan to save the coffers. What mattered was that he'd found the girl of his dreams, and he didn't intend to lose her.

Thank you, Lord!

～

*V*eronica closed the door and leaned against it, touching her cheek where Edward had kissed her. Goodness! The man stirred something within her, something she'd experienced with Henry a few years ago. She had to admit, she liked Edward's kiss, but she didn't dare let him worm his way into her heart the way she had let Henry, only to end up broken beyond repair.

However, she'd come to her senses. If she didn't want to shrivel into an old maid like her two Lexington aunts, she needed to take this small step in the right direction. It didn't mean she had to give him her heart necessarily. A marriage with Edward did not mean she had to love him. She could preserve her heart within the confines of the relationship. That, she might be able to do, for sensible reasons all the way around.

Oh bother. Why was love such a complicated matter? In any case, she would have plenty of time to ponder the answer to that question on the train. Right now, she needed to find Grace or Frances to help her pack her trunks, and let Mama know she would be traveling to New York.

CHAPTER TWELVE

Whoever thinks they are something when they are not, deceive themselves.
— Galatians 6:3, ESV

JUNE OF 1901, MANHATTAN, NEW YORK

Veronica met her estranged paternal aunt at the train station. Aunt Mae peered at her through a pair of lorgnettes she held up to her eyes after lifting the veil draped over her black hat. Her aunt clasped a silver decorative handle to one side of the elegant lenses with her pleasantly plump gloved hands. With her pale but smooth complexion, she showed little signs of aging except for a full face, robust figure, and a widow's apparel.

"I hardly recognize you. Goodness, the last time I saw you, you were this high. Well, don't stand there in the road dawdling. Get inside the carriage so we can be on our way, Veronica."

"Yes, Aunt Mae. It was kind of you to meet me at the station." She'd expected her to send a servant. She waited for

Edward while he finished securing her trunk with Aunt Mae's carriage driver. When He returned to her side, she introduced him. "I'd like you to meet Edward Beckett, my intended." She'd chosen to say *intended* after giving his introduction a great deal of thought. She refused to refer to him as her fiancé yet since he had not officially proposed, but they were obviously more than friends at this point.

Aunt Mae harrumphed, offering a curt nod and another toward Rupert and Mr. Beckett while they stood nearby, guarding their stack of trunks. "Yes, I know who he is, but it's nearly time for tea, and we must be on our way. The traffic will be horrendous otherwise."

Veronica overlooked her aunt's impolite greeting since perhaps she had good reason to fear the traffic. Assuming Edward would understand the ways of elderly folk, she tried not to take offense. It wouldn't do to start off on the wrong foot with her relation.

Turning to Edward, Veronica clasped his hand with her gloved one as she placed a booted Spencer heel onto the first step of the carriage. "I look forward to when you'll call upon me so we can discuss when I should meet your family."

"I'll call on you in a day or two when you're settled and rested from the journey." He smiled, firmly keeping hold of her hand until she settled inside the carriage after Frances scooted over to make room for her on the seat across from Aunt Mae. Mama had spared Frances to be Veronica's personal maid, chaperone, and companion on the trip.

Aunt Mae tapped her cane on the carriage floor three times, and the conveyance lurched forward. Veronica felt terrible about missing the opportunity for Aunt Mae to greet Mr. Beckett and Rupert, but she could only wave and hope they understood her aunt's desire to hurry home.

She only wanted to close her eyes and rest, but Aunt Mae chose the moment to lay ground rules instead of making small talk about their travels or inquiring about the health of her family back in Kentucky. "We'll be home in fifteen minutes if the traffic isn't too terrible. Your maid can unpack for you, and we'll have dinner at five o'clock sharp. Breakfast is served at seven o'clock every morning in the formal dining room. Church is every Sunday at ten-thirty, and lunch is always served at noon, except on Sunday afternoon, when it's served at twelve-thirty after we arrive home from church and change. I seldom receive any visitors on Sundays, but I suppose your Edward may call." Finally, the woman took a breath.

"Thank you, Aunt Mae. That's very kind of you. By the way, Mama sent some blackberry jam from Velvet Brooks."

"I'm glad to hear she remembered my favorite preserves. As I was saying, bed is at nine o'clock, unless you have a ball to attend, and then your curfew is midnight. Tea is served in the afternoons, usually around three. I expect you'll be bringing Frances along on your outings, unless you are accompanied by those insipid and foolish Beckett sisters."

As Frances stared at Aunt Mae with wide eyes, Veronica lifted a brow. Insipid and foolish? Might that explain her aunt's cool demeanor toward the Beckett men?

"I expect you'll avoid going out in public with only Edward until after you are married, and I expect you to adhere to always keeping a chaperone with you and maintaining a proper distance from your intended. Has he officially proposed yet?"

"Yes, ma'am—I mean, yes, I agree to follow all of the rules, and no, not exactly." Veronica sat up straighter. "We are on a sort of trial period, to see if I like his family and all New York has to offer. We haven't exactly worked out all of the details yet, but it is my hope we'll live most of the year at Velvet Brooks."

"Do you gamble, young lady?" Aunt Mae fussed with her veil again, returning the lorgnettes to her eyes as the carriage continued its journey toward a fashionable district in Manhattan, navigating behind a great many other carriages. She leveled her gaze in Veronica's direction.

"I assure you, Aunt Mae, I've never placed a bet in my life." Mama said true ladies could not do anything of the sort. Veronica knew ways around it, such as handing betting funds over to her father or any of the employees at Velvet Brooks who would place a bet on her behalf, but she had never done so, nor would she. She did try to behave as a lady should.

"Good. I cannot stand horseracing and gambling. These are useless and sinful frivolities for the idle and wealthy, and I frown upon the very mention of them. It's why I seldom visit Kentucky."

"Yes ma'am, Aunt Mae. Father said you did not care for such activities." Veronica bit her lip. Could she eventually win her aunt over with kindness?

"Did he, now?" She harrumphed again. "I do miss my brother. I'm very glad to hear you are in a sort of trial period with Edward. It is good to make a man show himself worthy of your hand. But I suppose I should congratulate you. Edward Beckett is a fine catch for a husband."

"Thank you." New York society belles considered Edward desirable? The thought made her smile.

"You'll be the envy of all of New York, but I'm not impressed with his mother or sisters. Don't ask me what I mean by that statement. You'll find out for yourself soon enough."

Veronica swallowed hard and her smile faded. What did her aunt know?

Her aunt tilted her head to one side. "I assume you know Edward is expected to inherit his father's stock brokerage company. You said it is your hope you will live at Velvet Brooks, but I would imagine you'll need to split your time between both states once you are wed. In any case, you should prepare yourself for that possibility."

"I suppose you are right, Aunt Mae. Edward and I are still sorting out those matters." Veronica bit her lower lip.

"Very good. A happy marriage requires sacrifice and compromise." The older woman had already turned her attention to Frances. "The staff gathers in the kitchen for meals and have most of the third floor to themselves."

Frances nodded and spoke up quickly in reply. "Yes, ma'am, thank you."

When they arrived at Aunt Mae's home, Frances unpacked Veronica's belongings and let her enjoy a cup of soothing tea followed by a long hot soak in Aunt Mae's modern bathing tub. Then she rested and did her best to assimilate to her aunt's routine. With so many rules to follow, waiting to see Edward again, and her nerves kicking in about meeting his family, she experienced an odd mixture of worry and excitement.

She also quickly missed her morning horseback rides and the countryside. Adapting to life in a busy city made her feel much like Edward must have felt at Velvet Brooks. Carriages drove by at all hours of the night, the hustle and bustle never ended, and where on earth did folks gather to go horseback riding? Why were the horses so slow and large? And the enormously tall buildings blocked out the sunshine.

Had she made a mistake in coming to New York?

~

A few days later, Edward invited Aunt Mae to join him and Veronica for her first evening out on the town. He escorted them to a steak dinner at Delmonico's, a popular restaurant her aunt approved of. Afterwards, they took in a performance from the Becketts' private box at one of the many Manhattan theaters. The next day, he charmed them with a visit to a tea shop and bookstore. Though the outings seemed to soften Aunt Mae toward Edward, Veronica couldn't help but be disappointed that his family hadn't joined them, and equally disappointed they hadn't yet invited her to dine with them. Was the snub deliberate? How could it not be?

A couple of days later, an invitation to tea arrived, and the day after that, she and her aunt sat with Edward's mother and sisters in the drawing room of the Beckett family brownstone near the corner of Lafayette Street and Fifth Avenue. Aunt Mae lived around the corner on Grosvenor, close enough for walking, but better accessed by a short buggy ride.

Edward, however, had yet to make his promised appearance. Perhaps he found himself delayed by the considerable amount of city traffic her aunt always moaned about.

"How are you enjoying Manhattan now that you've had a chance to settle in with your Aunt Fay?" Gloria Beckett, Edward's mother, peered at Veronica from the elegant parlor settee in the drawing room. Veronica barely remembered Mrs. Beckett and her daughters from their first meeting during her teenage years, but Mrs. Beckett had excellent taste in her furnishings. The settee and chairs featured pinstriped satin cushions which contrasted nicely with velvet drapes.

"My Aunt Mae." Veronica glanced nervously at her aunt, seated in the chair beside her. "Mae Wilson. She was a Lyndon before her marriage to my Uncle George, God rest his soul."

"Aunt *Mae*. How lovely you and your niece were able to join us for tea today, Mrs. Wilson." Edward's mother sipped her tea and surveyed Veronica's aunt before turning her attention back to Veronica. "And now that you've had a nice visit with her, I assume you can't wait to return to the countryside."

She had only just arrived and yet Edward's mother mentioned she could hardly wait to return to the countryside in such a snide tone? Was she trying to get rid of her? Dismiss her from Edward's life? Doubtful that the remark had been made in an effort to be polite, judging by the sour look on the woman's face. And had she forgotten her aunt's name on purpose?

Veronica immediately felt sorry for Edward having a mother who seemed icy cold and indifferent to his future bride —if she ultimately agreed to marry him—not for her own sake, but for his. Now she could understand why Mrs. Beckett and Edward's sisters hadn't accompanied Mr. Beckett and his sons on their visit to Kentucky.

"I do admit a certain fondness and preference for Velvet Brooks, my family home, and the countryside." Veronica focused on maintaining her composure despite the distinct chill in the ornate drawing room.

Surely, at any moment, Edward would arrive and rescue her. At least she had Aunt Mae, but Veronica struggled with what to say and remaining alert. The perpetual racket below her second-floor bedroom window as carriages, vendor carts, modern automobiles, and pedestrians passed Aunt Mae's residence disrupted her sleep at night and her thoughts during the day.

In truth, she could not agree more with Gloria Beckett's statement. She did long to return to Kentucky after she'd had her fill of adventure in Manhattan—only, she and Edward hadn't discussed where they would live if they married or where a wedding would take place. He had also mentioned joining his family for a visit at their South Carolina estate. At some point—if she agreed to marry him—she hoped to convince Edward a Kentucky wedding would be best, but she didn't want to put the cart before the horse. He hadn't officially proposed yet, nor had she accepted him.

Edward had said that after gently breaking the news about the match, his father had told his mother they could soon expect news of an official engagement. Perhaps what Edward had really meant by informing her of this was that he would soon propose. And she'd decided on the train that if things went well, she could say yes. But the Beckett women looked as if they might devour her with their stares alone. None of them smiled at her, and so far, the visit had only made her apprehensive.

Henrietta, Edward's twenty-four-year-old sister, the second-born daughter of the Beckett family, gave her mother a sideways glance and cleared her throat. "I think Mother meant to ask if you've enjoyed seeing any of Manhattan since your arrival."

"Yes, thank you, I have. Edward took my aunt and me to dine at Delmonico's one evening. We saw a play at the new Theatre Republic." Veronica had enjoyed the stunning interior featuring marble staircases, carved balustrades, and a gilded dome rimmed by lyre-playing cherubs. And how nice it had been to have Edward rest his hand comfortingly on hers during one of the acts when the lights were low.

Sophie, the next daughter in the Beckett family and only a year older than Rupert at twenty-two, brightened. Funny, but except for their blue eyes, Edward's sisters didn't look anything like him with their blond hair and thin, aristocratic noses. "Oh, yes. We have a box at the Theatre Republic. What play did you see?"

"Shakespeare's comedy, 'Much Ado About Nothing.'" Veronica offered her most winning smile. At twenty-three, she fit right between the sisters in age. She could surely find some common ground with them.

"An excellent play, I'm told. Leviticus and I plan to see it soon." Mrs. Beckett glanced at the timepiece pinned to her pigeon-front blouse. "Dear me, I wonder what is keeping our boys."

Aunt Mae lifted a shoulder. "The traffic must be horrendous today, or perhaps something at the office has delayed them. As for the play, it was one of the most exciting things we've done since my niece arrived. And we look forward to more excitement with Edward as a most attentive escort, ensuring Veronica has a splendid visit. I can't have my niece visit Manhattan and sit at home when there's so much to do and see here. In fact, our social calendar is filling up quite nicely. I'm starting to worry we won't have enough time to shop for her wedding dress before she returns to Kentucky to finalize the details." She turned to Veronica. "I do think a wedding in the white chapel in Lexington where your maternal grandfather was the preacher for so many years would be lovely. The event of the year."

"The more I think about it, the more I believe you are right, Aunt Mae. A small wedding at my home church sounds divine, but Edward and I haven't had this conversation yet." Veronica tried to hide her smile behind the teacup she held to her lips. How clever of Aunt Mae to mention a Kentucky wedding since Edward's mother wanted to dismiss her so soon and see her return to Velvet Brooks.

Everything seemed to be falling in place, and now Aunt Mae surprised her by rallying to her side—the very last thing Veronica had expected, given her rather tart first words to Veronica on the subject.

"A Kentucky wedding?" Mrs. Beckett's mouth dropped open. "That simply won't do."

Edward chose that moment to appear with his father and Rupert, and Veronica couldn't help but release a thankful sigh. Had he heard his mother's comment? Perhaps he would respond and then she would finally know what he had in mind about where they should marry. It had seemed improper to raise the matter until he gave her a ring.

Aunt Mae raised her chin, ignoring the arrival of the Beckett men. "Why not a Kentucky wedding? At twenty-eight and twenty-three, they are more than old enough to decide where they'd like their wedding, and I'm sure the bride's mother will have something to say about it as well. Veronica is the eldest daughter and the most popular belle of Lexington society. I know this for a fact since her Lyndon grandmother, my mother, who lives in Lexington, sends me letters on a regular basis about everything going on."

Mr. Beckett gave his wife a kiss on the cheek before accepting his tea, but she barely glanced at her husband. He settled onto the settee beside Mrs. Beckett. "Tell me when and where to show up, and I'll be there."

"Of course, you'd say such a ridiculous thing, Levi." Mrs. Beckett set his input aside with a wave of her hand. "But *Edward* is considered one of the most eligible bachelors in New York. He can't just get married anywhere. His place is here."

With little more than a raised brow, Edward pulled a chair up beside Veronica and seated himself, covering her hand with his. "I'm sorry we're late, darling." He'd taken to calling her sweet names. As long as he didn't refer to her as *adorable*, she enjoyed his indulgent nature.

"I'm sure they'll figure it out, Gloria," Mr. Beckett said.

Mrs. Beckett's brows furrowed, her lips pressing into a thin, firm line between sips of tea.

Sadly, Veronica was not off to a great start with her future mother-in-law. She would need to write to her mother at once. She still had yet to meet Edward's Aunt Lavinia at Chesapeake Manor. Hopefully, that would go better.

"Hello, Veronica, Mrs. Wilson." Rupert nodded toward them as his sisters scooted over on the sofa to make room for him. He sat down, smiling warmly at Veronica while balancing a cup of tea with some degree of caution.

"Hello, Rupert." Veronica returned his smile. "Good to see you again."

How nice it was to see a familiar face, someone who could always be counted upon to cheer everyone up. How on earth he'd convinced Leviticus Beckett to permit him to get his degree in veterinarian medical studies and Edward in fine arts remained a mystery, as Mr. Beckett wanted his sons to eventually take over at Beckett, Reed & Johnston. Such a shame that the man allowed his sons to pursue their interests in their studies, but not in their careers. He tantalized them with what they loved but refused to give them the freedom to live their dreams.

"You as well. Are you enjoying Manhattan?" Rupert asked.

As much as she wanted to know Edward's thoughts on where the wedding would take place, it was just as well that the topic had been diverted for now. Should it come up again, she would refuse to comment until she had more time to consider the matter. She had never imagined a New York wedding, not in her wildest dreams—though no doubt, it meant a great deal to Edward's family. What would her mother say?

"Yes, thank you for asking. I haven't seen much of it yet, but we have tea with a Mrs. Cleave tomorrow, and I've accepted invitations to two balls since Edward told me one is a debutante ball. The other is for a ball hosted by Mrs. Cleave. Did I get that right?" When Veronica glanced at her, Aunt Mae nodded. "Oh, and we plan to order my trousseau and wedding gown while I'm here, so a great deal of shopping is ahead of us." Perhaps she shouldn't speak of ordering a wedding gown yet, but she and Edward had been discussing marriage for several weeks now. "With church every Sunday and outings with Edward, I'm sure to see everything important and to stay quite busy."

"Tea with Mrs. Cleave?" Henrietta repeated, her small mouth remaining open in surprise.

"You did say, 'Mrs. Cleave,' as in the Mrs. Cleave on Fifth Avenue?" Sophie echoed her sister's question.

Veronica looked to her aunt for help. Why did they seem so interested in Mrs. Cleave?

"Yes, she is referring to my good friend Evangeline Cleave," Aunt Mae clarified as she returned her teacup to its saucer.

"H-how very nice," Mrs. Beckett muttered under her breath before heaving a heavy sigh and taking another sip of tea. She did not seem happy to hear this news.

"Yes, well, for some odd reason, we can't seem to secure an

invitation from her despite numerous attempts," Sophia began, but when Henrietta elbowed her, she clamped her mouth shut.

"We are looking forward to the debutante ball, although Sophie and I have each had our coming out balls a few years ago. Have you had your coming out?" Henrietta asked.

Veronica dipped her chin. "Yes, I had my coming out ball as a debutante after graduating from the Lexington Finishing School for Young Ladies."

Clearly, Henrietta asked the question partly to avoid the matter Sophie had brought up, but what reason might Mrs. Cleave have for not inviting the Beckett ladies to tea or the ball? Hadn't Edward said he would attend the Cleave ball? Apparently, his invitation did not include his sisters or parents. She could only surmise it had something to do with the fact that Mrs. Beckett appeared quite sour and her daughters somewhat dimwitted and frivolous, judging by the number of frills on their frocks.

"Have you had a chance to see Central Park yet?" Rupert asked Veronica.

"Central Park? Not yet, but I'm eager to see it. Aunt Mae has told me all about it."

Henrietta piped up with unexpected enthusiasm. "Perhaps you'd like to join us for a carriage ride to visit Central Park tomorrow, then, after your tea. We can pick you up in front of Mrs. Cleave's mansion at four o'clock in time for the procession."

Veronica looked at her aunt for approval.

Aunt Mae shrugged and nodded, a reluctant gleam in her eye as she sipped her tea and stared at the Beckett sisters from over the brim of the teacup with some degree of skepticism. Veronica half expected her aunt to produce her lorgnettes and peer through the fashionable lenses at Henrietta with one of her piercing stares.

She could hardly wait to thank Aunt Mae for her support

today, but perhaps she shouldn't say anything at all lest her aunt revoke such excellent behavior. Her paternal relation didn't strike her as the type who would value a compliment until she had truly earned it.

"Tomorrow at four o'clock. I'll be ready and waiting." Veronica welcomed the opportunity to become better acquainted with Edward's sisters—though she dreaded it a bit too. "It's a shame Edward has to work tomorrow, but we'll go again together on another day." Veronica looked over into Edward's blue eyes and smiled as he nodded. She had almost begun to think of him as her fiancé, but she still had to become accustomed to the idea after spending so much time fighting it. As things stood now, she could use his help handling his mother.

Edward set his teacup aside and took her cup from her hands. Then he took her by the hand and surprised her again, pulling her to her feet. "Everyone, you must forgive us for excusing ourselves for a moment. I promised to show Veronica my art studio and some of my artwork."

She smiled as he led her away, a great flood of relief washing over her. She could hardly wait. Could Aunt Mae fend for herself for a few minutes? Then she smothered a laugh at the idea of her aunt having any trouble with the Beckett ladies. She had a feeling her aunt could wrangle a tiger with her bare hands.

CHAPTER THIRTEEN

...Perhaps...love unfolded naturally out of a beautiful friendship, as a golden-hearted rose slipping from its green sheath.
—Lucy Maude Montgomery

Edward pulled Veronica aside the minute they reached the hall, cornering her against the wall beside an enormous mirror hanging above a marble-topped side table. The giggle that escaped her lips suggested she was as relieved as he to escape the stuffy drawing room.

He reveled in the joy of having her to himself, if only for a moment, placing his hands on each side of the wall on either side of her shoulders. "I must ask if you will let me have a kiss, Miss Lyndon. I've thought of little but you today at the office. I could hardly wait to see you."

"A kiss on the cheek. Edward, I would die if your parents found us here, and mind you, they are only around the corner," she whispered.

He brushed his lips against her cheek and then tugged her toward the staircase. He led her so quickly to the next floor that both of them were breathless by the time they arrived.

On the second story, he stopped her beside a potted fern. "One more kiss?" Under Aunt Mae's watchful eyes, he hadn't been able to kiss her, nor on the train journey with Frances constantly at her side. "We are only a few doors from my bedroom. Each time I pass this spot, I shall remember this moment before I close my eyes to pray for you."

She smirked and then batted her eyelashes at him. "Edward, I had no idea you would turn out to be such a romantic at heart, and I see your ankle has fully healed."

She smiled at him in a way that told him she enjoyed his attention. Good! Maybe she would soon begin to trust him with her heart too. He must continue to find little ways to help her open up to him.

He chuckled. "I'll take that as a yes." And since she didn't turn her cheek toward him, she must be granting him permission to kiss her on the lips this time. His heart thundered in his chest. His breath hitched. Ever so slowly, he lowered his head—and she didn't withdraw. Those lash-studded chocolate eyes stared into his trustingly. Amazing!

Edward's eyes fluttered shut as his lips finally contacted hers, sweetly, gently. Pure, unadulterated happiness swept over him in a tingling current from head to toe. As much as he could've lingered, he quickly pulled back. He mustn't scare her away.

"Your kisses feel like heaven must feel."

His eyes opened to behold her lovely smile. "You're happy too?"

She nodded.

"Then I am certain we have taken a step in the right direction...toward being together forever." He took her by the hand again and led her up the next flight of steps to the third floor. Slower this time, lest she trip on that pretty gown.

"You pray for me?" she asked breathlessly as he directed her toward the final set of steps to the garret.

Edward stopped to let her catch her breath, turning to smile at her so she'd see the sincerity in his eyes. "Of course. Ever since you agreed to come to New York, I've been praying for you every night. And visions of you dance in my mind. I thank the Lord for bringing us together, even though it seems to have happened in a way neither of us expected."

"Oh, Edward. I think that's one of the sweetest things you've ever said to me." She smiled, looking a little dazed, her cheeks reminding him of the sweet country roses blooming in the little garden behind her Kentucky home.

He squeezed her hand gently, lifting it to his lips to graze the back. "I don't know about you, but I'm looking forward to a time when I can hold you and kiss you as much as we like, as often as we like, without looking over our shoulders or sneaking away. No worrying about chaperones or aunts."

Veronica smiled, though she cast her lashes down. "I'm beginning to look forward to it, too," she said, "and if I can find the right dress, I'll feel perfectly ready. My sisters can be my maids of honor, and Rupert could be your best man, and maybe your friend Jack could be a groomsman."

"Sounds perfect. I'll tell Jack next time I see him at the office."

Edward led her up the shorter flight of stairs to the garret, and when he opened the door, she flew from one picture to the next, examining each with exclamations of delight. He stood back with his arms crossed over his chest, awaiting her reactions.

"A lighthouse! Oh, look at this one of the seashore. And is this your family estate, Chesapeake Manor, overlooking another beach?" She held the canvas up to the light.

He nodded, smiling. "How did you guess?"

"I don't know. I must have imagined it from what you've told me. Oh, goodness, this horse painting! I love these, Edward. You are so talented. And this space...it's an artist's dream." As a budding artist herself, she would know. Veronica hastened to assess the view from each of the windows.

Edward's chest swelled. He rarely allowed anyone into his garret except family and staff. Jack had visited a time or two, but his family had little interest in his work and seldom entered his domain.

He had more paintings in the closet but not enough time to show them all to her. Yet her approval was evident in her smile and the way her eyes lit up as she held one of his portraits. That's what he cared about. If she approved of his work, it meant more to him than strangers purchasing a painting here and there.

"How do you choose which window to paint beside?" She returned the painting to its proper place, handling it with great care, and crossed to look out over the garden. "I would be so torn. One has the garden, the other the city street below, and so many rooftops to look over with the ocean in the distance. Such a view from up here!"

He shrugged. "I guess it depends on my mood."

"I really love this barn landscape. I would have trouble imagining the countryside from here. I don't know how you do it." Veronica, a radiant and approving expression on her face, held a vivid Flemish-style painting. Her head tilted to one side, a smile playing on her lips. "You must have an amazing imagination."

"Sometimes I find inspiration in picture books or museums, the city streets, past experiences. All sorts of ideas come to me." She came to his side, the admiration he'd longed for shining in her gaze, and he took her hand in his. "My darling Veronica Josephine, someday, after we are married, we will paint up here together."

Her lashes fluttered. "Oh...yes."

Had he detected a bit of hesitation in her answer? He wanted to explore that, but a glance at his pocket watch showed that they were out of time. He needed to return her to Aunt Mae. His mother would be glancing at her timepiece too. So he settled for a kiss on her forehead, his lips lingering a few seconds as he attempted to memorize the feel of her creamy skin, before he led her back downstairs.

When had he fallen for the beautiful creature at his side? Maybe from the first time he'd seen her, so angry with him. But her determination and strength of spirit drew him to her. She was so unlike any other girls he'd met in New York. Not stuffy and superficial. Would he ever be able to truly win her love and trust, or would their marriage be without her whole heart? He needed to work hard to earn her trust, and then in time, love would surely come.

～

How this man stirred Veronica's heart. But how could she tell him she saw trouble ahead in dealing with his family members? Did he want a New York wedding like his mother wanted? And there he went again, assuming they would live in New York after they married. Would he be willing to consider splitting their time between New York and Kentucky?

Questions ran through her mind, but she kept them to herself, not wanting to take a chance on an argument during the sacred time of him sharing his studio. The place contained his hopes and dreams. She knew all too well the importance of the moment when revealing one's work to another soul. No, her questions would have to wait for another time.

～

The next day after tea with Aunt Mae and Mrs. Cleave, at three minutes after four, Veronica stepped onto the front porch of the Cleave mansion. It had taken her several minutes to find her way to the door again since she had followed her aunt and Mrs. Cleave down a different staircase from the second-floor parlor of the grand mansion as the older ladies departed for their own drive in the park. She spotted the Beckett carriage with Edward's sisters at once. She had worried she might miss them, but their ostentatious hats drew her attention.

With a wave and a smile, Sophie began to open the carriage door, and Veronica stepped forward to board. But an automobile horn bellowed three long blasts from behind them. The Beckett driver snapped the reins in frustration and pulled away into the heavy traffic, leaving her standing there on the side of the road.

The automobile moved on, too, and she stepped back onto the sidewalk before she might find herself splayed flat on the road. The plumes in the Beckett sisters' hats waved as they drove away. From what Veronica could tell, the women did nothing to stop the driver. A long line of carriages, all heading in the direction of Central Park, she presumed, followed behind.

She let out an indignant puff of air. "Well, I never!"

How could she send word to Aunt Mae, who had surely left with Mrs. Cleave by now? What was she to do?

The next moment, a carriage pulled up in front of her with another pair of footmen and an elaborate crest that looked strikingly familiar. This time, a footman climbed down from the seat beside the driver without delay. Ignoring the traffic behind them, he promptly opened the door, calmly released the carriage steps, and held out a hand to assist her inside.

So taken by surprise at this turn of events was she, Veronica had yet to look at the faces of the passengers inviting her to climb aboard.

"Don't dawdle, Veronica," she heard Aunt Mae say.

A wide smile overtook her face. She accepted the footman's hand and settled into the carriage. "Aunt Mae, Mrs. Cleave, you've rescued me from disaster. Thank you!" Of course. She'd seen Mrs. Cleave's crest embroidered on a pillow inside her parlor.

"I thought something like this might happen," Aunt Mae remarked as the footman returned to his seat. "Don't say I didn't warn you about those two."

"It doesn't surprise me either." Mrs. Cleave snapped her fan open. "Your aunt and I thought we should make sure you were all right, just in case. I can see we made the right decision."

"I'm so glad you did. I'm not sure what happened. Their footmen seemed concerned about the heavy traffic, but one would think he'd be accustomed to it." The carriage merged into the long line of conveyances on the avenue, and Veronica sighed with relief. She would see the park after all, and without worrying about offending Edward's sisters. Smiling at her fellow passengers, she added, "I can't think of any finer company."

Except perhaps if Edward were to join them one day. The memory of his sweet kisses made her shiver with delight.

They soon feasted on the glorious sight of the park's green lawn. Romantic couples at leisure drifted in rowing boats on a lake shared with gliding swans. A cascading water fountain caught Veronica's attention. Friends strolled throughout the park, arm in arm as they basked in the afternoon sunshine. She exclaimed over elaborate arches and feats of architecture and admired rows of wrought iron gates bearing hanging baskets with flowers spilling over their edges.

She also learned a little more about Mrs. Evangeline Cleave. Apparently, Mr. Charles Cleave owned a number of hotels throughout the States, three of them in New York. Folks in Manhattan considered him one of the wealthiest gentlemen in America. He'd built the Cleave mansion for his wife, a Philadelphia socialite back in the day. Aunt Mae had attended finishing school with Evangeline in that fair city, and she remembered when Charles had begun his courtship with her friend at about the same time Aunt Mae had begun courting Uncle George. Like Aunt Mae, Mrs. Cleave had no children.

On their way home, Aunt Mae added more insight. "Here in New York, Charles quickly became friends with Cornelius Vanderbilt, J.P. Morgan, the Astors, and he's even done business with the Rockefellers. These families frequently stay at his hotels, and they look out for each other."

"Ah, I see." Veronica's eyes widened at this impressive list of names.

"In any case, suffice it to say, I wouldn't want to cross Evangeline or any of her friends. She's fiercely protective, and don't let her poodle fool you. Roosevelt is even more ferocious."

"I did think he was awfully cute, but does our vice president know her dog is named after him?"

"He does, and when Mrs. Cleave brought him along on a visit for tea, he and Alice laughed and thought it quite an honor. Evangeline's dog and our vice president remain good friends."

Veronica had a feeling Aunt Mae and Mrs. Cleave could put New York society at her feet if she wished for it. But what she wished for more and more every day...was a future with Edward. Would he soon secure that future with a proposal?

~

Edward waited for his father and brother to leave the dining room the next morning after breakfast. His sisters slept in later than usual, but this worked in his favor. Hopefully, his mother would linger at the table after his father left for the office with Rupert. Today was his day to work in his studio, or spend it with Veronica, but at the moment, he had something important on his mind. Something he hoped Veronica would very much like if all went according to plan.

"Have a nice day, dear." His father leaned down to drop a kiss on his mother's cheek. "Remember, tonight is the night I take the train after work to convince Jacob Hartman of why he should purchase one of our tenements. If he says yes, we'll make an enormous profit. Enough to consider investing in a larger tenement someday."

"Yes, of course, dear. If you're sure this is the right move..." Mother sighed. "You've never let us down before."

"I'm sure. I'll send a telegram before my return so you can make arrangements for someone to pick me up at the station."

"I'll be here fending off rumors. I don't know what I'm going to tell Henrietta and Sophie." Mother sulked, shaking her head, her hand trembling a little as it held the letter she'd received from her supposed friend.

"Don't let Agatha's letter bother you." Father wiped his brow with his handkerchief. "And you'll think of something to tell the girls."

Edward frowned. Had he seen sweat on his father's brow? How would Father have a way to purchase a new tenement, even if the sale went through, and even if it did provide a tidy sum?

"I'll do my best to manage while you're gone, but this is really getting out of hand." Mother stared at the letter in her hands. "We simply must find a way to put an end to these dreadful rumors."

"Come along, Rupert, or we'll be late. See you later, Edward." Father darted away from the dining room faster than Edward had seen him move in ages.

Rupert gulped down his coffee, set the cup aside, and reached for two more slices of bacon. He took a large bite of one of the strips and winked at Edward—indicating that he wouldn't let on that he knew anything about their troubles.

"Paint something good. It's not my day off, sadly, but I'll see you at the office next time."

Edward nodded. "Thank you. Have a good day, Rupe."

His brother paused beside Mother's chair and placed a comforting hand on her shoulder. "Have a wonderful day, Mother. Don't listen to Agatha. She was always a little too gossipy for my liking, anyhow."

His brother dashed through the arched door and out into the main hall while jamming the remaining bacon in his mouth, hurrying to catch up with Father.

Their mother had gone on and on all through breakfast, troubled about Agatha's letter bearing more rumors about the decline of their financial status and stating Agatha would no longer permit her daughters to associate with Edward's sisters. A friend no more. Did everything in New York revolve around social status? Didn't anyone offer friendship with real and lasting loyalty these days?

Yet another reason to ponder leaving New York behind someday. But with his father's expectations and the pressure of saving his family from financial disaster, the idea hardly seemed worth considering any time in the near future. Except... Veronica clearly wanted to spend a great deal of time in Kentucky, and the closer they got to a wedding, the more that troubled him.

Could he somehow split his time between New York and Velvet Brooks? That seemed like the only answer to his dilemma if Veronica ultimately said yes to marrying him. And now seemed like the perfect time to find out if she *would* say yes. Hence, his plan.

He swallowed more coffee and laid the newspaper aside. He hadn't managed to concentrate on it. He almost wished his sisters had joined them for breakfast so they might catch on to some of the troubles they faced.

When a servant cleared away his plate, he leaned forward. "Might I have a word, Mother?"

Mother looked over at him. "I'm not sure now is the time with all of this on my mind, but go ahead, Edward."

He cleared his throat, mindful of being cautious in what he said to his mother since Father had never admitted the truth behind the rumors to her or his sisters in an effort to spare them from worry. And Mother had only agreed to consider him marrying a bride from Kentucky because of the rumors. "Yes, well, I've heard about these rumors, too, and I don't like them anymore than you do. I think what we need is a wedding. If I ask Veronica to marry me, you can leak out the news of our engagement. And then people will be so excited about our pending nuptials, most of them will forget about this other gossip." He paused, giving her a chance to absorb what he'd said.

"Hmm, you may be right, Edward." His mother perked up a bit and set Agatha's letter aside. "People do love weddings."

Before she could interject any of her other thoughts, he plunged forward. "I remember you told me that when the time came for me to marry, you wanted me to present the tiara and the matching set to my prospective bride as an engagement ring and wedding jewelry. The one you said had been passed down through your family to the eldest child." There, he'd said all he needed to say.

His mother's mouth dropped open. "Why, Edward, you clever son. You remembered my request. And I think you are right. We must do everything we can to deflect these horrid rumors. An engagement announcement should squash these rumors entirely. You must ask her at once. I'll retrieve the jewelry." She pushed her chair back and rose. "I do hope you can convince Miss Lyndon of a New York wedding, but in any case, wait right here."

Edward relaxed in his chair as his mother made a beeline

for the safe in the upstairs master bedroom. Hopefully, Veronica would like the set. At least his father hadn't sold it—at least not as far as he knew. His mother would never let his father sell precious family heirlooms without her consent.

He drummed his fingers softly on the white linen tablecloth, waiting for her to reappear with the jewelry. Maybe now he could also find a day at the office without his father around to have a closer look at the business records to see how bad things were. Perhaps he could even find a solution to their current problems if he had more of a clear picture of their financial situation.

Instead of telling him what he wanted to know, his father talked in circles. He avoided answering specific questions and told Edward he didn't need to know all of the particulars. Yet he expected Edward to simply hand over Veronica's dowry and commit to carrying on what could be a failing business. He deserved to know more, but as usual, his father had to control everything, even if it meant shrouding important details in secrecy.

When his mother returned with the square jewelry case, a smile on her face, he breathed a sigh of relief. She placed it on the table and opened it, revealing the sparkling gems. Today would not be the day for searching through his father's business records. No, today he would need to make a reservation at a fine dining establishment, cement his plans, find all of the right words, and prepare a proper proposal. He prayed Veronica would say yes, because at this point, his heart would never be the same again if she declined him.

CHAPTER FOURTEEN

... Isaiah was right when he prophesied about you hypocrites; as it is written: these people honor me with their lips, but their hearts are far from me.
—Mark 7:6, ESV

Veronica answered Edward's telephone call on Aunt Mae's modern telephone the next morning. He asked if she and her aunt might like to join him for an evening of dinner and dancing at the rooftop garden of the Waldorf Hotel. He said he would bring his brother and invited her aunt to join them.

"Wear something nice. It's bound to be a very special evening," he added.

Did she detect a little more excitement than usual in his voice?

"It sounds perfect." Looking toward Aunt Mae for permission, she smiled to find her aunt nodding with approval.

"I heard everything he said. Tell him yes," Aunt Mae insisted as she leaned toward the receiver in Veronica's hands. "But I won't be dancing with Rupert."

Turning back to the telephone, Veronica replied, "We'll be ready at seven."

Frances laid out her evening attire and styled her hair in an elegant updo. Veronica dressed in a flowing evening gown, an ivory and mauve concoction with a scooped neckline in the back, draping in folds to a ruched waist before spreading into an elegant demi-train. She pulled on long evening gloves and donned a simple pearl necklace and drop earrings to complete her look.

Would Edward finally pop the question and make her his fiancée? Why did she want this ring so much when she had so adamantly opposed it only a month ago?

When had she begun to fall in love with Edward? Did she dare admit it to herself? Could she trust him with her heart?

Frances whistled, making her laugh. "You'll be the prettiest lady there. I do wish your mother and sisters could see how lovely you look."

"Thank you, Frances," she said.

Most satisfying of all was how approving Edward looked when she came down the staircase. He helped her and Aunt Mae into the carriage with Rupert, then his driver navigated them to a stunning venue.

After Edward and Rupert escorted them to one of the very few empty tables with a stunning view of the city skyline, she ordered a Waldorf salad, salmon glazed in brown sugar, and green beans almondine. Each table was a dreamscape with some positioned under floral arches, others flanked by flowering trees, and some near flickering candelabras standing five or six feet tall. Surrounded by potted plants, elegant garden beds, and palms waving gently in the occasional breeze, a sinfonia played waltzes and classical pieces mingled with one or two modern love songs. Couples danced in the central garden, its dance floor a mosaic of Italian tiles.

Edward couldn't have chosen a more romantic environment, and the feeling inside Veronica that this evening would hold a special place etched forever in her memory intensified. She had never imagined eating on the rooftop of a tall building as the splendor of the sunset turned to moonlight. Waiters kept glasses full at linen-covered tables dressed with glass goblets and fine china, surrounded by containers of roses, lilies, and orchids.

Conversation flowed as they finished the meal under a blanket of stars, all of it making Veronica feel dizzy and spoiled. Rupert pulled her aunt into a discussion about Velvet Brooks. Aunt Mae appeared to enjoy hearing about her childhood home from his perspective. She even asked Rupert questions.

Edward's gaze rested on hers throughout the evening. Eventually, he asked about her visit to Central Park.

"It didn't go exactly as planned," she explained, relaying the story of how she'd missed the carriage with his sisters by mere seconds.

"I'm surprised Henrietta and Sophie didn't mention it at dinner yesterday." Edward's brows furrowed. "Did they mention it to you, Rupe?"

Rupert shook his head as he reached for a crystal pepper shaker and proceeded to season his potatoes julienne. "No, I don't recall them saying anything."

Edward pulled Veronica's hand into his. "I'm sorry. I will speak to them and make sure this doesn't happen again. In fact, I will make sure they call upon you to issue an apology."

"That's very kind of you, Edward." Aunt Mae nodded approvingly.

Veronica didn't want to spoil the evening by criticizing his sisters, and Edward's apology made her heart swell with appreciation. "I ended up in Mrs. Cleave's carriage with Aunt Mae." She lifted her shoulder in a nonchalant gesture. "Mrs. Cleave was an excellent hostess, quite knowledgeable about everything in the park."

"Yes, we certainly did have a lovely outing," her aunt agreed before tasting some of her asparagus toast.

"I'm glad it all worked out." Edward let the matter drop, but the way he flattened his mouth and the furrow in his brows showed her he held some degree of concern about the incident.

When she'd finished her meal, Edward stood, extending his hand toward her. "May I have this dance, Miss Lyndon?"

Her heart fluttered at how debonair he looked in his black tailcoat and white vest and cravat. "Yes, you may, Mr. Beckett." She allowed him to pull her to her feet. Had the moment finally come?

He drew away from Aunt Mae and Rupert, but instead of escorting her to the dance floor, he led her toward a cascading waterfall flowing into a pond with a fountain bordered by more potted flowers and greenery, all of it lit up with candles floating on the water along with lily pads and purple crocus. More lights displayed a variety of colors from behind the waterfall, reflecting on the pond. He took her to one side of the waterfall behind some tall potted palms where they had some degree of privacy.

"Before we dance, I'd like to give you something." He withdrew a thin but wide velvet box from his pocket and opened it. "I'd like to make you my wife, Veronica. You deserve a ring and a proper proposal to make it official."

Edward dropped onto bended knee, and Veronica's eyes grew misty.

"I promise I'll do everything in my power to make you happy all the days of your life. You'll always remain my number one priority, my God-given gift, the woman I'd like to create a family with. Will you marry me, Veronica Josephine? I know we have many details to work out, but I assure you, we can."

Hearing the words from Edward set some part of her heart free. Her heart soared. "Oh, Edward!"

Captive by his blue eyes, she finally glanced at the dazzling jewelry he held out in the silk-lined box. The set must have belonged to his family for generations. There was a diamond ring in rose gold with two ruby gems flanking each side. A matching bracelet, earrings, necklace, and a small tiara accompanied the ring, each with more stunning rubies, dangling pearls, and diamonds.

Veronica clasped a hand over her mouth. "It's beautiful, Edward. Yes, of course, I will marry you."

Joy and relief blazed across his features. "You will?"

"I will! I could never have imagined all of this. However did you acquire such magnificent items?"

Edward rose. "These were my mother's, and her mother's before her, and so on, although they have had some updates since then. I thought you might like to use some of the jewelry on our wedding day."

"Thank you! Yes, I'll wear all of this on our wedding day. Such a beautiful gift to begin our engagement with ..."

He removed the ring from the box. "Shall we see if it fits?" She nodded, and he reached for her hand to slide it on.

"It fits perfectly." She held out her hand to admire the ring as the lights all around them caused it to shimmer and sparkle. Then she stood on tiptoe and kissed his cheek. "I have a feeling we will be very happy together."

"I believe we will too. Each time we are together, I learn something new and more beautiful about you. Would you like to dance now?" he asked, studying her face.

"Yes, I would very much love to dance with you."

They floated on a cloud of happiness, every step leading them over a rainbow of joy as he took her by the hand and led her to the dance floor.

Could this really be happening? This was much better than she'd imagined. Was she finally in love? Her heart felt so full and free as she twirled in his arms. Though a few doubts swirled in her mind, Edward's character was nothing like

Henry's. Maybe she could finally put her fears to rest and trust this man with her whole heart.

~

*E*dward's sisters called on Veronica and Aunt Mae the next afternoon, gushing with apologies about what had happened in front of the Cleave mansion. Just as Edward had promised, their arrival indicated he'd taken his sisters to task over the carriage incident.

"We are sincerely sorry for what happened with our driver." Sophie tucked a stray curl back into place in her fashionable updo.

"Yes, it ruined our chances for our Central Park outing." Henrietta's lower lip protruded, conveying a rather fake pout.

"It's all right," Veronica assured them. "No harm has come of it. I had a splendid time riding with Mrs. Cleave and my aunt."

Aunt Mae brushed some crumbs from her lips after eating a croissant. "Mrs. Cleave and I saw the whole thing. We happened to be directly behind the rude fellow honking his horn."

Henrietta and Sophie exchanged disappointed looks, perhaps realizing they'd likely forever secured a cut from any of Mrs. Cleave's future invitations.

Henrietta shifted in her seat. "I do hope you can be of some assistance to us in clearing up the matter, Mrs. Wilson, since it happened through no fault of our own."

Aunt Mae's lips remained firmly pressed into a thin line. Her eyes narrowed, imparting her lack of trust with a powerful gaze, enough to make even Veronica squirm.

When Veronica's aunt did not take the bait, Sophie perked up. "Do let us see your engagement ring. Mother told us—and Edward confirmed at breakfast—he popped the question last night at the Waldorf Hotel, and the happy news that you've accepted him."

"Yes, it is happy news, indeed, that you are now officially engaged to our dear brother." Henrietta sipped more of her tea.

Veronica held out her hand and leaned forward so they could have a look at the glittering gem on her ring finger. "Thank you. It was a perfectly romantic evening."

"It certainly was," Aunt Mae said.

"Now that we'll be family, all the more reason for you to help us find grace with Mrs. Cleave." A glint radiated from Henrietta's eyes.

When Aunt Mae met this with silence, too, Sophie asked, "Have you set a date or decided where the wedding will be? We'd like to assist, of course, if you decide on a New York wedding. I'm sure you'll need help choosing the right gown and the best tips on a bakery from which to order a cake, who to invite, that sort of thing..."

Aunt Mae chuckled. "I'm sure they haven't had time to discuss all of those details yet, but if Veronica and I or her mother need your help, which I absolutely do not expect, we will let you know."

While Veronica was still struggling to control her amusement at Aunt Mae and her horror at the notion of Edward's sisters assisting with wedding planning, Sophie rushed on. "And Mother wanted me to mention, you simply must sit with us at the ball."

She sat up straighter. This was the first form of any communication from Edward's mother. "Sit with you at the ball?" She glanced at Aunt Mae for guidance, knowing she might prefer not to sit too close to Edward's sisters.

"If your family sits near Edward, we'll all end up close together. I'm certain of one thing. We won't be able to keep Edward and Veronica apart. They are absolutely smitten with each other." Aunt Mae winked lightly at Veronica.

This answer produced light smiles, but something in the way the sisters exchanged glances made Veronica wary. If she didn't know better, she'd think they were up to something.

After that, Edward's sisters moved from one subject to another while leaving little room for either Veronica or her aunt to utter a reply. They spoke about the weather, hinted at the possibility Aunt Mae might have enough power of persuasion to secure them invitations to the Cleave Ball, and mentioned their mother would soon invite them to dinner. Next, they spoke of their plans to vacate the city soon for a long summer retreat at Chesapeake Manor. This led to a discussion about their seashell collection.

As soon as Edward's sisters departed, chatting all the way to the front door, Veronica returned to the drawing room to find Aunt Mae furiously fanning herself. "Heaven help us. Those two are the chattiest girls I ever did meet. I don't recommend sitting too close to them at the ball unless you wish some sort of self-inflicted punishment."

Veronica laughed and sat down in a nearby chair, but Aunt Mae set her fan aside and rose, making a dash toward the staircase. "No time to dawdle. Come along, Veronica."

She dutifully rose and followed her aunt, trying to shake feelings of doom concerning Edward's sisters. "Where are we going?"

Aunt Mae lifted her skirts, climbing the staircase. She'd never seen her aunt move so quickly. "Put on your best day dress. We're going to Ladies' Mile."

"Ladies' Mile?"

"Yes, a visit to my seamstress, Nell, then Bloomingdale's, and then the Bergdorf Goodman department store."

"A day of shopping?" Veronica reached the top of the staircase and paused to catch her breath. Aunt Mae had already flung open the door to her bedroom and rang a bell pull to summon her personal maid.

"Yes, and we'll have dinner out. I'll be too famished to wait until we're home."

Aunt Mae swung open her wardrobe doors to reveal several black dresses like the one she now wore as Veronica leaned against the frame of her aunt's bedroom door. Her aunt rummaged through the black dresses until she found the one she wanted, her back to Veronica as she spoke. "I'm thinking if we don't purchase your wedding gown and a proper wedding trousseau at once, Edward's family will look down their noses and attempt to take over your wardrobe *and* your wedding."

Veronica couldn't help but smile. "Mother did send some funds for shopping." She could hardly wait to write to tell her parents how much she loved Aunt Mae.

"Nonsense. This will be entirely my pleasure. Call it an early wedding gift. Do tell Frances she'll accompany us. We need someone to help carry our packages. Meet me downstairs in twenty minutes. And cancel everything on your schedule for tomorrow. I'm not foolish enough to think we can accomplish all of what we have before us in a single day."

"Thank you, Aunt Mae." She turned toward her guest bedroom but spun and crossed the oriental carpet to where her aunt now sat at the dressing table powdering her face. Leaning down, she hugged her aunt and dropped a quick kiss on her cheek. "You are an answer to prayers I hadn't even thought to pray yet and the very best aunt in the world."

Aunt Mae looked a bit flustered and let out a harrumph, but a half smile curved her lips upward before disappearing again as she waved Veronica away with her powder puff. "None of that mushy stuff. Now off with you to change into something more suitable, and don't dawdle!"

hree hours later, Veronica had ordered a few items for her trousseau from her aunt's seamstress. She had also tried on a half-dozen ready-to-wear ball gowns from a rack in a private sitting room behind Nell's front room. Aunt Mae shook her head at all of the wrong choices and nodded at all of the right ones.

Nell also penciled them in for an appointment in the morning to continue where they'd left off. Then, on to Bloomingdales, where her aunt pointed out the right kinds of lace shawls, a fashionable waist-length silk cape, and new evening gloves. Bergdorf Goodman's provided new shoes and two fascinators, headpieces appropriate for both balls.

"I think you're finally almost ready to make your mark on New York," her aunt said approvingly. "Time for Dinner."

Starving from all of the shopping, Veronica and Frances followed Aunt Mae to the lift, and the maître de led them to a table in the restaurant on one of the upper floors. Frances rearranged their packages while Aunt Mae ordered high tea, salads, and bowls of beef consommé. The tea included a full pot of steaming brew, five small scones, a dish of raspberry jam and another of clotted cream, a variety of finger sandwiches, and tiny dishes of custard puddings and chocolate mousse.

"A fine way to end a busy and wonderful day," Veronica said. "Shall I say the blessing?"

"Yes, please do." Aunt Mae surveyed the feast through the lenses of her lorgnettes. "Would you mind keeping it a short prayer? I'm about to faint from lack of sustenance."

Veronica nodded, folded her hands, and bowed her head. "Dear Heavenly Father, thank You for this wonderful day, for my generous aunt, and for Edward, though I didn't at first see him as coming from Your hand, for I do now recognize and greatly appreciate Your provision, even if it did come through the meddling ways of my matchmaking mother, and ..."

Aunt Mae cleared her throat. "Short, Veronica Josephine. Short."

"Yes, ma'am." Veronica sped up to the end. "We'll continue our discussion during my bedtime prayers, Lord, and in the meantime, we bless this food for which we are eternally thankful, especially since someone could have dropped it in the kitchen, and we would never know but for your omnipotent presence. In Jesus's name we pray, Amen."

"Good grief, child. I have noticed your prayers are quite... detailed." Aunt Mae reached for a scone and began applying some of the raspberry jam with great vigor.

Frances did little to hide a smile at this remark.

"Pa says, and Mama agrees, we must at times pray very specific prayers to the Lord if we wish to receive and recognize the answers when they come," Veronica explained as she reached for a scone.

"A solid Spencer belief, I'm sure, and one I happen to agree with, except when I'm this close to fainting from hunger." Her aunt tasted some of the scone and sighed. "These are my favorite in all of Manhattan, except, of course, the ones my cook prepares." She sat back from the table a bit and stretched. "Oh, my aching, throbbing feet. They object to the number of miles we've traipsed over today, but I believe it was for a good cause."

"I guess I am a bit of a cause since I am in a strange new world," Veronica confessed.

"And a very good cause you are, my dear. Would you kindly pass me a chicken salad sandwich? I can't wait to see the look on Edward's face when he sees you at the ball." Her aunt eyed the scone in Veronica's hand. "At least we don't have to worry about gaining any weight from this meal. We'll walk it all off tomorrow."

"Tomorrow?" She swallowed the bite of her scone and gulped. She had been looking forward to sleeping in.

"Yes, you didn't forget about tomorrow morning's appointment with Nell, did you?" Her aunt's eyes widened, and she raised her chin..

"Oh drat, yes, I forgot." Somewhere in the fuss of trying on a half-dozen pair of shoes and even more hats. But she squared her shoulders. "Fear not. I will be ready."

"Good, because I'm determined we shall order your custom-made wedding gown from Nell and most of your trousseau. Then we have all of the accessories to shop for."

"Yes, and what a relief it will be to have ordered my wedding dress. Mama will be very happy to hear we can cross it off the list. Do tell me she can ship it to Kentucky."

"Of course. She can ship it anywhere in the world." Aunt Mae reached for a fork to try her salad. "Please pass the vinaigrette. I've got to lose some more weight before your wedding, so none of that country buttermilk dressing for me. I want to look my best."

Veronica smiled and passed the vinaigrette decanter. If Aunt Mae intended to attend her wedding, she had most certainly made an ally. She could only remember her aunt traveling to Kentucky on a couple of occasions. Veronica's Lyndon grandparents would be overjoyed to see their daughter again—not to mention, the rest of the family. Perhaps she could point out these things to Edward and persuade him to agree to a Kentucky wedding.

But first, she had to manage not to embarrass Edward with her appearance or behavior at the ball. Would she remember the right dance steps and all of the proper etiquette to make a fine impression on New York society? Perhaps his family would finally accept her too.

CHAPTER FIFTEEN

Woe to you, scribes and Pharisees, hypocrites! For you tithe mint,
and dill, and cumin, and have neglected the weightier matters of the
law: justice, mercy, and faithfulness.
These ye ought to have done, without neglecting the others.
—Matthew 23:23, ESV

E dward caught sight of his fiancée entering the rented ball
room at the Astoria with Aunt Mae. She looked so lovely,
he stared at her for a few moments before moving toward them.
They had agreed to arrive separately since Veronica had said
she needed extra time to dress. Consequently, he had arrived a
few minutes earlier with his family.

Captivated by her demure look, he took in the pale-pink
summery creation she wore. Her curls tumbled over one
shoulder of the sleeveless gown, trailing from her stylish updo.
Elegant white lace cascaded at the bodice's neckline, the only
embellishment to the gown with its modest train. The dress
hugged her figure in all the right places. He had to admit, he
liked the straighter skirts these days since they revealed Veronica's curves.

The gown's simplicity caused a sensation of whispers as she stepped into the room. Seeing how many gentlemen turned their eyes upon her, he hurried to her side. He would ensure she had a wonderful evening at her first ball in New York. Out of all the admiring bachelors present, he would make certain they knew he was the one for her.

As he navigated through the sea of guests, several friends stopped to greet him. After the third interruption, he determined to push past the rest of the people blocking his path. Finally, he reached Veronica, but now he had to stand aside while she finished greeting their hosts in a reception line he'd already completed. They made eye contact a few times, exchanging sweet smiles as he waited patiently for her.

When she finally stepped out of the line, he leaned close to plant a kiss on her cheek. He wanted to tell the whole room she belonged to him, and his kiss seemed the quickest way to do so. "Hello, darling. You look marvelous. Stunning!"

"You look handsome, too, Edward. I hope we didn't keep you waiting too long."

"Not at all. I just arrived a few minutes ago."

She smiled up at him, and her elegant earrings with sparkling gems dangling from her delicate earlobes reminded him of the color of pink champagne. A glance at her gloved hands revealed she wore the pearl bracelet from the engagement collection he'd given her. Had she worn the ring as well? She began peeling off her gloves, and he smiled to see her wearing it as she snapped her fan open to ward off the relentless summer heat.

He greeted her aunt and held out his arm to Veronica. "May I escort you both to some seats near my family?"

"Yes, please. The crowd is larger than we expected," her aunt said. "We'll sit with you if you've managed to save us some seats."

Veronica placed her hand on his arm. Was that concern

flickering over her face? He chalked it up to nerves at meeting so many new people and patted her hand as they progressed through the crowd.

Edward led the way to his family's table. His sisters and mother, decked in their finery, glowed with happiness at being out and about among New York society. Rupert and his father wore jovial smiles, looking dapper in their best formalwear. Seeing they engaged Veronica and her aunt in a number of introductions and kept conversation flowing smoothly, he excused himself to fetch some refreshments for them. It took an unusually long time to cross the crowded room to the table laden with sweets and punch.

When he managed to return, Veronica had disappeared. Aunt Mae pressed her lips together and pointed to the dance floor, where her niece swirled in the arms of some gentleman he didn't recognize. Did he detect a look of slight distress on her face?

Edward's heart fell. He'd hoped to have the first waltz with her, but now he could only wait until the dance ended. Things were not off to a good start.

His mother waved her ostrich feather fan at him. "Oh, Edward, there you are. Would you mind going to find your father? He went to bring your sisters and me some punch, but he's been gone a very long time. I suspect one of his business cronies may have snagged him."

His stomach clenched. "All right. Would you tell Veronica I'll return as soon as I can?" He had to dismiss his concern about his fiancée for the moment.

～

*V*eronica sighed in the arms of a gentleman named George Eaton who had pulled her away for her first dance of the evening—at Sophie's insistence. She had trouble thinking of anything to say to the man, and she longed to dance with Edward. When George had asked her to dance, she hadn't wanted to appear rude. Without Edward at her side, she had little recourse but to oblige.

Besides George, Edward's sisters had already introduced her to at least five gentlemen. At least they had done so by saying she was Edward's fiancée. Now Sophie stood off to one side with Henrietta, where the two could observe George swirling her about while they talked behind their fans. Were they up to something?

When the gentleman returned Veronica to her seat, Aunt Mae, standing near Edward's mother, leaned toward her. "You've just missed Edward, but he brought us both glasses of punch." She nodded toward the small table near their chairs, bearing crystal glasses of fruit punch.

"Oh no," Veronica murmured, a sigh escaping her lips. "I had hoped to save the first dance for him, and now I've missed him again."

Mrs. Beckett, overhearing the exchange, stepped closer. "I'm sorry, dear. I've sent him to find Leviticus, who has surely been delayed while fetching punch. There must be quite a line for refreshments." She turned to Veronica's aunt as two ladies approached. "Mrs. Wilson, have I introduced you to my good friends, Mrs. Logan and Mrs. Nottingham? Perhaps you know them."

"Why yes, we are acquainted. How nice to see you ladies here tonight." Aunt Mae allowed Mrs. Beckett to pull her closer to the ladies to engage in polite chatter.

Hopefully, Edward would return soon. Naturally, Mrs. Beckett would want Mr. Beckett at her side for such an important event, so she must find patience for her future mother-in-law's sake. It did please her to see Aunt Mae getting along with Mrs. Beckett and her friends.

And where had Rupert gone? Lost in the crowd with his friends, she assumed. Maybe dancing in the sea of couples.

Veronica resigned herself to her seat and sipped some punch while she listened with half an ear to Mrs. Beckett, Aunt Mae, and their mutual acquaintances. If another gentleman asked her to dance, she would simply decline. No doubt, Henrietta and Sophie would appreciate having her remain in her seat, out of their way so they could fill up their own dance cards.

When the crowd thinned, she caught another glimpse of Edward's sisters, now surrounded by a growing flock of gentlemen. Perhaps a dozen, but why did they keep glancing in her direction? Veronica snapped her fan open. Surely, she only imagined their looks.

Just as Aunt Mae took her seat beside Veronica with a contented sigh, clearly invigorated by her chat, Sophie reappeared, her face alight. She took Veronica by the hand, pulling her onto her feet. "Come with me, Veronica. Henrietta and I have more gentlemen to introduce you to."

"I'd much prefer to wait for Edward..." Veronica barely had time to set the glass of punch down, let alone resist being pulled from her seat.

Maintaining a firm grip, Sophie tugged her toward Henrietta's side. Henrietta scribbled names onto the dance cards she held, pausing to look up and smile in her direction. Why did she have a bad feeling about this? Maybe because the smile seemed false.

"Put Clarence down." The gentleman who spoke glanced at Veronica with a coy grin.

"Clarence." Henrietta added the name to the dance cards in her hands.

When the gentleman kept grinning at Veronica with a shy, downward tilt of his head, she returned a weak smile. After all, she must make a good impression for Edward's and his family's sake. It was nice to see Henrietta and Sophie securing dances for themselves, but couldn't she return to her seat? What if she missed Edward again?

"Did you get Milton?" Henrietta scribbled this name down.

"Frank Crandall. Do you need me to spell it?"

"I know how to spell your name, dearest Frank." Henrietta batted her lashes at the suitor before she jotted his name down.

Another gentleman clasped the lapels of his suit. "Arthur Lewiston as well."

Veronica did her best to hang back, trying to discern which gentleman they wished her to meet. Henrietta and Sophie had introduced her to a few of them prior to her dance with George, but many more clamored about them.

Sophie turned from facing Henrietta and drew Veronica closer to her side, placing an arm around her. "Gentlemen, may I present Miss Veronica Lyndon, to those who have not met her yet."

Oh. Perhaps Sophie simply wanted to introduce her to all of them. Why didn't she announce her as Edward's fiancée? Veronica bit her lower lip as a knot formed in her stomach. At the same time, some of the men chimed in with broad smiles, staring with flirtatious twinkles in their eyes, showing little interest for her future sisters-in-law.

"Hello, Miss Lyndon."

"Nice to meet you."

"I would love a dance, Miss Lyndon."

"Can I get you a glass of punch, Miss Lyndon?"

Who to respond to first? Back in Kentucky, single, she would have known exactly what to do. She would have walked away with some excuse or another, leaving them in the dust. But Sophie had her arm around her and wasn't letting her off the hook so easily. And maybe the men just wanted to meet the newcomer. "Thank you, but I already have a glass of punch." Perhaps if she ignored the one who'd requested a dance...

Henrietta wrote another name on the dance cards before looking up at the gentlemen. "As we promised, you've met our dear Veronica. I assure you, she will be most happy to dance with each of you. Now, who is next? Two dances for us in exchange for every one dance with her, just as we said."

What? Now their ruse became clear. Completely clear. She could hardly believe her ears. Her mouth dropped open. No, this couldn't be happening. How dare they assume she would agree to this! And why couldn't she get any words to come out?

"No, no...I'm saving my..." Veronica shook her head, but her denial was drowned out by the gentlemen in the back of the group talking over each other, arguing over who would be next to have their name written on those dance cards in Henrietta's hands.

Veronica's mouth went dry, preventing other words from escaping her parched throat. A surge of heat rose to her cheeks. She forced herself to bite her lower lip to keep from shouting. She resisted the urge to stomp her foot, but presently, the idea of landing a heel on the feet of the gentlemen nearest her or Edward's sisters didn't sound so bad. *Stay calm. Refrain from disgracing yourself and Edward, Aunt Mae, the other Becketts...*

"Who's next? I believe Mortimer, Charles, then Fred." Henrietta pointed to each and scribbled their names down. Before the men swarmed closer to Henrietta, blocking Veronica's view, she counted the dance cards Henrietta held. Three, not two.

Veronica's fists clenched. With her aunt and Edward's mother seated only ten feet away and many high society patrons at the ball, how could she stop Henrietta and Sophie or the supposed gentlemen participating in this affront to her personal wishes?

Henrietta smiled sweetly toward her, as if aware her future sister-in-law threatened to boil over. "Fear not, Veronica. We'll have your card full in just a moment. You won't have to miss a single dance or any of the fun."

Sophie fluttered her fan with her free hand, maintaining a hold on Veronica. "Have we missed anyone?"

If only she could push through the gentlemen, snag her fake dance card from Henrietta, and rip it to shreds. But how would that look? Would the gentlemen think she had cheated them out of a promised dance? Would it ruin her reputation, or worse, Edward's? Would Sophie and Henrietta be left without any dance partners if Veronica refused to honor the arrangements? Could they not secure dance partners on their own merits?

What a mess!

Veronica had to find Edward. Perhaps he could discern a way to end this nonsense. She looked back toward where Aunt Mae waited, but she couldn't see her aunt or any of the other Beckett family members through the crowd. The only blessing was that the orchestra was performing a gallop, a dance so boisterous others might not notice what the Beckett sisters were doing.

"And the last dance..." Henrietta's announcement was accompanied by a smirk of satisfaction as she stared at Veronica.

"Stop!" Veronica simply had to save the last dance for Edward. She spun around, extricating herself from Sophie's hold. She managed to reach Henrietta and snatch one of the cards from her hands. Was it hers? She looked down, relieved and alarmed to see her name at the top. She tilted her chin. "The last dance I am saving for Edward, my *fiancé*."

Groans rose from a few of the gentlemen. Perhaps some of them had not realized she was engaged. Did they also realize the Beckett sisters had not acquired her consent?

With the replica of her card in her hands, Veronica pushed past the gentlemen. Perhaps she could go to the hostess sponsoring the ball and explain that these dances were not granted with her permission or penciled in by her hand. She'd heard a story once of someone who'd had something similar happen, but the result had consisted of a great amount of gossip and disgruntled gentlemen. Edward might not like the unwanted attention, but she wasn't sure she cared at this point.

Reaching Aunt Mae, she plopped into her seat in a most unladylike fashion, hardly caring what New York thought of her at this point.

Her aunt surveyed her with an open mouth and wide eyes. "Oh dear, whatever is the matter? You look positively put out!"

"Aunt Mae, something dreadful has…" Her voice caught. "Have you seen Edward?" When her aunt shook her head, Veronica waved the dance card. "I take no pleasure in telling you what his sisters have done, filling up a dance card in my name in exchange for dances for themselves."

"They did what?" Aunt Mae snapped her fan open and began fanning herself furiously. "If I understand you correctly, they must be terribly desperate for dance partners, but this by no means excuses such wretched behavior."

"Yes, you understand me correctly."

Aunt Mae leaned closer. "I think I see Edward making his way here. Whatever you do, don't tell their parents. It will only make them implacable. Wait for Edward. He'll know what to do."

Veronica nodded, tears misting her eyes.

"Oh, dear me." Aunt Mae suddenly twisted in her seat. "I seem to have lost one of my pearl earrings. Such a treasure…an anniversary gift from my George. Do be a dear and see if you can discreetly look around on the floor behind our chairs to recover it. It can't be far…I've only been right here this whole time."

"Yes, Aunt. I'll find it." What choice did she have after all her aunt had done for her? She'd find the earring, and surely, by then, Edward would appear with Mr. Beckett. Perhaps Edward could take her home early.

~

*A*s Edward weaved through the crowd with his father finally in tow, carrying three cups of punch between them for his mother and sisters, he caught a glimpse of Veronica seated beside her aunt. Aunt Mae dropped something over her shoulder and then whispered to Veronica. His fiancée rose from her seat. However, the crowd thickened again, preventing him from seeing where she went. When he finally emerged almost directly in front of her aunt, there was no fiancée in sight.

"Levi, there you are. Thank you, Edward, for finding him," his mother said, clutching Father's arm. She began prattling to some of her friends as she leaned on Father, a wide smile on her face.

At last, he could find Veronica. Aunt Mae beckoned him closer. What had she thrown over her shoulder? She was up to something, but what, and why?

Aunt Mae placed her hand on his arm, a wary and concerned expression on her face, and he bent to hear what she had to say. "Edward, I am ever so glad to see you. A most concerning situation has arisen. I'll let Veronica explain. I've deliberately lost one of my earrings so you two might have a chance to speak to each other without interruption...but you'll need to hide her from that gentleman with the hideous side-burns standing over there who is in line to dance with her..." She paused to glance in the fellow's direction and take a breath. "Not this song, but the next."

Edward raked a hand through his hair. In line to dance with her? What was Aunt Mae talking about?

"As soon as he turns his head, you'll need to draw Veronica

away to sort things out." She nodded to the area behind their seats where Veronica was indeed searching for her aunt's "missing" earring. At least her chair and the dim lighting mostly shielded her from view.

Edward's brows furrowed, but he nodded. "Thank you, Mrs. Wilson."

What had happened while he'd been gone?

Slipping past the fellow who stood shifting his weight as he apparently waited for Veronica to appear, Edward glowered. The space behind Aunt Mae did not provide much room, but he managed to squeeze in next to his fiancée. "Looking for something?"

"Edward! Where have you been?"

"I might ask the same question." He shifted onto bended knee.

"My aunt's earring, but honestly, I'm thinking about making a grand escape. Would you mind terribly?"

Edward's heart skipped a beat. Whatever would have made his spirited Veronica want to flee? "But we've only just arrived. What's happened?" And were those tears in her eyes?

"Would you like the short answer...or the horrid details?" Veronica drew her legs to one side, arranging her skirt over them.

Edward winced. "My knees would prefer the shortest possible version, but I have a better location in mind." He peeked over the edge of the chairs. The man had finally turned to observe the dance floor. "We can escape to the alcove over there if we hurry." He nodded toward a recessed area where they could sit down properly. "I'll have a servant find your aunt's earring after we talk."

Relief replaced her flustered look. "Very well, the alcove. If you will be so kind as to help me up in this fitted dress, perhaps I can join you in a more dignified manner."

Once he pulled Veronica to her feet, he guided her into the

nearest alcove. They sat on cushioned benches, facing each other. "This is much better."

She nodded. "It is. Thank you."

"Now, tell me what happened." Edward leaned forward, hands on his knees.

"While your mother and my aunt were turned away speaking to someone, your sisters obtained a blank dance card —from the hostess table, I suppose—and wrote my name on it. Never mind the fact I already had my own which I was saving for you to fill with the dances you wanted." She held up the blank card dangling from her wrist. "Meanwhile, they offered their extra card up to the highest bidders among gentlemen who saw their chance after you stepped away." She produced another card from her pocket. Sadly, he recognized Henrietta's penmanship, and the card looked quite full.

Hot indignation flooded him. "They took bids?" That seemed extreme, even for his selfish sisters.

Veronica swiped at the corner of her eye. "Not for money. For dances with themselves. One dance with each of them for a third with me. They scribbled down nine names on my card and theirs in a matter of minutes."

"Lord, have mercy." Edward clenched his jaw tight. He had failed her terribly. He'd let his mother send him off on an errand he should have declined in favor of staying at her side. His sisters wouldn't have dared to carry out their plan directly under his nose. He had so much to make up for.

"I did manage to save the last dance for you."

"You did?" He touched her arm. "I'm glad."

"And we mustn't forget to send a servant to find Aunt Mae's pearl earring—a gift from my dearly departed Uncle George. I confess, I was hoping the gentleman on my dance card would not see me, or if he did, I prayed he'd give up and go away. But he is waiting this very minute."

Edward frowned. The man standing near the table. "You

shouldn't leave. You deserve to enjoy your first ball in Manhattan. The new debutantes haven't been introduced yet, and I wanted to introduce you to my friends at dinner." He pursed his lips in thought, then smiled as an idea struck. "I think I have a plan. Will you trust me?"

Veronica let out a gusty sigh. "If you think you can salvage this disaster, then I'll give you that chance."

"Yes, as a matter of fact, I do think I can salvage this disaster." Edward slid closer to give her a quick kiss on the cheek. "Thank you for trusting me. I love you, Veronica."

Edward caught his breath. Had he said that aloud? Her stunned expression confirmed it. Had he scared her off?

~

*V*eronica's spirit soared for the first time since she'd arrived. He'd said those words she hadn't realized she needed to hear. And it couldn't have come at a better time, lifting her from despair and anger to joy. "I love you, too, Edward."

He leaned toward her and softly kissed her on the lips. She sighed with contentment. And where had her words come from? Was she ready for this step? Had she truly fallen in love with him? Perhaps she had.

"Are you ready?" He stood and arched his brow as he offered his hand.

"Ready." She allowed Edward to pull her onto her feet.

Edward peeked out into the ball room. "The first man waiting to dance with you has given up and wandered away. Another has appeared, though, and seems to be looking for you. I'll go and get a servant to recover your aunt's earring, then make my way to you as soon as possible. Go and enjoy the next dance or two until I find you again."

"All right." She nodded, stepping out of the alcove and

making her way to the waiting gentleman. How odd this night had become.

As her new partner took her hand, Veronica glanced over her shoulder at Edward. He nodded, dispelling her reluctance. Then she allowed the gentleman to lead her onto the floor.

When the dance ended, before the fellow could return her to Aunt Mae and their seats, the next partner arrived. About halfway into the waltz, Edward tapped on the man's shoulder. Veronica stifled a smile. Her partner frowned, but he couldn't do anything to prevent her fiancé from cutting in. He left them to dance.

Edward pulled her into his arms and began swirling her about the dance floor, his eyes locking onto hers. The presence of his hand on her back and her other hand in his were all she needed to begin feeling secure and her happiness returning.

"I tried to hurry," he said by way of apology.

"Where did you go after you found someone to locate my aunt's earring?"

"I cut in on Henrietta's dance and then Sophie's to reprimand both very sternly." A glower accompanied his words while he led her around the dance floor almost effortlessly.

Veronica relaxed in the security of his arms. "What did you say?"

"I told them exactly what I thought."

"Which was what?"

"That their actions were reprehensible, and that they owe you yet another apology. I let them know I am disappointed in their behavior and that it won't be tolerated."

Veronica sighed with relief. "Thank you, Edward."

"And now I will share the rest of my plan. I will cut in on every single dance partner who presumes to claim a dance with you for the rest of the evening." He leaned closer to her, giving her a secret wink.

Veronica returned his affectionate smile. "I would love to

see you cut in on every one of those men who dare call themselves gentlemen after participating in that despicable dance auction." She wouldn't dwell on it any longer. Why let it spoil their evening when he had come up with a perfect plan to put those men in their place? In fact, the more she thought about it, the more giggles escaped. "I'm laughing, but won't that scheme draw attention? People will think…"

"That I'm madly in love with you and can't stand the idea of someone else dancing with my future wife?" Edward's chin lifted.

His plan made her giddy with happiness, as did this sign of his protective nature. "Yes, I suppose that is exactly what they will think, and I must say, I love it."

Far better than complaining to the hostess or causing a scene by refusing to dance with all the men on the card, and then contending with the flurry of gossip that either of those scenarios would certainly ignite. And despite the chaos of the evening, they had also exchanged professions of love. Things were definitely looking up.

She especially appreciated that Edward had taken his sisters to task. Far more effective than if she had done so, since not only would doing so make her appear retaliatory, but it could cause a greater rift between family members. Nonetheless, she would prefer to ignore them for the remainder of the evening as much as possible. She did not trust her tongue, though the fact she hadn't stomped on their feet or shouted before all of New York perhaps indicated some growth on her part.

Had Edward leaned a tad closer as they danced? Yes. He pressed his hand more firmly on the small of her back. Inhaling, she enjoyed the scent of his musky cologne. And did she detect a determination in his blue eyes she hadn't seen before? A change had come over him that made him look stronger and somehow, more appealing. Maybe his protective side emerging, a side of which she very much approved.

When the orchestra interlude began, he drew her close as they left the dance floor together, tucking her hand into the crook of his elbow. "Mind if I introduce you to some of my friends before dinner?"

Now that she had him to herself again, she was eager to meet them. "How nice. And there is Rupert...leaving the dance floor with someone I don't recognize."

"Excellent. Let me introduce you to his dance partner, Mirabel Salisbury. Then we'll find Jack Curzon, Stephen Galloway, and the Wheatland sisters, Dora and Emma."

Thankfully, none of the men he mentioned had taken part in the dance card scheme. When they caught up to Rupert, Veronica smiled warmly at his partner.

"There you are, Rupe. If I may introduce my fiancée to Mirabel... Miss Veronica Lyndon of Lexington, meet Miss Mirabel Salisbury, a longtime friend."

"How have you managed to escape us all evening, Edward?" Mirabel turned her attention to Veronica and offered a warm smile. "It's a pleasure to meet you, Miss Lyndon. Congratulations on your engagement, both of you. New York is glowing with happiness that Edward has found the love of his life. Everyone wants to meet you, Miss Lyndon."

"Thank you. I'll try not to disappoint them. It's very nice to meet you too."

Mirabel turned to Rupert. "It's dreadfully hot this evening. Shall we head outside for some fresh air before dinner?"

Veronica had wanted to converse with her a little more, but Rupert led her away. Edward began introducing her to his friend she'd heard so much about, Jack Curzon, and then some others who joined them.

From then on, all seemed right in the world. Rupert and Jack made her laugh, cracking jokes about how it took Edward less than twenty seconds to cut in on all of Veronica's eager dance partners.

$\sim$

When Edward finally climbed inside his carriage to go home, he looked at his family with fresh eyes. He needed to make some changes. He must never let family members come between him and Veronica again.

With his father back in town and his partners constantly interrupting him, he hadn't been able to find out much about what had happened to the family coffers. Hopefully, when Father left on business again soon, presumably to sell off another piece of real estate, he could uncover answers.

He needed to come up with an excuse to sort through Father's files in case anyone stumbled upon him in his father's corner office again. The last time he'd made an attempt, one of the senior partners had encountered him there and had raised a curious brow. He'd had to abandon the search, but if Jack could help him, he would be better prepared this time.

CHAPTER SIXTEEN

Beware of false prophets who come to you in sheep's clothing
but inwardly are ravenous wolves.
—Matthew 7:15, ESV

About a week after the ball, as they sat in Aunt Mae's drawing room, Veronica cautiously and optimistically approached the subject of a Kentucky wedding with Edward. While he'd taken her on a couple of outings with her aunt, this was the first she'd been able to spend time alone with him. Since Edward had been working long days at the office to cover for his father, who was out of town to meet with another buyer for some real estate, she had taken the opportunity to finish her shopping with Aunt Mae. Her aunt spoiled her far too much. Her sisters would simply drool over all of her new things, but their turn would come.

"It would mean so much to me, Edward. You do remember how I told you Grandfather Spencer preached there for so many years, don't you?" She set down her teacup. "And all four of my grandparents would be able to witness the exchange of our vows. My mother can organize the reception. It will be far less grand than a New York society wedding, but so sweet, surrounded by all of our closest friends and family…" Having presented her plea, she reached for the teapot to refill Edward's cup.

"I'm all for it, darling."

"Truly?" As joy darted through her, she turned to search his eyes.

"Truly. A small church wedding in Lexington sounds much less stressful than a New York society wedding. I only need time to figure out a way to break the news to Mother." Edward held his teacup out to receive his refill.

How smoothly that had gone! It gave her courage for her next question.

"Before we speak of when this wedding will take place, I must know, where shall we live once we are wed, Edward? I miss horses. As exciting as Manhattan is with balls and the theater, Central Park, grand museums, and bookstores, I'm wilting, Edward. I need the countryside. I miss Velvet Brooks and my family." She was missing out on so much. Delia had written to tell her of her growing romance with Thaddeus Sullivan, and she'd included an update about Gladdie's blossoming relationship with Clay Grinstead.

"I know you do." Edward sipped some of his tea and leaned forward. "I've been thinking about this too. Would you consider a compromise of splitting our time between the two states? Six months here, six months there? I'd have to work more days at the office when we are here, but it's the only thing I can think of that might appeal to my father. And I do have a connection to a friend who has a riding trail for horses in New York. We might be able to make excursions there on weekends."

The man was willing to give up more of his precious time with his artwork in order to make their marriage work. Veronica's heart soared. Maybe once they married, when they were in

New York, she could find ways to encourage his art in the evenings and on weekends.

"I, too, have been thinking a compromise of this sort might be our only option. Would we perhaps be able to find a house with a garden, maybe something not too far from your office?"

"Of course." His brow furrowed. He set his tea aside and then raked a hand through his hair. "I'm not sure how I'll break the news to my father, but I'll try to convince him this is the best and only way forward for us. Let's keep this matter to ourselves for now, until I can find the right time to talk to him and the right approach."

"I understand. Your father has certain expectations." She patted his leg, though she pushed aside a twinge of unease.

She had faith in Edward, but what might happen if his parents put their foot down? Would Edward stand his ground? Would his parents threaten to cut him out of the family business or do away with his share of the profits or the family fortune in order to get whatever they wanted from him?

~

Since Edward indicated he would be buried in work for a few days, Aunt Mae took advantage of the time to help Veronica finish her wedding shopping. Half of the trousseau would come to her aunt's home in New York, and had indeed already begun to arrive, ensuring Veronica looked smart at every type of event she attended. The trousseau included two shirtwaist dresses, walking suits, reception frocks, a tea dress, a visiting dress, two new bell-shaped skirts and lace-collared blouses, two evening gowns, one black mourning dress—just in case one might have to attend a funeral, Aunt Mae had said—and one more ball gown.

The seamstress, Nell, would ship the dress and veil to Lexington along with the portion of her trousseau that wouldn't be ready when they departed with the Becketts for Chesapeake Manor. While Nell's team of seamstresses worked hard to fill the order, Veronica sent a letter to her mother, advising her to remain vigilant for the shipment.

It made Veronica a bit nervous. What if Edward failed to convince his parents of their wishes? What if she had to comply with her future mother-in-law's hopes for a New York society wedding? Even her mother, who had many friends in New York, had written to say she preferred a simpler Kentucky wedding with their Lexington friends. What if his father refused to let him live half of each year at Velvet Brooks?

Meanwhile, they had the Cleaves ball to look forward to. After all of their wedding shopping, Aunt Mae had earned an afternoon luncheon at the Waldorf with Mrs. Cleave, and Veronica reveled in the opportunity to relax in her aunt's drawing room with a book.

Mrs. Cleave had brought a furry little visitor to sit with Veronica, however. "I simply don't know what's wrong with him, Veronica," Mrs. Cleave had said as she handed the sweet little pup over. "He just doesn't seem like himself. Perhaps an afternoon adventure with you would do wonders for him."

Veronica had smiled as she snuggled the pet. "I'm sure we'll have a perfectly ordinary time reading my book together, but he can sit here on my lap until you return. No need to hurry. I don't plan on going out."

Veronica patted Roosevelt, and he curled up in her lap. Then she opened a copy of *Jane Eyre* to read to her heart's content. Alone at last...

Not half an hour later, Frances interrupted Veronica's pleasant afternoon to announce the arrival of Henrietta and Sophie. Veronica sighed, in no mood to deal with Edward's sisters, but they'd practically followed Frances into her aunt's drawing room instead of waiting in the hall. After the way they had behaved at the ball, Veronica had wrestled greatly to achieve forgiveness during her earnest bedtime prayers. But now, her aunt's absence left her to face them alone.

Frances brought a tea tray in since the cook had gone to pick up some items at the market. Edward's sisters gushed about the cute little dog in her lap. When Sophie attempted to come near to pet Roosevelt, he growled, and she retreated to the sofa.

Henrietta prattled on while Veronica eyed the tea tray, reluctant to make the customary offering. "We are dreadfully sorry about filling up your dance card, and especially for bargaining with it for dance partners for ourselves. It was a dreadful thing to do. I don't know what came over us. I guess in retrospect, we partly thought you might appreciate meeting more of the fine bachelors Manhattan has to offer. Poor Edward tends to hide from society, and we thought it would help if you didn't have to sit out so many dances. We hope you can forgive us for such ill-mannered and thoughtless behavior."

"Yes, we are terribly sorry," Sophie echoed. "It was reckless, indeed. Edward has made us see the error of our ways."

She knew he had also bade them offer an apology, though his sisters' version came off as backhanded. What had their mother thought of their behavior? Or had she even been apprised of it?

Veronica bit her lip, choosing her words with care, not trusting his sisters nor believing them repentant. While Edward had mentioned he had hidden from the ladies his mother had tried to entice him to consider as prospects for marriage, he hadn't shown this side at all to her. "In fact, he seemed eager to dance with me all evening."

Henrietta tittered quietly. "Being eager doesn't mean he is skillful."

Veronica sat up straighter. "On the contrary...Edward knew all the steps. He was a perfect gentleman, and I thought he led me magnificently on the dance floor. I can't imagine why you would think I would wish to draw the attention of other dance partners when I am perfectly happy and in love with Edward."

"Of course. Clearly, you are." Henrietta exchanged a muted glance with Sophie.

Veronica sipped some of her tea and patted Roosevelt, unsettled by the girls' reaction. For Edward's sake, she took note of their somber looks and added, "Your apology is accepted, although I must say your scheme placed your brother and me in a predicament. I wanted to save most of my card for him to fill in the dances he wanted. Since he is my fiancé, I had hoped to give him the benefit of penciling his name in before anyone else. Unfortunately, because of your actions, I couldn't give your brother that courtesy, and as you know, he had to resort to unusual methods to dance with me."

"I thought it ended up being quite romantic, the way he cut in on every dance to be with you." Sophie's blue eyes widened as she tucked some of her blond curls in place. "Everyone noticed his efforts. But you shouldn't feel bad about not saving dances for Edward. I sincerely doubt he would do the same for you."

Veronica held the teapot out, ready to pour, but this remark struck her as odd, and she set it down. "What makes you say such a thing about your brother?" Where could Sophie's statement lead? She implied Edward did not value Veronica to the degree she valued him.

"Oh dear, another blunder on my part. It's probably something we shouldn't mention in polite society." Sophie shook her head and covered her mouth, looking away.

"No, I wouldn't tell her, Sophie." Henrietta shot her sister a stern glance. "It will only upset her."

Veronica looked from Henrietta to Sophie and back again. "What would upset me?"

"I shouldn't have brought it up." Sophie sighed, waving her hand as if she could take back her remarks.

"Since you did, why bother to keep it a secret? But if you don't wish to tell me, I think we should conclude your visit." Veronica's heart hammered as she patted Roosevelt...as though that would calm her.

"You had best tell her. Seeing as how you've gone and upset her, Sophie." Henrietta's tone conveyed aggravation.

The little dog in Veronica's lap growled again. Veronica kept her hand around him in case he decided to dive at their company.

Sophie looked up at the ceiling and then at her hem, where the tips of her white summer ankle boots peeked out from under her fashionable skirts. Finally, she directed her gaze toward Veronica. "All right, I'll tell, but you mustn't breathe a word."

"Go on." She would not offer tea, after all. She could only imagine what would come next, but she had a feeling she would regret the visit. Little Roosevelt's tiny growls increased in volume and frequency, but she could hardly blame his instincts.

"I'm afraid you may not want to marry Edward after what I share..." Sophie pulled at the gloves on each of her fingers as she spoke, loosening them as if she now planned to stay for a while. "And I certainly wouldn't blame you for abandoning him once you know, but if I were in your shoes, I would want someone to tell me. As his future bride and our future sister-in-law, you have every right to know. If it were me, I would cast him aside ..."

"I thought we had already established the fact you would tell me, and if it concerns my fiancé, your brother, our dearest Edward, I believe you should indeed tell me." Veronica braced herself, her hands wrapping around the arms of her chair.

"Well, you may recall meeting Edward's friends at the ball. You met Dora and her sister, Emma, the Wheatland sisters," Sophie reminded her.

"Yes, I did. Very nice girls." Veronica gave a curt nod. What did his friends have to do with Sophie's news?

"And you met Edward's closest friend, Jack Curzon. And you met the Galloways, Stephen and his sister Jane, the girl who wore the powder-blue ball gown with the rosettes on her neckline. But the last girl you met in Edward's set, the debutante in the white gown, Mirabel Salisbury? Well, I suspect he introduced her last because she means the most to him."

"Wh-what do you mean, she means the most to him?" Veronica's voice wavered.

Henrietta huffed, casting her sister an impatient glance. "What Sophie means to say is, Mirabel Salisbury, the daughter of James and Wallace Salisbury, our dear South Carolina neighbors and mother's good friends at Chesapeake Manor, is Edward's...mistress."

The walls seemed to close in on Veronica, squeezing the life out of her. "Ed-Edward...has a m-mistress?"

Henrietta pressed her lips together. "Perhaps I should say, she will become his mistress once the two of you are married, since I am absolutely certain he will never give her up. Her family has a townhouse here in Manhattan, so she and Edward will never lack the means to be apart, not to mention, he is solidly smitten with her."

"I cannot believe it." Veronica held her hand to her heart, which seemed determined to hammer right out of her chest.

This did not sound like the Edward she knew, but how well did she know him? Could he have hidden his true love, his true nature, from her? And after having spent so much time with him in recent weeks, during which he'd seemed so genuine and honest, Veronica could hardly fathom it.

As for Mirabel, she seemed like a sweet young lady, but Veronica had only met her briefly. The girl had danced a good bit—more than once with Rupert.

Henrietta fluttered her lashes. "I'm afraid it's true, but

please don't let it bother you too deeply. It's nothing personal, I'm sure. It's common among men, especially among the elite of New York society, unfortunately. It's best to accept it and get over it early on."

"And better you find out now than *after* you are married," Sophie offered in a low, steady voice.

Veronica looked from one to the other and shook her head. "I don't believe you. It cannot possibly be true. Why doesn't Edward ask Mirabel to marry him if there is any shred of truth to what you say?"

"Edward secretly wanted to ask her to marry him, but she would have had to refuse him for another arrangement her parents have in mind," Henrietta explained with a tilt of her chin and a triumphant gleam in her eye. "A gentleman from England with a title and a great deal of money, much more money than either of our families have, or so we have heard. Although she would marry Edward in a heartbeat if she could..."

Sophie nodded emphatically.

Could any truth exist in what Sophie and Henrietta shared? Veronica couldn't seem to catch her breath.

"Believe whatever you like, but don't say we didn't warn you," Sophie added nonchalantly with an indignant tone as she crossed her legs and swayed one of her pretty boots. "Are you going to offer tea? If not, I suppose we should be going. I wanted to surprise Father when he returns from his business trip by bringing fresh flowers to spruce up his office. Shall we tell Edward you said hello if we see him? He has been working so hard, I haven't even seen him for dinner lately."

"No, we haven't," Henrietta said as though just realizing it. "Perhaps he has been having dinner with you, Veronica." She toyed with a glove in her lap.

Henrietta's remark stung. Indeed, Veronica hadn't seen Edward for the past few evenings. He'd indicated he would be working late to cover for his father's absence, but was it possible he had been with Mirabel? Had Edward lied to her?

"N-no. I'm not in the mood for tea anymore. I think we are done for today." Her throat felt as though it might close up. Veronica reached for the little gold bell her aunt used to summon the help and rang it. What if some shred of truth existed in what his sisters shared? Would Edward turn out to be like Henry, after all? Had she made a terrible mistake in coming to New York?

Frances appeared in seconds with a concerned look on her face as Henrietta and Sophia began to gather their belongings while casting pitying glances in Veronica's direction. Had Frances waited nearby, close enough to have overheard the disturbing news?

"Frances, if you would escort Edward's sisters to the door, they won't be able to stay for tea." Veronica rose, her voice as firm as she could maintain it, tucking Roosevelt under one arm as she smoothed her skirts. Ready to burst, she did her best to hold her head high, blinking back tears. She could not let them witness the loss of her composure.

CHAPTER SEVENTEEN

The shattering of a heart when being broken is the loudest
quiet ever.
—Carroll Bryant

Edward closed the ledger book he'd finally found. His
father had buried it in the lowest right-hand drawer of
his massive desk. He'd hidden the key to the drawer, and it had
taken attempts with two different letter openers on two sepa-
rate occasions to unlock. Then, as now, his co-worker and
friend Jack Curzon kept watch.

Returning the heavy book to its place, Edward sat back in
his father's leather chair and stared at a photograph of his
parents taken during a second-honeymoon trip to Europe. How
could his family make it through the tough times ahead of
them?

He had finally found the information he needed about his
father's predicament. He'd uncovered statements for a bank
loan tucked into the back of the ledger. Everything had gone
haywire when his father made a disastrous short sale on the
Elkins Cotton Conglomerates stock.

A series of fires started by mysterious explosions had caused Elkins to lose several East Coast textile plants. Father's plan to sell the stock quickly had almost gone off without a hitch. But then news of the fires had turned up in headlines all over the country the next morning. Edward, away at Princeton at the time, hadn't known about any of it. He'd found newspaper clippings about the mysterious fires tucked inside the ledger book too.

The short sale on the Elkins stock had backfired, and Father had to buy back all of it at a much higher price. His partners couldn't bail him out. Edward's father had made tough business decisions and liquidated other valuable stocks to survive the ordeal and tide them over. After draining his savings, Father had dipped into the account containing the dowries for his sisters. Edward had found his father's penciled notes entered in neat lines of the ledger book about each of these transactions, along with notations about his actions to reverse the damages. *Check with partners for help*, for example. *Balance from savings applied to short sale*, was another.

When these moves hadn't covered the losses, he'd taken out a ridiculously large loan with high interest. No wonder he'd sold one of their tenements and now tried to sell another. Father needed to not only pay back the loan, but replace the dowries for his daughters and the savings he'd drained. At the same time, he needed to increase sales and find ways to bring in more clients for Beckett Reed. It was also clear that his father was struggling to make the monthly payments on the loan... until Edward could hand over some of the dowry from his marriage to Veronica.

The outstanding loan balance would indeed come down with the profits from the sale of the first tenement. But even if Father managed to sell more property on his current trip, he still wouldn't be able to pay the loan completely off. This also left Edward's parents with nothing to retire on and no dowries for his sisters. In addition, they'd need to continue cutting expenses as much as possible to climb out of their current hole.

Edward shuddered at all that he'd discovered. He rose from the desk, glancing around to make sure everything looked tidy. The flowers his sisters had brought to welcome Father home looked nice, but if they only knew their dowries had entirely disappeared! They might not feel much like bringing flowers to their father's office if they knew their bleak future and the reasons behind it.

On second thought, his sisters might have hopes of Father returning early, but they didn't know how desperately Father needed to sweet talk and entertain his potential buyer in order for the sale to close. May as well make good use of the flowers and give them to Veronica. He swiped the summer bouquet from the vase and an empty file folder from the desktop he'd use as cover for his foray into Father's office. Returning to his own office down the hall, he laid them aside.

Jack poked his head around the corner, tapping on Edward's door with his knuckles. "Glad to see you're back." He kept his voice low. "No one stepped out into the hall while you were gone. I kept the secretary distracted by asking her questions about where we order our coffee, as you suggested."

"Thanks. I appreciate it."

Jack peeked out into the hall and raised his voice. "Did you find the file? Careless of us to misplace something so important."

"Yes, I found it." Edward grinned and handed him the file.

"Good. Can you try to be more careful next time?" Still spoken loudly.

"Okay, you can close the door." Edward waved Jack inside. He offered a polite chuckle, though in truth, he was in no mood to laugh. His father's financial situation looked bad, bleaker than he'd imagined. No wonder Father had pressed him to marry Veronica.

188

Jack closed the door and sat in the chair in front of Edward's desk. "Just wanted to let you know, I've picked up three new clients in the past two days. I'm hoping you can mention it to your father when he returns."

"Still hoping for that promotion to a senior-level partner?"

Jack nodded. "Beckett, Reed, Johnston & Curzon has a nice ring to it, don't you think? Nothing would make me happier. It's what I've been working toward, putting in all these extra hours."

"I'll slide in a good word, on one condition." Edward shot him a sly grin.

"What's that?"

"You'll let me borrow your horseless carriage so I can take Veronica for a drive. I've spent too much time at the office lately." He dreaded the place and longed for his garret, his artwork, and time with his fiancée. "I need to impress her tonight with something fun and different."

"I think we can arrange that. I'll be in the Adirondacks for a couple of weeks. Just don't forget to put in a good word for me with your father." Jack winked.

Edward smiled, though for that to do any good, he'd need to find a miraculous solution.

~

*A*fter Henrietta and Sophia left, Veronica repeatedly swiped tears away, perched on the edge of her bed. She tried to talk some sort of sense to herself. If she'd seen Edward at all over the past few days, perhaps she would not have so many doubts swimming through her mind, but she hadn't, and his sisters had filled her head with doubts and questions. Did he have poor character, like the ones she saw in his sisters? Like the one Henry Sullivan had shown?

Had Edward dined with Mirabel in secret, behind her back?

It seemed unlikely he would tell her if he had a mistress, so she would simply have to conduct her own investigation. If the answers led to her discovering he had a compromised heart, she would return his ring and refuse him.

She trembled and wiped more tears from her eyes, reeling as her entire world came to a crashing halt. Maybe Edward didn't truly love her. Maybe he only wanted her dowry. Perhaps everything they'd built together stood on a lie instead of the truth and the trust she thought they shared.

But she couldn't assume anything until she discovered the truth.

She patted Roosevelt. The little dog sat on the edge of the bed, content to cuddle up beside her, his tail wagging every now and then. She needed fresh air to clear the thoughts swirling through her mind.

Donning her favorite purple riding habit, she pinned her hat in place and arranged the long white veil to trail properly from the brim of the black hat, over her chignon and down her back. Satisfied with her outfit, she used a hook to button her riding boots.

She located a canvas shopping tote from the wardrobe of her guest room. Then she tucked Roosevelt inside it so only his fluffy white face peeked over the edge. She slung the handle over her head so that it rested from one shoulder to her opposite hip, patted her furry friend, and headed downstairs.

Finding Frances in the dining room, polishing the silver for Aunt Mae, she paused in the door frame. "Frances, I'm going for a ride on one of Aunt Mae's horses. I'll be taking Roosevelt with me, but I'll return in about an hour."

"Do you want company?" Frances asked with an arched brow as she set aside a gleaming silver spoon.

"No. Someone should be here to tell Aunt Mae and Mrs. Cleave I won't be gone long, in case they return earlier than expected. I need a little time alone and some fresh air. A short ride will do me good."

"All right, Miss Veronica, I understand. The saddles in your aunt's stable are much heavier and wider than the ones we have in Kentucky. It's because of these great big horses," Frances warned her. "Arthur, your aunt's groundskeeper, left early today. It seems we're the only ones around at the moment. Do you want my help saddling one of those huge horses?"

"I figured the saddles would be enormous." She shook her head. "No need to help. You know me—tough Kentucky girl."

A few minutes later, Veronica bridled and hoisted a proper side saddle over Aunt Mae's chestnut stallion in the narrow stable behind the house. She managed to buckle the belt under his girth and found the stepstool. She despised riding sidesaddle, but she couldn't exactly ride through Manhattan streets as though she owned the place as she did at Velvet Brooks. Even so, it would feel marvelous to get out and about.

"Here we go, Roosevelt," she said, patting the sweet dog. She took a moment to speak gently to the horse, stroking his long neck and enjoying the feel of the reins in her hand. "Ready, Cornwall?" At least she remembered the horse's name from hearing her aunt's groundskeeper, who also functioned as a groom and occasionally a driver, speak to him. She snapped the reins, urging him forward. "Yaw, boy."

Cornwall's hooves clicked on the stable floor, moving them forward and down the drive. The poor fellow probably hadn't been ridden in a coon's age. "You'll love this, old boy. Show me New York. Take me anywhere you'd like to go, since I feel utterly lost and filled with despair today."

Naturally, Cornwall turned of his own accord from Grosvenor onto Fifth Avenue, toward Central Park, putting a weak smile on her face.

Veronica hardly noticed the mansions they passed, unable to acknowledge any of the beauty around them. The little dog, however, eagerly looked around, taking in everything with bright eyes. Her own eyes misted with tears as they plodded down the avenue, the traffic thickening the farther they traveled.

As they yielded onto Broadway, Roosevelt peeked his head out of the tote, and before Veronica could stop him, he scurried out and leapt into the air at a remarkable height. A cry left Veronica's throat. Thankfully, he landed safely on all four paws, but she gasped, seeing him in the middle of the road. What was he doing?

Roosevelt had spotted a stray cat.

As the little dog sprinted toward the feline on the sidewalk, Veronica called out, "No, no, Roosevelt! Come back!" But there was no way he would hear her over the commotion of traffic.

A freight wagon rumbled past, blocking her view. For a moment, she lost sight of the precious cargo Evangeline Cleave had entrusted her with, and she released another frightened gasp.

By the time her view cleared, the little doggie had already covered a great amount of distance. But thank the Lord, he'd somehow made it safely across the oncoming traffic.

She eyed the conveyances coming toward her in the opposite lane, and as soon as a lull occurred in the steady stream of wagons, buggies, and carriages, she hollered, "Yaw!"

Commanding the horse with all of her might, she nudged a heel into Cornwall's girth, steering him at a diagonal angle across the street and onto the sidewalk. They flew past a grand hotel as they tried to catch up with Roosevelt's head start. When nearly a whole block with few people on the sidewalk appeared before them, she urged Cornwall to gain speed. His trot turned into a gallop, his hooves clicking in glorious motion beneath her. They had to catch that dog!

Veronica leaned into his mane as low as she could, holding tightly to the reins, her skirts whipping in the wind. Ahead, a number of people stood in line to purchase produce from a vendor's cart. At the speed they traveled, her only hope lay in Cornwall's ability to jump over the cart. If she steered right, she risked a head-on collision with some fancy carriages. If she steered left, she risked trampling innocent and unaware pedestrians. She could still just see Roosevelt up ahead, but if she didn't get past that vendor cart, she would probably lose Evangeline's darling dog.

"All right, old boy," she whispered to Cornwall's ear. "Let's see what you've got." She snapped the reins again. Cornwall gave her what she asked for, sailing over the vegetable cart as people scrambled to her right and left.

～

*H*alf an hour after leaving the office, Edward sat behind the wheel of the idling horseless carriage in the drive of Jack's family's Fifth Avenue home and tried to think of somewhere he could take Veronica for dinner. Maybe he'd let her choose. She had probably heard about some place to try, but he'd best hurry before the traffic grew any worse.

He steered the Oldsmobile to the left in the half-circle drive, bringing him back to facing Fifth Avenue. And stopped with his mouth falling open. A woman was galloping a horse at the end of Fifth Avenue where the street forked, connecting to Broadway at Madison Square.

Edward would know that purple riding habit anywhere. *Veronica!*

He pulled onto Fifth Avenue and followed, pushing the pedal to the floor. What could have caused her to break into a full gallop on one of the busiest streets in Manhattan? Obviously, something urgent.

His astonishment quickly turned to fear at seeing her cross

at a crazy angle onto the sidewalk. What on earth? Would he forever find himself chasing his fiancée down on a horse?

A vegetable cart loomed in her path. His palms began to sweat as he gripped the steering wheel. Surely, she would stop. But no! She was going to jump it. Edward forced himself to relax his grip. If anyone could land the risky jump, she could.

But only when she succeeded did he release the breath he hadn't even realized he'd held. "Oh, Veronica! What are you up to, my love?" he muttered, still trying to keep up with her. The wagon ahead of him stopped to turn, and now he had to wait, his foot on the brake when he wanted to move forward.

Suddenly, just past Weber's Music Hall and Daly's Theatre on 30th Street, she cut left. He intended to follow—as soon as another oncoming buggy cleared out of his way. She steered her horse to the right on Seventh Avenue, still traveling by sidewalk, scaring lots of folk who stopped to turn and look at her ride past them with their mouths wide open. The horse continued at a gallop, thundering down the sidewalk.

As she neared the Metropolitan Opera House, a constable on horseback blew his whistle. The officer managed to pull up alongside her, bringing her to a stop for the first time since Edward had spotted her back on Fifth Avenue. He shook his head and prayed the officer wouldn't haul his fiancée off to jail.

Edward tapped his fingers on the steering wheel as he waited for traffic to move. Veronica pointed out something up ahead and said a few words to the uniformed man, her steed breathing hard and swishing his tail. She waited for the constable to respond. Then the two of them took off at an even greater speed on the sidewalk—toward a little white dog.

At least now some of her actions made sense, though Edward didn't recall Aunt Mae having a dog. It looked like a fluffy poodle, maybe wearing a bit of blue ribbon, but for whatever reason, it must be awfully important.

This time, the constable pulled slightly ahead of Veronica,

blowing his whistle, clearing the way through the busy sidewalk, alerting passersby to step out of their way as their horses thundered past shops, hotels, restaurants, and a few more vendor carts. At least Veronica didn't have to jump over anything else.

Whatever she'd said to the constable, it had garnered her the help she needed. Edward did his best to keep up without wrecking Jack's shiny red Oldsmobile.

When the dog stopped to rest, perhaps giving up on its chase, the constable and Veronica finally caught up with it. Edward found a place to park on the side of the road and jumped out of his conveyance. He raced across the street as Veronica dismounted.

"Roosevelt! Here, little guy!" Veronica's voice rang out as she fell to her knees and the fluffy poodle leapt into her arms.

Still some distance behind them, Edward reached her panting horse and took the reins. The officer knelt next to Veronica, shaking his head as she introduced him to the dog. A moment later, the constable helped her to her feet, patted the white dog, and bid them farewell.

When the officer mounted and rode away, Veronica turned and spotted Edward. As her surprise receded, tears pooled in her eyes. He'd missed her, too, badly...but was that hurt in her big brown eyes? Whatever it was, she tried to hide it from him as she approached, then fell into his arms. Then it was as though a dam broke, and tears rolled down her cheeks.

"What is it, Veronica?"

She gulped, and hard crying ensued, the kind where she couldn't utter a word. He clasped her close in the middle of the sidewalk, still holding the reins to her horse, the little dog between them.

When she regained her composure, he stepped back. "Are you all right?"

She looked deep into his eyes and shook her head. "No, but I will be."

He nodded, knowing she couldn't talk about it yet. "Who is this fella?" he asked. "And what did you say to the officer to engage his help?"

"That part was easy. I told him this was Mrs. Cleave's dog." She smiled for the first time and held the poodle up, the two of them rubbing noses. "This adventurer is Roosevelt, and I was in charge when he made his grand escape."

"He's a cute fella. And I can see why the constable would help you. Everyone knows Mrs. Cleave." He patted the poodle between his ears, and the dog wagged his tail.

"Let's get him home before Aunt Mae and Mrs. Cleave have a conniption. Where did you come from, anyway?" She glanced around.

"I happened to recognize you when I was driving back on Fifth, but let me help you mount," he said as she tucked the dog inside a tote she wore over her shoulder. He assisted her into the saddle, earning a weak smile of gratitude.

"Thank you, Edward. I've missed you." She took the reins in her hands with a strange and deeply contemplative look.

"I missed you, too, more than I can say. Jack loaned me his Runabout." He motioned toward where he'd parked the conveyance. "I was headed to your place to see if you wanted to have dinner. I have the automobile for a couple weeks while he visits the Adirondacks with his family."

"Oh." She patted Roosevelt. "Yes to dinner, but maybe something quiet, just us, at my aunt's. I'm not up to going out."

"That sounds terrific. I'll meet you there." What was wrong with Veronica? She didn't seem her usual chipper self, especially after such a spirited ride. "Promise me you won't gallop down the sidewalk? I'm too tired to bail you out of jail."

"Deal." She smiled, but the gesture was too weak to

convince him that everything was okay. She hadn't even laughed at his attempt to joke. Could he find a way to encourage her to trust him with whatever was bothering her?

CHAPTER EIGHTEEN

The heart is deceitful above all things, and desperately sick;
who can understand it?
—Jeremiah 17:9, ESV

Seated at a small round garden table amid her aunt's well-tended roses and hollyhocks, Veronica attempted to unwind from the Great Chase of Roosevelt. But the nagging need to ask Edward about his sisters' sordid, wicked accusation quite kept her from enjoying the Oysters Rockefeller, salad greens with vinaigrette, asparagus, and roast beef Hattie had prepared for them.

Finally, she said, "I'm curious about how well you know Mirabel. She seemed like a nice girl, perhaps someone I could trust as a friend in New York."

Edward nodded before drinking some of his strawberry lemonade. "Our families go way back."

"I'm sure you must know her quite well, then. I noticed her dancing with Rupert at the ball..." She cocked her head and managed to look at him as she awaited his response.

Edward shot her a quick glance, then pushed his salad

greens around. "She has seemed trustworthy for as long as we have known her. Her family has a summer retreat neighboring ours. We all grew up together."

That meant Edward might be closer to Mirabel than he let on. It only compounded her worries.

When she didn't respond, he added, "I sure have missed you these past few days, and I'm looking forward to spending time with you at the Cleave ball."

He peeked at Aunt Mae. To see if she approved? Her aunt didn't bat an eyelash.

"So am I." Not knowing for certain where Edward stood with this Mirabel—alleged friend of the family—she refused to sound mushy about spending time with him. What if she had completely missed a flaw in his character? "My ball gown is ready. Are you ready, Aunt Mae?"

"I believe I am." Aunt Mae reached for the decanter of vinaigrette and drizzled some onto her salad.

Her aunt had imparted nearly every detail about her luncheon with her friend, and thankfully, Mrs. Cleave had taken their story about the day's events in stride, even chuckling about it. Veronica hated to think what might have happened to her aunt's friendship with Mrs. Cleave if Veronica had lost the furry companion. She had enough to deal with where Mirabel was concerned.

Aunt Mae leaned forward, excitement in her eyes. "Wait until you see all of the flowers Evangeline plans to use as summer décor for the event."

Veronica drooped as the conversation moved away from her targeted topic.

Edward paused his fork in midair. "Are you sure you're feeling all right, Veronica? You don't seem your usual self."

She could hardly obtain further information about him and Mirabel in the presence of her aunt, so she attempted to put him at ease for the time being. "I'm just a little homesick. Nothing a good night's rest won't remedy."

Tomorrow she would try again.

~

The next evening, Edward arrived to ride with Veronica and Aunt Mae to the ball.

"I'm sorely tempted to have you drive us in your Merry Oldsmobile." Aunt Mae rather wistfully surveyed the shiny red automobile through her lorgnettes as they pulled away in the carriage. "But appearing at my dear friend's ball in a carriage seems more dignified."

"I agree, but I am enjoying driving about in it until James returns." Edward checked a cufflink on his dinner jacket. Turning to Veronica at his side, he said, "You look lovely in peach silk, darling. It's beautiful with your dark hair."

"Thank you, Edward. My mother says peach is my color." And indeed, Aunt Mae had paid a great deal for the gown, with its elaborate cream lace and gold satin motifs. Veronica waved a small lace fan with a pearl handle in the stifling July heat as the carriage turned onto Fifth Avenue. "You're looking handsome yourself. I will have to fight away the ladies who want to dance with you."

Would he dance with Mirabel this evening? Then again, one dance would really not give grounds for her drawing a conclusion to the matter of his fidelity.

Inside the Cleave ballroom, guests climbed a wide set of plush carpeted steps on an impressive mahogany staircase to a spacious second-floor ballroom. Mrs. Cleave had outdone herself, decorating the opulent space with fragrant rose-covered arches, potted ferns and rose shrubs, and vases of roses adorning corners and tables in every direction. The French doors thrown wide open to the balcony and all of the arched windows open let cool air circulate among guests while waiters offered fancy hors d'oeuvres on silver platters. Guests feasted on caviar, oysters, clams, stuffed mushroom caps, and salmon croquettes. But with Veronica's world falling apart before her very eyes, she had little appetite.

Their hosts welcomed guests in a long reception line. Shortly thereafter, Edward escorted Veronica to her seat in the dining room, then he went in search of his assigned seat. The elegant dinner included a menu that ordinarily would have seemed like a treat. It began with turtle soup, followed by lamb with mint sauce or broiled teal duck. Another course of red raspberry ice was followed by pickled tomatoes, lobster, and currant jelly. Then came lady fingers or custard pie. Brie and water crackers with coffee completed the supper before dancing. Veronica could only eat a few bites of each course.

Thankfully, Edward didn't look around for Mirabel at all, seated at some other table behind him. But his conversation with Aunt Mae and the elderly gentleman seated to Veronica's left who regaled her with stories from his days as a colonel leading a regiment in the "War of the Rebellion" prevented her from making any progress with her investigation.

As the evening commenced, between her dances with Edward, she kept a steady eye on Mirabel and Edward. But Edward did not dance with Mirabel a single time. In fact, they barely exchanged more than a nod—though, of course, that *would* be the case if they were trying to hide their affair.

Veronica accepted only a few dances with any of the gentlemen who flocked to her side, saying her aunt needed her, which was partly true. Aunt Mae sat nearby, and after all she'd done for her, Veronica felt obligated to stay close. Edward didn't dance with any other ladies, either, preferring to speak to her or his friends between dances with her.

Halfway through the evening, a gentleman Veronica did not know led Mirabel off the dance floor and to a vacant chair next to Veronica. Mirabel fluttered her fan before her flushed face. "May I join you, Miss Lyndon?"

"O-of course." Veronica sat straighter and tugged her skirt away from the chair Mirabel sank down onto. Uncomfortable as it might be, this could be her opportunity.

Mirabel thanked her escort for the dance before turning to Veronica. "I'm so fascinated by Kentucky. I would love to visit sometime and have always admired thoroughbred racing."

"Is that so?" This she had not expected.

Mirabel nodded, her curls bouncing. "I assume you know Edward's mother despises horseracing and gambling, but it doesn't bother my family in the least. It's why you will seldom see Edward or Rupert seated at a gambling table in their mother's presence. Their mother won't stand for it, but I do know Mr. Beckett, their father, sometimes takes them to Pimlico. My father takes us there for the races annually. My mother and I look forward to it every year."

"Actually, I didn't know Edward's mother despised horseracing and gambling." This news could potentially explain why Gloria Beckett had never sent her and Aunt Mae a dinner invitation, though she tried to give Edward's mother the benefit of the doubt.

"Oh yes, she can't abide it. I do hope she is kind to you in spite of her aversion to it. My mother says to ignore her when she gets a bee up her bonnet." Mirabel looked genuinely sincere rather than smug as she shared her knowledge.

"Thank you for letting me know." Things began to make a little more sense now. Perhaps Edward's sisters felt the same way.

But then again, what if Mirabel only told her these things to scare her away from Edward and his family? What if they weren't even true?

Once Mirabel excused herself, Veronica simply had to find the balcony to cool down and collect her thoughts. Perhaps she should locate Edward. Where had he gone? Ah, speaking with Rupert and some other gentlemen about the revolution of motor carriages a few feet away.

After she stepped into the cooler air on the balcony, she stood between two enormous potted palms and behind a wall of rose bushes to fan herself. A few moments later, to her left, she spotted Mirabel looking for someone. From the right, Edward approached her.

And that was how Veronica ended up crouching behind the wall of roses with several palm branches in her face. Perhaps she could overhear a discussion between the two and discover the truth once and for all. She braced herself for the worst.

"Hello there, Edward. Are you enjoying the evening?" Mirabel inquired as the pair met on the other side of the shrubs.

"Yes, thank you. Have you seen Veronica anywhere?" Edward inquired.

A pang of guilt at hiding from him stabbed her somewhere around her breastbone, but she had to know the truth.

"Not since a few dances ago. Have you seen Rupert?" Mirabel asked. "I wanted to…" Whatever she said became muffled. "…give him this note for me."

What was going on? Veronica peeked over the wall of roses…and came face to face with a pair of bumblebees. They flitted from one rose petal to another, inches from her nose.

Oh no! No, no, no. Not bees!

Her lips parted as terror took hold of her. She *had* to escape. But then Mirabel tucked a folded note into Edward's hand, and he placed it in his wallet with a nod. Veronica sucked in a sharp breath.

Unfortunately, that delivered a strong waft of the fragrance of roses, and the sensation of someone tickling Veronica's nose resulted in a loud, "*Achoo!*"

And that was how she landed on her bottom and, a

moment later, found herself looking up directly into Edward's face. Her cheeks heated with a deep blush.

"*Veronica?*" Edward blinked and his brows furrowed.

"Hello, Edward." Veronica smiled up at him as Mirabel leaned over the wall of peach and pink flowers to peer down at her. Veronica tried to appear natural and opened her fan again. At least she no longer teetered on her heels.

"Hello, Veronica. What are you doing down there?" Mirabel whispered with amusement in her voice. "Are you hiding? Oh yes, I know. You are hiding from Colonel Deering. You are such fun! I must think of a better hiding place for you."

"Colonel Deering?" Veronica didn't know any Colonel Deering. Then she remembered her dinner companion and nodded profusely. "Oh yes...yes, I am hiding from the colonel."

Mirabel laughed sweetly. "I saw him giving you a rendition of the war. I've had to sit beside him before. He's a perfectly nice gentleman, but it can be a tad boring to listen to him go on about military maneuvers."

Consternation plagued Veronica. Mirabel struck her as a perfectly innocent and pure girl who might turn out to be a good friend. But why were she and Edward both on the balcony? Had Mirabel passed a message to Rupert through Edward? Or was the note meant for Edward himself?

The bees distracted her as they chased each other, landing on a peach rose mere inches away, so close she could feel herself turning blue.

"And here I am again, doing a poor job of defending you from unwanted circumstances." Edward hurried around the rose wall and extended a hand. "May I help you up? I don't know how you keep ending up on the floor, but I digress—it is entirely my fault. Please forgive my inattentiveness, but I confess I had hoped to find you out here."

"It is nice here with a view of the rear gardens and all of the romantic couples below strolling hand in hand." Mirabel sighed, a dreamy look on her face. "Much cooler than indoors, though we should probably return before the next waltz begins. I had hoped to dance with Rupert at least one more time."

Veronica couldn't take her eyes off the two bumblebees buzzing from rose to rose, circulating almost in time with the notes of the waltz pouring out of the French doors. She clasped Edward's hand and maneuvered away from the bees as she struggled to her feet. She was just about to straighten and release a sigh of relief when one of the insects landed on her cheek. She froze, her heart skipping a beat.

A stinger sunk into her skin, and she let out as ladylike a scream as possible while tears filled her eyes.

CHAPTER NINETEEN

It is the glory of God to conceal a thing, but the honor of kings
is to search out a matter.
—Proverbs 25:2

MID-JULY 1901

The balcony incident offered inconclusive evidence in
Veronica's effort to seek truth about her fiancé. Veronica's
severe allergy to beestings had caused an immediate fainting fit.
Thankfully, Edward had scooped her up into his arms—or so
Aunt Mae had told her later. A servant had led him as he
carried Veronica to a drawing room, with Aunt Mae, Mrs.
Cleave, Mirabel, and Rupert on his heels. This had caused
quite a stir among the guests at the ball, according to
Aunt Mae.

The only thing Veronica remembered was waking up in
Edward's arms to his blue eyes looking at her with such adora-
tion that she found it harder and harder to believe the accusation of his sisters. Edward had insisted upon carrying her to
Aunt Mae's carriage. And so off they went—Aunt Mae,

Edward, and Veronica—the note all but forgotten in the ensuing chaos.

Frances had tended her sting, knowing exactly what to do. Grace had equipped her well. Consequently, Veronica hadn't attended church on Sunday morning, not with a welt smothered in baking soda paste still healing on her face.

To make matters worse, the incident delayed her and Aunt Mae from leaving with Edward's family on the train the following Monday for Chesapeake Manor. Edward had agreed to remain behind and make the journey with them a few days later, while his family went on ahead.

Meanwhile, Veronica took the opportunity to pray and ask the Lord to reveal the truth about Edward and Mirabel to her during their time in South Carolina. She had too much invested in the relationship to simply walk away now, and she deserved to know why Mirabel had passed Edward a note, allegedly to deliver to Rupert.

What had Mirabel written in the note? Was it truly for Rupert? Had Edward's sisters fabricated their story, and if so, why? Or did Mirabel and Edward use Rupert as a cover for their own affections? This seemed unlikely given the amount of affection Veronica sensed from Edward toward herself, leaving her stumped. Since she had found no other clues to corroborate the supposed clandestine affair, and it seemed so out of character for Edward, she desperately wanted to believe him innocent in the matter. Nonetheless, duped by Henry Sullivan before, she would not rest her case until she knew for certain.

~

Shortly after settling into a private compartment neighboring that of the women in their party on the train bound for Chesapeake Manor, Edward knocked on the door to the space Veronica shared with the ladies—Frances

Ellis, Aunt Mae, and Aunt Mae's personal maid, Adeline. They'd had to switch over to a ferry taking them to the mainland before transferring their trunks to the train. He had managed to herd all of the women onto the train without losing anyone or their belongings.

Once Aunt Mae bid him enter, he slid the pocket door open and sought Veronica's gaze. "Care to join me at a table in the dining car for breakfast?"

Veronica offered a strangely weak smile, but her aunt waved them away, returning to reading a book and enjoying a hard-boiled egg. Frances looked up from a sampler she stitched with a nod before refocusing on her needlework. Adeline's eyes were closed, occasional snores escaping her open mouth.

In the dining car, they settled at a table for two. A waiter brought them coffee and orange juice while they waited for their orders of scrambled eggs and bacon to arrive. The train sped past miles of farmland, carrying them farther from the city. "I can see you've healed from the bee sting." Edward doctored his coffee. "You look beautiful, as ever. Maybe a little pale. Are you sure you're all right?"

"The sunshine and ocean air will do me some good, and thank you for delaying the journey." Despite her words, Veronica's brows furrowed.

Was she on edge about something? She hadn't behaved like herself since the day he'd spotted her on horseback on Fifth Avenue.

The waiter arrived with their plates, and Edward reached for a pepper shaker and seasoned his eggs. Then he began buttering the biscuit, but Veronica only stared at him. Finally, despite his growling stomach, he put his knife down. "Something's troubling you. You haven't touched your breakfast."

"Edward, the note Mirabel gave you on the balcony to give Rupert—have you given it to him yet?" Veronica clutched her coffee cup.

"Oh, drat! When you passed out from the bee sting, I forgot about it."

That was what had troubled her? He reached inside his wallet and rummaged about. Producing the note, he unfolded it and read it silently, hoping it hadn't contained anything too important. All good. He smiled. Then he handed it to her.

"I may as well share it with you. I can't keep Rupert's secret any longer. He's sworn me to secrecy, for reasons which I will explain. But please keep this to yourself. Our parents don't know yet. They are friends with Mirabel's parents, and Rupert thinks they won't be eager to support him if it means defying her parents and their wishes."

Had Veronica thought him deceptive in some way? He'd only tried to shield his brother.

~

*V*eronica stared at the note. Rupert had a secret? Edward had been helping him keep a secret that had something to do with Mirabel? Defying her parents? Mirabel had said her mother was friends with his mother. How wonderful that Edward had not attempted to deny that he'd accepted the note from Mirabel—he'd forgotten about it! How could Mirabel be that important to Edward if he'd forgotten about it?

And even more wonderful, he'd still had it in his wallet, and now she held it in her trembling hands. If he'd had something to hide, surely, he would have made up some sort of excuse, but instead, he handed it over to her to see for herself. She read quickly, silently.

Dearest Rupert,

Yes, I will marry you, even if it means we will be poor as church mice and live in the countryside in some small town with

*you as the veterinarian for the community. You have my undying
love and devotion.*

    Sincerely Yours Forever,
    Mirabel

Her mouth popped open. Why hadn't she seen it before? Mirabel and Rupert had fallen in love. How foolish of her to believe Edward's sisters. Veronica covered her mouth so no one could hear her laughter as the Lord freed her from her doubts in one sweet, glorious moment.

Edward raked a hand through his hair. He looked adorable with messy hair. She wanted to take him in her arms and kiss him. But she couldn't exactly reach across the table to do anything of the sort on a public train. Tears misted her eyes. Tears of relief. In the next instant, anger rose—not at Edward or Mirabel, but that his sisters had duped Veronica so easily.

"Don't cry, Veronica. What's all this about?" he asked, reaching across the table to comfort her by placing a hand over hers.

"Oh, Edward. These are happy tears. I'm happy for Mirabel and Rupert, but I'm also happy for us." She sniffled and then drew herself up straighter in her seat, relieved to shed all of her worries.

"Well, then. Do eat some of your breakfast. Your food is getting cold."

She nodded and obediently took a few bites of her scrambled eggs. Buttering her biscuit, she plunged onward, her eyes lowered. "I also have a confession to make. Please don't hate me."

"I could never hate you."

"Your sisters..."

"What have they done now?" He looked at her with exasperation in his blue eyes, about to take a bite of his biscuit.

"When they came to apologize about their behavior at the

first ball, they told me you were having an affair with Mirabel. Th-that she would become your mistress if we married."

Edward set the biscuit aside. "They said what?"

She nodded. "I know, it sounded unbelievable to me, too, but after what happened to me with Henry... And we haven't known each other for very long. And I know almost nothing about Mirabel..." Veronica fell silent at Edward's scowl. Had she done the wrong thing in telling him?

~

"*Y*es, I can see how it would upset you." Edward blew out a breath. Since he knew Henry had broken Veronica's heart, he couldn't be angry with her for wondering about the lie his sisters had told her. But anger stirred in him about what they'd done. "Nothing could be further from the truth, and I'm trying to figure out why they would say such a thing."

"I can understand they may feel some disappointment about Aunt Mae being unable or unwilling—I'm not sure which—to secure them invitations to the Cleave Ball, but all I can think is that for some reason, they're trying to scare me away from marrying you." Veronica stirred the eggs on her plate.

"To be perfectly honest, I'm steaming mad at my sisters. Once Father hears of this and all of the other incidents, he won't like it either. Now that he's back from his business trips, I just have to find the right time to discuss this and our other plans for a Kentucky wedding and splitting our time in two states. I will get to the bottom of this, Veronica. I apologize for my family. I hardly know what to say." He had only to find the right time to approach his father—about this and the other things on his mind. If he could finish sorting through them.

*E*dward spoke so sternly, Veronica caught sight of some other passengers looking their way. "It's all right, Edward. The Lord has shown me truth. That mattered more to me than anything else." God would surely deal with his sisters if she continued to forgive them in her heart.

"No, it's absolutely not all right. My father won't like any of it. I hope to approach him after he's had a chance to enjoy the beach and being with the family again." He balled his fist on the table. "As for Rupert, he and Mirabel have been sneaking around together for a while. Since she doesn't have much of a dowry and her parents want her to marry someone with a title and wealth, it's made it complicated for them."

"I think it's sweet Rupert and Mirabel want to be together. Does it sound as though he plans to abandon ship and move to the countryside to pursue his field of study someday?" Veronica reached for his hand, and he relaxed it to take hers.

Edward's brow arched. "It's hard to say from this note, but it does sound that way. It's his passion, like art is mine. But I'm sure he wants to graduate first."

She nodded, a wave of relief concerning Edward's loyalty washing over her soul. His sisters aside, wouldn't it be nice if Edward could fully pursue his passion too?

Lord, help dear Edward. He is so talented. I know his art can touch hearts for You.

*T*wo weeks later, after a picnic lunch, Veronica sat on a quilt spread out on a sandy dune overlooking the ocean with the Beckett siblings. Edward and Rupert played badminton about ten feet away.

When they first arrived, Edward had taken her on a tour of

their summer home. Chesapeake Manor, a glorious Greek revival mansion with Federalist influences seen in its columned front pillars, stood tall and proud, set back a distance from the ocean on a ridge. An hour's drive from the center of Charleston, they had miles of beach all to themselves with their nearest neighbors several miles away. As far as her eyes could see were only sandy dunes, long stretches of glistening beach, and foamy waves rolling in and out. Straight ahead, only the immense span of sea stretched into the horizon, not a ship in sight. She hadn't seen the ocean in years, but the waves lapping the stretch of beach bordering the ridge where Chesapeake Manor's lawn began had a calming effect.

She and her aunt had fallen into the Becketts' holiday routine. Mr. Beckett took long afternoon naps. Aunt Mae spent time with Edward's aunt and mother, and after big family dinners in the long formal dining room, Veronica took romantic walks with Edward on the beach at sunset. She strolled the gardens with Aunt Lavinia holding onto her arm, and nearly every afternoon, she read excerpts to her from Jane Austen, Louisa May Alcott, or Charles Dickens or accompanied her on a carriage ride. In fact, Aunt Mae, Adeline, and Frances had also helped find ways to occupy Lavinia's time. This spared Edward's sisters from having to act as a companion to their aunt, something they considered a chore. As it turned out, Aunt Lavinia wasn't the sour old lady they painted her to be.

A cool glass of sweet iced tea in her hands, wearing her nautical-style swimming suit with its matching cap, Veronica planted her toes in the sand while watching Edward and Rupert play a brotherly yet competitive game.

Sophie rose from her place and plopped down on the quilt next to Veronica. "You've hardly spoken a word to us since arriving, Veronica."

Henrietta scooted closer to them, onto the edge of the blanket, picking up some sand and letting it filter through her fingers and picking out a seashell for the collection she'd begun to gather for a craft project.

"I don't have much to say." Veronica glanced at them before returning her gaze to the ocean.

She regretted her curt reply almost immediately. Why couldn't she have said something such as she didn't possess a chatty nature? She'd come to visit them hoping Edward's family would accept her, hoping they would embrace and welcome her. She had hoped they would at least find happiness in their hearts for their brother.

"I don't blame you. We've behaved terribly. We can see our mother isn't very welcoming. Maybe her attitude has impacted us," Sophie offered in a quieter and more genuine voice than Veronica had ever heard her use before.

Still...hadn't life taught her not to trust everyone? It would take time. They would have to earn her trust. Only a kind of sympathy for them remained.

"You mean she doesn't like people like my family, like me. People with horseracing blood in their veins who had to build their empire, rather than being born with blue blood?" Veronica heard herself say in a tone that contained more than a little bitterness and hurt. If only they hadn't said anything of depth to her.

She would have to dig deeper to find a more complete forgiveness toward Edward's sisters and his mother. Hadn't the Lord said to forgive those who trespassed against her as He forgave her? She would keep trying, for Edward's sake. It might take a little more time and prayer.

"We can tell Edward is much happier with you by his side. It's obvious he's crazy about you." Henrietta plucked another seashell from the sand.

"I think you might need to tell him that," Veronica retorted. "I haven't seen anyone care to ask him what he thinks or wants in any of this."

"If you are referring to Mother's comment last night about having the wedding in New York, she *is* thinking of Edward and his friends." Sophie lifted her chin, sitting up straighter.

"No, she's thinking about herself and her friends." And Aunt Mae had said much the same in reply to Gloria Beckett at the dinner table. At least here, while they stayed in the main house with his family, Edward's mother *had* to invite them to supper each night. Veronica didn't want to discuss the matter with his sisters or his mother. They wouldn't change until Edward found a way to speak to his father.

"Well, if you want to win Mother over, continue helping her entertain Aunt Lavinia. She runs herself ragged looking after her." Henrietta nodded toward the manor house.

Veronica pressed her lips together. Of course, she would continue to spend time reading to Edward's aunt, taking her on short walks in the garden, and anything else she could think of. But just as much because Lavinia was precious and witty as to lighten Mrs. Beckett's load. She wasn't naïve enough to think anything she could do would win Mrs. Beckett over. Maybe only after a great passage of time. And she certainly wouldn't fall into the trap of believing Henrietta didn't have some alternative reason behind the suggestion. She probably hoped to drive a wedge between Veronica and Edward by keeping her too busy to spend time with him.

As for Mrs. Beckett? Why, no doubt she was merely biding her time until she could put someone else under Edward's nose.

Veronica set her tea aside and rose from the quilt.

"Veronica, where are you going?" Edward called as she walked away. "Come play badminton with us."

She placed a hand over her eyes to shade them from the bright sun. "I'm going inside to check on Aunt Mae and Aunt Lavinia, darling. I promised them a carriage ride sometime today. I need to change."

"I haven't seen Aunt Lavinia enjoy carriage rides in years." Rupert shook his head and wiped his sweaty brow. "You work wonders with her, Veronica."

Veronica smiled weakly.

"I'll join you." Edward shot his sisters a wary look and tossed his racquet aside. "We'll play tomorrow, Rupe." Then he hurried to catch up to Veronica.

After Veronica had changed into something suitable for their ride, she met Edward in the upstairs drawing room where their aunts had enjoyed tea with Mr. and Mrs. Beckett.

"There you are, Veronica. A telegram just arrived for you from Velvet Brooks," Aunt Mae said, handing her an envelope as Edward's siblings entered the drawing room. "Open it, please. Tell me everyone is all right."

Veronica tore the envelope open. She scanned the contents of the message. Delia had sent the telegram, begging her to return home. Clay Grinstead had jilted Gladdie. Her sister was in a state of complete despair. "It's Gladdie. She's suffered a heartbreaking situation, and I am needed at home." She looked up at Edward. "Forgive me, darling. I must go to her side at once."

Aunt Mae spoke over the murmurs in the room. "Praise be to God no one has died. She'll recover from a heartbreak, but nonetheless, you must go. Your sister needs you. Frances can pack your trunks. I have enjoyed my time here getting to know Lavinia. I'll stay another day or two and return to Manhattan until I hear about your wedding plans."

Veronica sighed and nodded in agreement. Though she would be glad to leave the Beckett women, she regretted parting abruptly from her aunt and especially Edward's company, but she was needed at Gladdie's side.

CHAPTER TWENTY

Woe to you, scribes and Pharisees, hypocrites! For you clean the outside of the cup and plate, but inside they are full of greed and self-indulgence.
—Matthew 23:25, ESV

"I'm going with you, Veronica," Edward announced. An overpowering fear seized him at the thought of parting from her so suddenly. Much had conspired against them, and he dare not let her out of his sight.

"But we return to New York next week, and I need you at the office," Father said before Veronica could respond.

"Whatever you and your father decide." Veronica neared the entrance to the hall but turned to look at Edward. "I haven't much time to spare if I'm going to catch one of the next trains. I'll find Frances and we'll begin packing. I assume you will have someone pack your trunks shortly if you plan to accompany us to Velvet Brooks."

She dashed away to her guest room, leaving him to work things out with his family.

"I'll go and help my niece pack," her Aunt Mae said, excusing herself too.

As soon as Veronica's aunt's footsteps faded, Edward's mother's petulant voice rang out. "I knew she would run away to Kentucky, Edward."

Edward didn't like his mother's words or her tone. Did she imply he should give up on the love of his life? He had come to a number of conclusions during his walks on the beach with Veronica and in his prayer time. Getting away from New York had helped him sort through things. The time had come to stand up to his family.

"Come sit beside me, Edward." Aunt Lavinia patted the empty seat where Veronica's aunt sat moments ago. "It's been a lovely couple of weeks getting to know your beautiful fiancée and her aunt. I think you should follow your heart to Kentucky. Miss Veronica loves you and makes you happy."

Truer words had never been spoken. But he couldn't sit at a time like this.

"She has likely changed her mind about marrying our Edward," Sophie said before he could utter a reply to his aunt. "It seems to me she has seized upon a weak excuse to cut our visit short—and it's such a vital time to get acquainted."

"It's probably for the best, Auntie," Henrietta put in, but when Edward turned toward her with fire in his eyes, she snapped her mouth shut.

He'd had to face the hard truth, the realizations he'd come to while gazing out at the ocean and praying for wisdom. He loved his family. He always would. But his family had not always shown him the same kind of love he held in his heart toward them. He had longed to come home from the military academy, but beyond the holidays, his parents hadn't made it possible. At least he had been able to choose his own major at Princeton.

He had been working hard to please them, to do the right

thing by them, to do the responsible thing since his graduation. To bail them out of the mess his father had put them in. In return, all they had ever shown him was that if he didn't please them, they would cast him out. It was time to listen to God's plan for his future with Veronica and follow the passions laid upon his heart. His two callings, to be a husband to Veronica and an artist for the Lord.

Filling the world with paintings of the beautiful things God had created and building his life with the woman God had led him to fall in love with meant more to him than all the riches in the world. His father might not understand, but his Heavenly Father's call rang louder than all of the other voices he heard. And Veronica had helped him realize it with her appreciation of his artwork and her desire to live at Velvet Brooks. There, he, too, could pursue his passions.

"Do you really think it's for the best to let her go, Henrietta?" His voice sounded calm, stern, and clear. A peace and determination rose inside him. He felt the Lord's hand, helping him say what he should have long ago.

Henrietta swiveled to face him. "Yes, Edward, I do. She isn't right for you, and you know very well why. Mother has said so many times. She comes from horseracing and gambling money. And none of our suitors will call on us because of it."

"And you, Sophie, do you think it's best to let her go?" He turned to his other sister.

Sophie bit her lip, obviously sensing something different in him. "Y-yes, I do. You know how Mother feels about gambling. And it's true—our suitors have disappeared ever since she arrived." The determination on her face wavered, and her lips quivered.

He clasped his hands behind his back. "It's a pity the two of you feel the way you do. You see, Father didn't want to worry either of you, or Mother, but it's time you know."

His father opened his mouth to protest, but Edward held up

a hand. Father closed his mouth like the lions roaring before Daniel when the angel silenced them. Maybe he wearied of keeping his problems from the women in the family.

"It's not Veronica causing you to lose your suitors, my dear sisters. It is the rumors about what has happened to your father's finances." As they stared at him with round eyes, Edward told them about the short sale with the Elkins stock. It was fortuitous that Rupert was there to hear everything too. "The worst of it is not just that Father's savings is gone, but he also had to use your dowries."

"Our dowries!" Henrietta gasped and Sophie clutched her throat.

Mother listened with her mouth gaping.

"And then he had to take out an enormous loan and sell off two of our tenement properties, which still won't pay back all of the loan. He concocted a plan, suggesting I marry Veronica to save your dowries and replenish some of the family coffers. In short, Veronica's dowry would have helped you a great deal, Henrietta, and you, too, Sophie."

"Oh dear, what have we done?" Henrietta groaned.

"We've treated her so terribly." Sophie raised her hand to her mouth.

"What exactly have you girls been up to?" Father leaned forward, his nostrils flaring like one of the horses in the stables at Velvet Brooks.

"I'll let them tell you since I must pack and leave." Now he knew the reason Sophie and Henrietta had whispered lies to Veronica about his involvement with Mirabel, especially since they had admitted to believing their suitors would not come around because of his fiancée's background. "Suffice it to say, in the meantime, I've fallen head over heels in love with Veronica, but it seems some of you don't care for her. And you think she and her money are tainted, though it would have replenished your dowries and secured you happy futures." He looked directly at his sisters, an attempt to convey his anger and disappointment.

"No, no, Edward. We are sorry. Please forgive us," Henrietta pleaded, Sophie echoing the sentiment.

"You really should forgive them, Edward. They didn't know," his mother said in a low voice. "I didn't know the extent of things either. Levi, you should have told us."

Father heaved a sigh, muttering something indistinguishable under his breath, lowering his head in shame.

"I do forgive them, Mother. And now you know everything, but it's too late. The damage has been done. Your dowries are gone, and only after you realize how much Veronica becoming part of the family could have helped you do you say you are sorry. Equally appalling, Father expects me to just hand half of her dowry over to him while I give up my passion for art and slave away in an industry I don't even like." Edward shook his head. "No, it's not going to work out that way. I am done with sacrificing my passion for all of you."

Mother's back stiffened. "But it's your duty, Edward."

"Yes, it is your duty to the family." Father's face reddened. "Your responsibility to carry on the family trade, our good name, everything I've worked so hard for."

"No, Father, I have a better plan." Edward turned toward him. "I'm going to marry Veronica at her home church if she'll still have me after all my family has put her through, live in Kentucky, and pursue my dream of becoming an artist. We'll use the dowry to become established somewhere near Velvet Brooks until my artwork begins selling. As for your situation, after a thorough search of our financial records, I've found a solution. I suggest you sell a parcel of our beachfront property here in South Carolina. There is plenty of land, and we're only here a few weeks in the summer and winter. Use those funds to pay off the rest of the loan. It should leave enough to replace Henrietta's and Sophie's dowries, albeit with small ones."

His mother's mouth dropped open. "But that land has been in my family for generations..."

Edward sighed. "It's the only way, Mother. Even with the sale of two of our tenements. You'll still have your summer home and the land around it. It is a very small price to pay to restore your finances and give my sisters a chance for futures of their own. In the meantime, you can promote Jack to a senior partner. And with his passion for our industry, he will help the business improve."

"Jack Curzon?" his father echoed, clearly aghast. "But I intended to make you and Rupert senior partners when I retired."

Edward waved his plan aside. "Jack loves working at Beckett Reed. Make it Beckett, Reed, Johnston & Curzon. He's brought three new clients in while you were gone. He'll make a fine senior partner. I don't want to be a partner, and although I can't speak for Rupert, my guess is he'd prefer to pursue his field of study someday too. Regardless, I'm moving to Kentucky."

Henrietta and Sophie burst into tears.

His mother rose and faced his father. "How could you have let this happen to us, Levi? It pains me to say it, but you must listen to Edward. I don't see any other way forward." She turned to comfort his sisters, who sobbed quietly.

Edward had rendered his father speechless. In time, he would come to accept the plan Edward had offered.

Rupert stood and thumped Edward on the back. "Good for you, brother. You are finally free." When Rupert finished school, he could be free from Beckett Reed also. "I'd still like to be your best man. And I hope you and Veronica have a wonderful life in Kentucky. I'd like nothing more than to see you happy."

"Thank you, Rupert. Your turn to stand strong is coming." Edward patted his brother on the shoulder. If he wanted to marry Mirabel and pursue his dreams, he needed to complete his education and stand up for himself too. Edward had passed along Mirabel's note shortly after their arrival.

Rupert mouthed a silent *thank you*. Edward's actions had paved an easier way forward for his brother's happiness too.

"Will you please send us an invitation to the wedding, Edward?" Aunt Lavinia's gentle query turned Edward back at the door. "I can't blame you one bit for the decisions you've come to, but I for one intend to support you by coming to the wedding, if Veronica's family won't mind after the way our family has treated her."

"Of course, Aunt Lavinia. You'll all be invited. Unlike the rest of my family, the Lyndons are horseracing royalty, and they behave like royalty too. I'm sure they'll send invitations. Perhaps by the time of our wedding, you will all remember to treat Veronica with respect. You must never forget that she and her family are highly esteemed where they come from." With this, Edward headed upstairs to pack.

Right now, what mattered most was being at Veronica's side, if she'd still have him. He could hardly believe she hadn't abandoned him entirely.

$\approx$

AUGUST, 1901

VELVET BROOKS

*V*eronica sat at the dining room table across the hall from Father's library, quietly tapping her foot. She'd wanted to be in the meeting between Pa and Edward. Her fiancé's plan had filled her with surprise and happiness when he shared it with her on the journey home.

She didn't know a woman could have this much happiness in her heart. This had turned out far better than she'd expected, and Edward was finally free to pursue his artwork.

And she wouldn't have to leave Velvet Brooks if things worked out the way she and Edward hoped. She would find out when his meeting with her pa finally concluded. What took them so long?

After hearing about the way Edward had stood up to his family, she trusted him to sort things out. If all went according to plan, she would marry Edward on the last Saturday in September.

The library door swung open, and she caught a glimpse of Pa shaking Edward's hand, smiles on their faces. Then Edward hurried across the hall toward her, and Pa went out the front door to handle some other matter.

When Edward reached her side, she stood, and he pulled her into his arms. Looking up into his blue eyes, which were sparkling with excitement, she asked, "Well? How did it go?"

He picked her up and spun her around. "It was perfect. Splendid. Everything we hoped for."

When he set her down again, she giggled. "I want every detail. Ten acres?"

He nodded. "Ten acres with one edge along Cornflower Road, and we can begin construction of our new home as soon as we like."

Her hand fluttered to her chest. "He'll sell it to us?"

"He already planned to give it to us as a wedding gift. With a deed in both of our names." He smiled.

"And what did he think of your idea for the name Glorious Day Dreamer for the new foal?" The birth of Glory's foal had lifted everyone's spirits—especially Gladdie, who loved Edward's name suggestion. The foal made her think of the fresh new beginning ahead for them.

"Loved it. But I'd like to know, do you want the house to sit back far from the road with a long lane leading to it? With sugar maples planted along both sides?"

She pursed her lips and stepped away from him, placing

her hands behind her back. "I don't know. I'm not sure if I like any of this plan."

"Wh-why not?" Edward looked puzzled, almost crestfallen.

"I don't know, city boy." Veronica placed her hands on her hips, her gaze hidden beneath her lashes, her voice coy. "Does the house you have in mind include matching easels, a piano, far too many books, a bunch of messy, noisy children who look just like you, a stable of our own, Jesus at the center of our world, and a rose garden to admire after church every Sunday?"

A grin a mile wide spread across his face. He reached out, catching her by the hand and pulling her into his arms for a sweet kiss. "Yes, yes, to everything on your list, my darling, but you are the only rose I'll ever need in our garden."

EPILOGUE

O n the last Saturday in September, Veronica married Edward at the little white church in Lexington before as many guests as the place could hold. Some townsfolk who couldn't fit into the building stood outside, wrapping around Church Avenue, all the way down to Meade Street and spilling onto Mulberry. Rupert stood beside Edward as his best man, and Jack Curzon was his groomsman. Veronica's sisters, Delia and Gladdie, were her bridesmaids.

Edward's family, including Aunt Lavinia, and Veronica's Aunt Mae had arrived a few days ahead to celebrate the wedding, and they would linger for the week-long celebration. While Edward's family lodged in rooms at the Phoenix Hotel, Aunt Mae stayed at her childhood home, clearly overjoyed to see it again.

Immediately following the ceremony, the crowds erupted with cheers for the couple as they came out of the church with the bridal party. A huge potluck picnic dinner occurred on the grounds, the size of which has seldom been seen again, since nearly all of Lexington's inhabitants were invited. The happy bride and groom drove away in a fine carriage decorated with flowers and ribbon, pulled by two matching bay stallions from the stables at Velvet Brooks.

Joseph Lyndon gave Veronica and Edward a wedding gift of ten acres on which to build their home. There they lived happily ever after, with an art studio for Edward, a heart-shaped piano, matching easels, a rose garden, a stable, far too many books, and several messy, noisy children.

The End

Did you enjoy this book? We hope so!
Would you take a quick minute to leave a review where you purchased the book?
It doesn't have to be long. Just a sentence or two telling what you liked about the story!

Receive a FREE ebook and get updates when new Wild Heart books release: https://wildheartbooks.org/newsletter

Don't miss the next book in the Kentucky Debutantes of the Gilded Age!

To Choose the Longshot
Releasing November 2024!

Chapter 1

SATURDAY, MAY 10, 1902
LEXINGTON, KENTUCKY

"Are you ready, Delia, sweetheart? It's almost time." Pa patted her hand with his large rough one. "You look a little nervous."

"I *am* nervous." Today she, Delaney Lyndon, would marry Thaddeus Sullivan, son of the wealthiest horse breeder in Fayette County. And yet she clung to her father's elbow at the foot of the steps outside the First Christian Church. He looked nice in his best suit with a peach rose pinned to his lapel. "I feel as though I'm forgetting something, but other than that, I think I'm ready."

Delia had used lip balm to hide the fact she'd bitten her lower lip too much, a physical manifestation of the overwhelming stress and anxiety consuming her since before the Kentucky Derby. Time had flown by since last weekend's race in a frenzy of last-minute preparations for her wedding, with deliveries and fittings in rapid succession. And now, at long last, her big day had arrived. Despite her mother's meticulous planning and her family's support, a bad case of the wedding jitters and a sense of dread plagued her. Her stomach churned and flipped, unable to keep down a single bite of breakfast. The echoes of a disturbing dream haunted her, leaving her unsettled and on edge.

But thanks to the unwavering dedication of Mama and her

trusted employees at their horse farm, Velvet Brooks, Delia had managed to make it through the morning without breaking down. Grace Mitchell and Frances Ellis, long-serving household staff, had kept everything running smoothly amid chaos. Grace filled the role of a lady's maid to the women at Velvet Brooks. Frances served mainly as a household maid, but she occasionally helped Grace or Willamena, their cook. Earlier today, Veronica and Gladdie, Delia's sisters, had tucked her shimmering white skirts, the long train of her gown, and her stunning veil into the carriage. Now she stood before the church steps, clinging for dear life to Pa's arm. She blinked several times as flashes of her dream echoed in her mind.

Pushing the dream away, she tried to focus on the day of sunshine the Lord had given. Her reception would take place at the Phoenix Hotel Ballroom. By now, Lexington's finest bakery would have delivered her three-tier wedding cake, placing it on a round marble-topped table in an elegant room to one side of the ballroom. She smiled to think of it. Their wedding cake would have a room unto itself. Such splendor awaited, if only she could make it through the ceremony without fainting.

Veronica, her oldest sister, acting as her matron of honor, stretched out her veil and the train of her wedding gown before dashing around her and Pa, lining up on the church steps with the other bridesmaids. The train of Delia's dress weighed more than expected, and she moved slowly in so much lace and satin. She could barely see through the filmy gauze of her veil, trimmed in elegant lace, shipped all the way from Paris.

Mama had slipped inside the church moments ago, taking her seat on the second pew on the left side, lovely in a sage-green concoction with a demi-train. Mama's seamstress in Lexington had designed it to complement Delia's peach wedding colors. The first few notes streamed through a few open windows as Aunt Celia Jane began playing Grandfather Spencer's favorite hymn on the piano, Charles Wesley's "Love

Divine, All Loves Excelling." Her aunt had arrived the day before from Louisville with Uncle James to attend the rehearsal since no one else they knew played the instrument as well as Delia's father's sister-in-law.

The church doors swung open, and she caught a glimpse of Uncle James, filling the role of an usher, positioning the doors to keep them in place. She gulped again, hearing the music perfectly now. Her bridesmaids stood up straighter, fidgeting with their dresses before they began to proceed up the aisle to the magnificent hymn. Each carried a bouquet of peach roses tied with a sage-green silk ribbon. Glancing down at the slightly larger bouquet in her own hands, she managed a weak smile at seeing the delicate petals.

Veronica had disappeared inside the church, followed by their younger sister, Gladdie. Then Thaddeus's sisters, Tilly and Mary Louise Sullivan, proceeded inside. Their Sullivan cousins, Hazel and Flora, filed in next. Mama had said five bridesmaids and one matron of honor constituted a fine number. Delia could picture them taking their places to the left of the altar, all wearing flowing peach satin with demi-trains swirling at their feet. Their dresses featured white sashes at their waists, three rows of white lace ruffles at their hems, and sage-green piping on their bodices. Exquisitely fitted, they looked like the first breath of summer, perfect for a May wedding.

Thaddeus, dressed in a black suit, would also stand at the front of the little white church with his older brother—Henry, the best man—Tilly's twin, Percival, and three of Thaddeus's best friends. Edward, Veronica's husband, completed the groom's party. They would have lined up on the right side of the church before the bridesmaids entered, all wearing black suits with a peach rose pinned to their lapels.

Pa stepped forward, and Delia willed her feet to move, but

they didn't budge. Joseph Lyndon stepped back as she clung to his elbow. "Time to go inside, princess."

A nervous laugh escaped her lips. "Oh, Pa, only you could make me laugh at a time like this. You haven't called me princess in a while."

"You do look like a princess today, and now you'll finally get to marry your prince."

"You don't look so bad yourself."

He grinned. "Your ma says I do clean up nice."

They climbed the steps. Aunt Celia Jane pounded out the traditional wedding march as if her very life depended on it. Delia kept her eyes forward, aware of the guests rising when they reached the doors. The pews creaked, and a sea of smiling faces turned toward them as she made her grand entrance on her father's arm. All of Lexington seemed crammed into the building.

A few feet down the aisle, she sought the face of her groom. Finding him, she relaxed a little when she met his blue eyes. Did he approve? His smile told her he did. Her heart pounded with an odd mixture of fear, apprehension, and excitement. Why did her lips quiver when she tried to return his smile?

They finally made it to the front of the church, and Pa let go, handing her over to Thaddeus. Just like that, as if she no longer belonged to him. Thaddeus tucked her hand into his elbow with another of his handsome smiles as he leaned toward her. She offered a weak smile in return.

Dizziness caused her to waver as the preacher, Reverend Burrows, said a short prayer and then began to address the congregation. Thaddeus steadied her. She couldn't hear many of the preacher's words, but she caught a few here and there. Something about dearly beloved gathering to witness. A moment later, she heard him asking if anyone knew of any reason these two should not be joined together in wedded matrimony. The dream flashed before her, and Delia stiffened.

Should *she* speak up? Had she arrived at the altar for the wrong reasons? Could marrying Thaddeus Sullivan finally put her fears to rest? No. She did not think it could, but she couldn't get any words out. Her mouth dry as the tail end of a summer drought, she swallowed.

She tugged her hand back, but Thaddeus wouldn't let go. She tugged again more firmly and managed to untuck her hand from the crook of his elbow. Twisting to her side, she picked up a handful of her white satin dress. A stirring of murmurs hummed from those in attendance, but she couldn't see many of their faces clearly through her veil. Her gaze locked on the doors as her means of escape. Her uncle had left them open. Like one of the horses from the Lyndon stables breaking into a gallop on Pa's racetrack, she broke into a run down the middle aisle, sucking in full breaths for perhaps the first time in the last thirty seconds. How could a girl breathe properly with a veil covering one's mouth, anyhow?

It didn't take long to reach the church doors. She burst through them and flew down the steps, shoes clacking and train rustling, as onlookers outside gasped. Behind her, commotion broke out. Someone sobbing—Mrs. Sullivan? Her father directing someone to go after Delia.

She ran toward the corner of the church, hoping to spot Pa's carriage, yet Mama would need it. But Charlie Ford, Velvet Brooks's jockey, had ridden Midnight Sunburst—one of her father's most prized horses—to the wedding. She'd seen Charlie arrive while waiting with Pa before entering the church. Presently, she needed Midnight Sunburst more than Charlie did.

Rounding the side the building, she hiked her skirts up a little farther in time to leap over several planters of more peach roses the florists had positioned along the perimeter. Delia landed safely, digging her heels into the ground as she teetered. Her train glided over the roses, and she kept going until something yanked her back. Drat! She stopped, twisting around to see what prevented her escape. Ah! The enormous holly shrub attempted to tangle with her dress.

She freed the train and turned back to the horses and carriages parked alongside the church her Spencer grandfather had helped to build. He'd preached there for most of his adult life until his retirement. Right now, he was likely fanning Grandmother Spencer to keep her calm. Both sets of grandparents, pillars in the Lexington community, would be mortified at her behavior.

She'd make them understand—once she did herself.

She hurried toward the beloved horse at the hitching post, tossing her bouquet of roses over one shoulder. Someone in the crowd caught it, and more gasps ensued.

Delia yanked at the lead until she managed to untie the horse. After a brief fight with her veil, she swiped it away, pushing the front layer up and over her coifed updo. She stuck one of her dainty heels into a stirrup and mounted. With a few quick sweeps of her hand, she arranged her skirts to hide the fact she would not flee sidesaddle. It could not be helped.

Feet clattered down the church steps, and voices she recognized called out. Some of her bridesmaids come to retrieve her? They would attempt to coerce her to exchange vows with her betrothed. No, she could not speak to them, nor allow anyone to convince her otherwise. She didn't know her own heart or what her dream meant, but she wrestled with an unshakeable sense of foreboding. Nonetheless, a few spectators pointed in her direction, apparently eager to help the bridesmaids catch up to her.

She tightened her hold on the reins as Veronica and Gladdie appeared at the corner of the church. Blocking her path to Church Avenue along with dozens of acquaintances who hadn't secured an invitation to the wedding stood a fancy Sullivan carriage with a team of striking white horses. Delia had no time to lament the fact someone had labored to decorate the carriage and the team with ribbons and flowers. It would have carried her and Thaddeus to their reception, but now she looked for a way around it.

"Delia, wait!" Gladdie lifted her skirts and waved her bouquet.

"Delia!" Veronica was right on Gladdie's heels.

More bridesmaids caught up to her sisters. A sea of peach dresses swarmed toward Delia.

To her right and left, a thick crowd of onlookers whispered at the spectacle as she urged Midnight Sunburst through them, steering the horse toward the road. Folks would have to step aside and let her horse pass. A couple of guests opened the church windows to observe her departure, but she paid them no mind.

"Let's go home, boy," she whispered in his ear. The towns-folk parted like the Red Sea.

When she cleared the thickest part of the crowd, she sat up straighter, digging her knees into her mount's haunches. She snapped the reins. "Yaw!"

Midnight Sunburst took off as her bridesmaids nearly caught up to her at the edge of Church Avenue. The horse broke into a powerful gallop, as if understanding the assign-ment. His strong muscles began to move in swift stride beneath the saddle, carrying her far from the scene.

As Midnight Sunburst's hooves thundered down Church Avenue, tears streamed down Delia's face—so many tears, not even the breeze could dry them as she sped along. Runaway bride or no, she refused to marry Thaddeus Sullivan today, or any other day—at least not until she sorted out the mess inside her head and heart.

Maybe Thaddeus would never forgive her for leaving him at the altar as Clay Grinstead had nearly done to Gladdie, but she would have to take her chances. At least Gladdie's episode had happened in private. Poor Thaddeus!

Riding hard toward Velvet Brooks, she told herself the town gossip did not matter. Well, it mattered a little, but they hadn't seen her dream. What did she care what they thought, anyhow? She'd rather face the wrath of her betrothed, her family, and her friends than contend with the consuming flames dancing in her dream. She'd witnessed a large building burning in the dream—one she didn't recognize—but why had it seemed like watching her future burn?

AUTHOR NOTE

Dear Readers,

Thank you so much for reading *An Arrangement with the Heiress*, the first book in my new series, Kentucky Debutantes of the Gilded Age. I thoroughly enjoyed immersing myself in the rich history and heritage of horseracing in the state of beautiful Kentucky where I live. My husband and I recently enjoyed touring a Lexington horse farm as part of my research. It made me giggle and laugh when one of the horses nudged me gently with his nose, asking for another peppermint from the candy stash the tour guide gave us to share with the horses. The books in this series have been a joy to write. I hope you love reading them as much as I have loved researching and writing them.

According to my research, from 1898 to 1904, Lexington didn't host a Phoenix Stakes race. This race is normally held in October, but prior to 1989, it ran during the spring meet. Consequently, I may have taken some fictional liberty in having a certain horse win a fictitious 1901 Phoenix Stakes in my story.

The Kentucky Derby didn't take place in May of 1901, but instead occurred on April 29th of 1901 as a horse named His Eminence, ridden by jockey Jimmy Winkfield, bred by Overton

H. Chenault of Kentucky, and trained and owned by Frank B. Van Meter, took first place in 2:07.75. The winner's purse of $4,850.00 in 1901 had the purchasing power of $175,185.42 in 2023, to give readers some idea of how lucrative it could be to win the Kentucky Derby during the Gilded Age. Many champion horses went on campaigns, winning several races in one season.

Everything about Colonel Blaze, Glory, and the other horses in the story are also fictionalized, including names. In fact, if there are any horses in history matching the names of the horses in my story, please keep in mind, my horse characters are purely figments of my imagination, some with names suggested by readers. Their personalities were incredibly fun to develop, and though fictional, I hope these horses seemed real for the story and enjoyable to read about.

I found it interesting to discover the Latonia Racetrack in the Covington area thrived in the early 1900s because they offered a purse with much higher winnings than many other tracks from 1915 to 1928, but the Latonia track slowed in the 1930s when horseracing went through another downturn due to the financial crisis of the Great Depression.

Horseracing continues to survive and thrive, but many said we were actually in another downturn because we haven't had as many astonishing horses such as Secretariat to appear on the scene and earn a Triple Crown—until American Pharaoh and Justify in 2015 and 2018, respectively. There have been some eighteen- and twenty-five year waits for Triple Crown winners to appear, to give horseracing enthusiasts some idea of what an extraordinary feat it is to capture the elusive title. Believe it or not, the Triple Crown hasn't been in existence as long as some may think, though England certainly had a Triple Crown. Meriwether Lewis Clark, Jr., the founder of Churchill Downs, and other race organizers in New York tried to promote a Triple

Crown, but these early efforts failed since each insisted their events were preeminent.

In American racing circles, though the "Triple Crown" term had long been coined in various articles and journalistic mentions, no winners were formally proclaimed until an annual awards dinner in December 1950 held by Thoroughbred Racing Associations in New York. The first winners to receive the award were named retroactively, with Sir Barton as the first horse to win all three races in 1919. Of the thirteen horses to win a Triple Crown, ten have been Kentucky horses.

I truly hope you enjoyed this series from my heart to yours. I can remember admiring the annual Kentucky Derby tradition even as a youth growing up in Ohio, sitting on the floor with my sisters, excited to watch the races, see all of the amazing hats, and cheer on the beautiful horses. Never in my wildest dreams did I think I'd have the privilege of living here one day.

I greatly appreciate your kind reviews of my attempt to do justice with this fascinating and fun, world-renowned equine theme in my Christian historical romance. I pray it has blessed you in some way.

Warmest Regards,

Lisa M. Prysock

ABOUT THE AUTHOR

Lisa M. Prysock is a *USA Today* Bestselling, Award-Winning Christian and Inspirational Author. She and her husband of more than twenty-five years reside in beautiful, rural Kentucky. They have five children, grown. Empty nesters, they are slowly reclaiming the house.

She writes in the genres of both Historical Christian Romance and Contemporary Christian Romance, including a multi-author Western Christian Romance series, "Whispers in Wyoming." She is also the author of a devotional. Lisa enjoys sharing her faith in Jesus through her writing and has authored more than 50 published books in both Contemporary and Historical Christian Romance. She loves to make readers laugh and enjoys writing humor in many of her stories.

Lisa has many interests, but a few of these include gardening, cooking, drawing, sewing, crochet, cross stitch, reading, swimming, biking, and walking. She loves dollhouses, cats, horses, butterflies, hats, boots, flip-flops, espadrilles, chocolate, coffee, tea, chocolate, the colors peach and purple, and everything old-fashioned.

She adopted the slogan of "The Old-Fashioned Everything Girl" because of her love for classic, traditional, and old-fashioned everything. When she isn't writing, she can sometimes be found teaching herself piano and violin but finds the process "a bit slow and painful." Lisa enjoys working with the children and youth in her local church creating human videos, plays, or programs incorporating her love for inspirational dance. A few of her favorite authors include Jane Austen, Lucy Maude Montgomery, Louisa May Alcott, Charlotte Brontë, and Laura Ingalls Wilder. You'll find "Food, Fashion, Faith, and Fun" in her novels. Occasionally, she includes her own illustrations.

She continues the joy and adventure of her writing journey as a member of ACFW (American Christian Fiction Writers) and LCW (Louisville Christian Writers). Lisa's books are clean and wholesome, inspirational, romantic, and family oriented. She gives a generous portion of the proceeds to missions.

Discover more about this author at **www.LisaPrysock.com** where you'll find the links to purchase more of her books, free recipes, devotionals, author video interviews, book trailers, giveaways, blog posts, and much more, including an invitation to sign up for her free newsletter.

Connect with Lisa:
  *Lisa's Author Website:
  https://www.LisaPrysock.com
  *Lisa's Facebook Reader & Friends Group:
  https://www.facebook.com/groups/500592113747995/
  *Follow Lisa on Goodreads:
  https://www.goodreads.com/author/show/7324280.
Lisa_M_Prysock
  *Get a Free Book When You Sign Up for Lisa's FREE Newsletter:

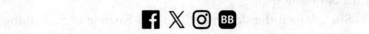

If you love historical romance, check out the other Wild Heart books!

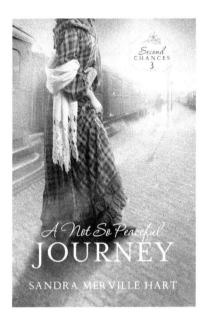

A Not So Peaceful Journey by Sandra Merville Hart

Dreams of adventure send him across the country. She prefers to keep her feet firmly planted in Ohio.

Rennie Hill has no illusions about the hardships in life, which is why it's so important her beau, John Welch, keeps his secure job with the newspaper. Though he hopes to write fiction, the unsteady pay would mean an end to their plans, wouldn't it?

John Welch dreams of adventure worthy of storybooks, like Mark Twain, and when two of his short stories are published, he sees it as a sign of future success. But while he's dreaming big with his head in the clouds, his girl has her feet firmly planted, and he can't help wondering if she really believes in him.

When Rennie must escort a little girl to her parents' home in San Francisco, John is forced to alter his plans to travel across the country with them. But the journey proves far more adventurous than either of them expect.

~

Ranger to the Rescue by Renae Brumbaugh Green

Amelia Cooper has sworn off lawmen for good.

Now any man who wants to claim the hand of the intrepid reporter had better have a safe job. Like attorney Evan Covington. Amelia is thrilled when the handsome lawyer comes courting. But when the town enlists him as a Texas Ranger, Amelia isn't sure she can handle losing another man to the perils of keeping the peace.

Evan never expected his temporary appointment to sink his relationship with Amelia. Or to instantly plunge them headlong into danger. But when Amelia and his sister are both kidnapped, the newly minted lawman must rescue them—if he's to have any chance at love

A Heart's Forever Home by Lena Nelson Dooley

A single lawyer whose clients think he needs a wife.
A woman who needs a forever home...or a forever family...or a forever love.

Although Traesa Killdare is a grown woman now, the discovery that her adoption wasn't finalized sends her reeling. Especially when her beloved grandmother dies and the only siblings she's ever known exile her from the family property without a penny to her name.

Wilson Pollard works hard for the best interest of his law clients, even those who think a marriage would make him more "suitable" in his career. And when the beloved granddaughter of a recently deceased client comes to him for help, he knows he must do whatever necessary to make her situation better.

As each of their circumstances worsen, a marriage of convenience seems the only answer for both. Traesa can't help but fall for her new husband—the man who's given her both his home and his name. But what will it take for Wilson to realize he loves her? Will a not-so-natural disaster open his eyes and heart?